T0354862

BUNYIP

Sid Stephenson
and
Aaron F Diebelius

authorHOUSE®

AuthorHouse™ UK
1663 Liberty Drive
Bloomington, IN 47403 USA
www.authorhouse.co.uk
Phone: UK TFN: 0800 0148641 (Toll Free inside the UK)
       UK Local: (02) 0369 56322 (+44 20 3695
       6322 from outside the UK)

Published by AuthorHouse 10/19/2022

ISBN: 978-1-7283-7605-9 (sc)
ISBN: 978-1-7283-7606-6 (hc)
ISBN: 978-1-7283-7604-2 (e)

LOG-LINE:

Powerful political lobbies and criminal forces relentlessly pursue the truth behind the 5000-year-old BUNYIP legend.

Co-Writers:

Sid Stephenson is a former Educationalist evolved into an Author and Screenwriter.
E: stephensonsid3@gmail.co.uk
www.sidstephenson.com

Aaron F Diebelius is a professional screenwriter and Author.
E: AaronFDiebelius@outlook.com

This book is written in a unique genre called 'SCROVEL'.

This is an amalgamation of a **SCREENPLAY** and a **NOVEL**. It tells the story in what can be seen and heard. All introspective text is removed. The intention is that the Reader experiences the story by 'playing the movie in their head' as they read.

Notes:
* SCENES replace CHAPTERS
* EXT: Exterior
* INT: Interior

BUNYIP:
A mythical creature from Australia's ancient history. It is believed by some that Bunyip flesh can massively speed healing processes.

SUMMARY:

In a remote cattle station in Australia's Simpson Desert a cattleman kills an unidentified creature that is slaughtering his cattle. Within hours the story that a BUNYIP has been shot, goes viral worldwide. For political reasons the story is given credibility by the Australian Government to divert public attention away from a potentially World shattering news announcement.

Powerful political lobbies and criminal forces relentlessly pursue the truth behind the 5000-year-old Bunyip legend. The story challenges and questions the issue of state sponsored assassination for the greater good - some possessions are simply too big to be owned by a single person.

Set in Australia's magnificent Simpson Desert isolation, this story questions whether myth can ever be suppressed or destroyed, where in comparison, reality is often tenuous and fragile.

BUNYIP

EXT. CORDILLO DOWNS HOMESTEAD. SIMPSON DESERT OUTBACK. STH AUSTRALIA. MORNING

The wool station at Cordillo Downs in the Simpson Desert sits in majestic scrub country 100 dry miles southeast of Birdsville. Built entirely of stone the crumbling building, in a homestead of smaller buildings, once saw 85,000 head of sheep shorn by itinerant shearers in relentless heat and dust and working conditions that today's workers could only guess at.

The long-time owner, the Beltano Cattle company, switched to beef farming in 1940 and since then the desert has gradually encroached on the homestead despite the family's continued attempts to restore the historic structure.

William Robert Mason,46, dressed for the desert, known as Billy Bob, worked in the deep shade of the old building loading equipment and fuel into a long-wheel-base Land Cruiser. Finishing his tasks, he spoke tersely into a Sat-phone.

> BILLY BOB MASON
> It's me. In leaving now. Guess I'll overnight at the MIKIRI, so don't hang around.
> (A beat)
> I'll ring if anything.

About to end the call, he stopped, listened.

                    BILLY BOB MASON (CONT'D)
                    (Impatient)
          PJ, I don't know yet, just what Jiemba
          Ngara told me, half dozen. He said
          they had been savaged, ripped up. Not
          pretty.
                    (A beat, listening)
          OK, roger that.

He disconnected, holstering the handset in
worn leather, winding his lanky frame into
the Cruiser, he headed south-east into vast
timeless scrub desert.

**EXT. SIMPSON DESERT OUTBACK. STH
AUSTRALIA. DAY**

4 HOURS LATER

Billy Bob sat with his boot heels hooked in
volcanic gravel on a ridge and glassed the vast
desert floor below him that stretched forever
into a horizon of orange shimmering haze. The
valley with the MIKIRI waterhole showed as a
slash of faint green in falling shapes of dunes
and a stand of Gidgee trees.

He lowered the binoculars, unscrewed a water
flask and studied the land. Far to the south,
lost in the shimmering haze were the Flinders
Ranges, vast ancient twirls of terracotta lava
mountains, dazzling white salt pans and broken
country, baking and raw, a magnet for the
more adventurous four-wheel drivers, and the
spiritual home of the Aboriginal Wankangurru
tribe. To the west and north lay the deep
rolling red of the endless Simpson Desert with
its parallel combs of north-west to south-east

ridges and sandbanks, some reaching 90M high and 200k long, making it almost impossible to travel in any other direction.

Focusing his binoculars, he picked up a small hunting pack of dingoes delicately pacing a low ridge in a single file. The dominant female and her mate leading, with a faint wind in his face, they had not scented him. They were heading towards the waterhole where he knew from Jiemba, that some of his cattle had met an untimely end.

He hefted his rifle, sighting on the dingoes with the high-definition rangefinder of his Hawke 8-25 scope. He studied the animals through the floating air motes and heat distortion. They were moving lazily, ears down and back, unhurried, approx. 7 hundred meters away. Too far for a shot even though that was not his intention.

His rifle was a Bull-barrel 270 Cal on a Mauser Bolt action with a laminated walnut stock dressed with an old leather sling bequeathed to him by his Father. The rifle would shoot a 100mm group at 700M, dropping 60mm, but he had nothing to prove, and he had other things to be concerned with.

The sun was behind him as the blazing afternoon wore on and, somewhere out there in front of him on the desert floor, his shadow moved imperceptibly. He hefted his rifle and shoulder pack and slid down in the gravel below the ridge line, then got to his feet, heading downwards.

When he got near to the foot of the ridge he looked again for the dingoes, they had not moved far but were still 500M away, pacing slow.

He wallowed down the gravel scree after them towards the waterhole hidden in a low haze of dull yellow cat claw pollen.

200M on and he bellied up on some smooth warm rocks, cradling the rifle and sighting through the scope. Strangely, the dingoes had now grouped, heads up, alert, ears up and forward, on both sides of their Leader. They were looking away from him and towards the waterhole. He felt vaguely troubled by what he was seeing, his senses prickled, involuntarily pushing off the rifle's safety catch.

In the valley below, the late sun glinted off the muddy waterhole, and laying randomly around were seven swollen flyblown carcasses of his cattle.

He stiffened, wiping away sweat and slowly traversing the high-def scope across the humped bodies of each of his dead cattle. They were all eviscerated, their intestines and ripped flesh spread across the mud and in the water in a primeval demonstration of a savage ferocity that he had never seen before.

He swung the scope back to the dingoes, the fine optics crystallizing into sharp focus. The animals were uncharacteristically standing totally still, staring transfixed towards the bodies of the cattle, noses raised, immobile.

Billy Bob was shocked, dingoes would normally be now stampeding towards meat, totally focused on a personal feeding frenzy, fighting each other for position, all caution gone.

This wasn't happening - weird or what?

Without warning, the dingoes suddenly bolted en masse away from the water hole, jinking, and yowling away in spurts of orange dust. Initially they ran towards him, then leaning gracefully away, passed him at full speed less the 100m away but strangely, didn't seem to register or look at him.

He watched them stream out of his sight, amazed, then they were gone, orange dust settling slowly, and the waterhole silent and empty in the falling afternoon sun as if nothing had occurred there at all. A rotten putrid iron scent he could not identify hung faintly in the air; it unsettled him.

Billy Bob remained in position, watchful, for several minutes, then stood, picked up his rifle and made it safe. It took him 15 minutes to make his way carefully closer to the waterhole. He kept looking back at where the dingoes had gone but saw nothing more of them. 50M away from the remains of his cattle something disquieting made him pause, even though he hadn't seen a movement. He sat on his shoulder pack for 20 minutes cradling his rifle, his back to a rock, sniffing the air, senses tingling, heart rate high. Something else was out there. For the first time in his 46 years living and hunting in the remote outback, a reptilian curl of fear squirmed in his gut.

The body of the cow furthest away from him was maybe 70M. Suddenly blowflies scattered, and it moved grotesquely, its ripped belly distorting and heaving wetly outwards, entrails flopping, a putrid iron stench reaching him. He watched in total horror as the shape of the dead cow changed, grew bigger. Then in a wet slosh of entrails, a black creature with a huge head, slippery with gore, emerged hunched and powerful. It raised its head, jaws dripping, shook it, and looked at Billy Bob for a long moment, white marble eyes flaring, then looked slowly around in all directions as if considering. Then abruptly with mind-numbing speed and power, took off, disappearing over a ridge leaving orange dust and the ferrous brass stink of blood hanging in the still air.

Billy Bob watched it go for a heartbeat, then lurched to his feet cursing, his hunter instincts surging. Wet with sweat he hiked fast along a sandbank with his rifle held high, knowing his heart rate was too fast for accurate shooting.

By the direction the creature had gone, he knew it would be crossing the parallel horizontal ridges, so it would offer a diminishing target at least once. He sank to his knees and settled himself for a shot, watching the nearest skyline point 100M away.

A movement. The creature suddenly broke the skyline, head down, its back hunched in a powerful bear-like shamble, but it was no bear. The rifle bucked in his hands and through the scope he saw a vertical plume of pale orange dust kick up from the hardpan, he cursed, missed. The long flat thud of the shot rolling across the ridges, repeating, fading. The creature was now out of his sight.

He leaned and spat with disgust, then lurched towards the next ridge, knowing his next shot, if indeed one presented itself, would be almost impossible. He crested the ridge expecting nothing, the creature was in front of him, injured, shuffling away from him in clear sight, limping, dragging its rear leg. He realized that his bullet must have skipped off the desert hard pan floor and hit the creature in the rear quarters.

The next shot was easy one. 50M, zero hold-over. Black fur and blood mist flew off the creature as the thud of his second shot rolled away. The impact of the heavy slug bounced the creature over several times, and it lay snorting, kicking up dust, making an unearthly mewling sound. Billy Bob did not approach the creature, but sat holding the scope onto it for a hour until his muscle-tone failed as the light began to drop.

Eventually it was dusk, and the creature lay still and quiet. He kept his rifle on his knee pointing down-range, the centre-aim point of the scope showing bright red. He rummaged for his sat phone.

On Sat-phone

> BILLY BOB MASON
> Louise, it's me.
> (A beat, listening)
> Look don't start on that now! OK, PJ it is then.

> No, I'm fine, no worries, it's OK. Look you need to come get me first thing. I'm at the MIKIRI waterhole half-way between Cordillo and Durham station. 50 miles south-east of you. Map reference 26.50N * 141.09N.
> (A beat, listening)
> I've shot something, I have no fucking idea what. I'm pretty sure it's dead

but I ain't going no-where near
it until you guys get here in the
morning - come mob-handed please,
this thing looks heavy.
(A beat, listening)
What I said before, I seriously do not
know what it is, but it slaughtered
seven cows before they could run,
and it scared the living shit out of
a hunting pack of dingoes who ain't
scared of nothing I know of, so I
ain't gonna take any risks with this
thing - whatever it is.
(A beat, listening)
OK, yes. Just get here please,
first light will be good. I don't
particularly want to spend the night
out here, but it's too late to get
back home safely now.
(A beat, listening)
See you in the morning babe, I mean
PJ - sorry.

Billy Bob retreated with care keeping an eye
on the still dark hump of the creature. A few
hundred meters away he put his back against a
warm rock and hunkered down. A swollen moon
was up bathing the desert in blue light with
scudding cloud shadows crossing the desert
floor. He sat with his boots crossed, feeling his
body subside, the rifle on his knees, sipping
water from his canteen, dreading the long night
in front of him.

He turned slowly, watching the black rim of the
land against the spectacular Milky Way as the
desert around him cooled.

As his body calmed the only thing he could hear was the beating of his own heart. He pulled a sleeping bag around and hunkered down. A long time later in the small hours an unearthly wail began somewhere out in the desert, starting low, then rising and falling away as if its owner was falling into an abyss.

Billy Bob shuddered in the cold, clutched his rifle and waited for the dawn.

FADE TO BLACK

EXT. DOWN-MARKET AREA. ADELAIDE, STH AUSTRALIA. DAY

Adelaide baked in 38c. The shops on the sunny side of the streets closed and shuttered. The Holden Kingswood saloon nosed through moderate traffic along Grove Avenue, taking a right onto Commercial St, cruised for a shaded parking place, gave up, finally parking in the sun.

JOHN

Fuck its hot. How long you gonna be?

Sarah, impossibly cool in the relentless mid-afternoon heat, rummaged in a voluminous bag, producing a black velvet wrapped package.

SARAH

Not sure, I guess he'll have to take measurements before he can alter it.

JOHN
(Grimace)

OK yes. Its OK, I can wait here, but I'll cook.

Sarah looked away, uncertain, perplexed.

                    SARAH
          Look, I can leave it...

                    JOHN
               (Snappy)
          It's fine! We are here now. Get it
          sorted babe.

Sarah got out of the car, stood by the open
window, leaning in, a manicured hand on the
sill.

                    SARAH
          I'll be as quick as I can Johnny, OK

John gestured, didn't answer and after a beat
she hurried off. He watched her along the
sidewalk thinking she looks bloody good still,
her dancer's natural athleticism and grace, tied
back hair bouncing like a teenager's in an 80s
rock movie.

He kicked back into the seat, glad of the sheep
fleece seat covers protecting his back and legs
from the fierce 38c heat. Waiting in the car
without it would have been impossible.

The street in the industrial area was quiet.
He watched an old BMW crawl along towards
him from the intersection. He idly anticipated
where it would stop, 80M away, just past an
alleyway and several innocuous doorways. It
lazily three-pointed and faced away towards
the intersection. A young Aboriginal in an
oversized BEARS T-shirt and tattered jeans
got out of the near-side, hands thrust deep
in pockets, standing looking both ways, then

strolled away from him, disappearing into a doorway. John noticed the car was idling, white smoke drifting sideways from the exhaust, air-con running.

In the mirror, John saw two white guys leaning, smoking in the shade outside a warehouse. One of them shouldered away from the wall, grinding out his cigarette stub, lighting another, and ambled towards John's Holden, passing it without a glance, walked on and leaned against the BMW. The window silently rolled down. The driver was a white man, mid-thirties, white shirt with sleeves ripped away, a tattoo, gold flashing. The two men talked for two minutes, then the smoker handed over some cash, folded over once. The driver palmed the bills like an expert, then gestured further down the street to the innocuous doors. The smoker ambled away, the window rolled back up to preserve the air-con. The street was still again, the heat shimmering, relentless.

John noticed that the BMW driver was watching him in his mirror, saw him reach up, adjusting it, so he could watch from his semi-reclined position. After a few minutes, the driver stirred, then got out of the car, stood beside it, tossing back a mane of jet-black hair, adjusting a pony tail, all the while staring along the pavement at John.

The air crackled with sudden tension; John shivered. The driver was a testament to leashed power, solitary, separate from the world around him, yet entirely capable of ruling it.

John glanced at his watch, checked the street where Sarah had gone. No sign.

A movement. The younger Aboriginal in the BEARS T shirt emerged from the doorway, looked both ways, and ambled back to the car. The two men conferred, both looking at John, then they get into the BMW, the driver athletic, his powerful back muscles flexing as he pulled the door shut. The car rumbled, deep, animalist, then it moved away majestically towards the intersection.

John leaned back into the sheepskin, feeling his tension ebb away in a shaky outward breath. Somewhere across town, the wail of emergency sirens sounds, diminishing into distance. Silence again.

The sudden thud of vehicle tires over a manhole cover behind, then a multi-coloured Ford pickup passed slow, the roar of suppressed power loud, then diminishing. The driver leaned over, looked curiously across at John. The car slowed, it looked like it would pull into the kerb, then inexplicably, it pulled back to the centre of the street, accelerated away and indicated left at the intersection 200M away, orange indicator pulsing.

John's watch showed that Sarah had been 25 minutes.

A movement flickered in his mirror, noise, and the sound of someone running. A man emerged at speed from an alleyway, turned hard towards John's car, pounded down the sidewalk, running strangely wide-legged, his arms crossed over, hugging his chest.

John moved in his seat, suddenly alert, leaned into his mirror. The man came level with the car and suddenly wrenched open the near-side door, tumbled into the passenger seat. He and John stared into each other's faces with shock - horror.

                    JOHN
          What the fuck... Who...

                    RUNNING MAN
               (Urgently)
          Get fucking moving man...

John did a double take at the man as he hugged his chest. There was fresh blood covering his entire chest area, and down his tattered blue jeans. At closer glance, the man was hugging a large slab of fresh abattoir meat to his chest, white bones showing stark, translucent meat, blueish beneath the blood.

                    RUNNING MAN (CONT'D)
          Who the fuck are you mate? You
          are not...
               (A beat, then looking behind)
          Oh fuck, fuck, fuck...

The man wrenched open the door again, legs pistoning him out onto the pavement. He ran towards the intersection with the same comical wide-legged gait as before, hugging the slab of meat. John watched him as he disappeared into an alleyway.

John reached over to close his car door as an angry Chinese man with a meat cleaver appeared. The man grabbed the door, peering fiercely down into the car at John.

John pointed along the street.

                    JOHN
        There, he went along there, then into
        the alleyway to the right.

The Chinese man slammed the car door with
unnecessary force, and ran along the street,
boots pounding, disappeared into the same
alleyway as the meat thief. John leaned back
into the sheepskin seat cover, eyes stinging
with sweat, heart thumping.

Sarah appeared on the street, cool, fresh, and
feminine, pony-tail dancing, smiling brightly,
her boots tapping as she pulled open the
passenger door. She dropped gracefully into the
seat in an intoxicating cloud of Chanel No5.

                    SARAH
        I wasn't too long, was I? Sorry baby.

She paused, sensing something, eyes wide,
searching John's, glancing both ways.

                 SARAH (CONT'D)
        What...? are you OK?

John checked his mirror, pulled out into the
street, pulling the car in a squealing U-turn
on the hot bitumen. He drove away from the
intersection, turned left into Sherrington St,
hunched down watching the mirror.

                 SARAH (CONT'D)
            (Buckling up)
        John, what the hell? You are acting
        very strange. What's going on?

                    JOHN
          (Testy)
     There's nothing going on, absolutely
     nothing.
          (A beat)
     Did you get your fucking bracelet
     sorted out then?
          (A beat, then more reasonable
          tone)
     Sorry, baby, it's been so bloody hot.
     Did you get everything sorted?

Sarah leaned back, crossing an elegant leg,
placing her hand flat to her knee, critically
examined her newly fitted bracelet.

                    SARAH
     Looks good huh.

                              FADE OUT

EXT. UPPER SHEEN RD. WEST LONDON. DAY.

The Bentley slid smoothly to the kerb next to
Sheen Rd Tube entrance. Andrei Lebov (56) got
out and stretched, waving away the driver who
was half out of his door.

                 ANDREI LEBOV
     Cruise around, I'll ring you.

The driver closed his door and the car merged
into the West London melee, indicators and
brake lights pulsing. Andrei pulled his coat
around him, crossed the pavement, and entered
a glass door under a shopfront named 'Tandoori
Knights'.

He passed straight through the sparsely populated restaurant area and through sprung doors into the kitchen. It was stifling. The extractor fan wheezed, pans sizzled, garlic and ginger competed with the smell of frying onions, shouts, and metallic clashes everywhere. He made eye contact with a pony-tailed wok-slinger who indicated a doorway with a sideways nod.

The back alley led to a building site where a long-coated thug leaned against a door-less opening in a concrete wall. He walked past the man without a word, stepping into a grated site escalator. The lift sped rapidly upwards through floors of frenetic construction activity, finally, noise dropping away, through three floors of empty concrete framework, open to the London roof-scape.

Andrei exited the escalator, walking to a windy unprotected edge and gazed out over the grey rain-swept city. He lit a cigarette and looked down at his shoes, stepping purposely forward, the toes over the dizzy edge of the 17th floor. A voice behind him.

                    SERGEI
     Boss, you OK?
          (A beat. Respectfully)
     You shouldn't stand so near that edge.
     They haven't put any safety rails up
     here yet.

                 ANDREI LEBOV
          (Vague smile)
     It would be so easy Sergei, just a
     single step forward huh? All this
     shit would just disappear

Sergei stood respectfully several feet away, he didn't respond. Somewhere nearby came a muted scream, quickly cut off. Andrei turned, catching Sergei's eye.

                    SERGEI
            (Sideways twitch of head)
        This way Boss, over here

Sergei walked to a hanging plastic curtain, holding it back for his boss to walk through. Andrei stopped before he got there, his cigarette glowing bright red, narrowed eyes searching Sergei's face. Sergei shook his head minutely, his eyes casting downwards.

                ANDREI LEBOV
            (Quietly, resigned)
        Sergei, I spend my days now coming
        to terms with the consequences of my
        deeds or trying. I'm weary of it my
        friend.

He turned slightly.

            ANDREI LEBOV (CONT'D)
        Over there is the abyss, my personal
        one. 17 floors straight down, I just
        gazed into it.

Andrei shook his head, stared sightlessly across the city landscape for several beats, then turned, ground out his cigarette. He nodded through the plastic sheet.

            ANDREI LEBOV (CONT'D)
        Is he any use to us at all?

Sergei shook his head again, eyes down.

                    17

                    ANDREI LEBOV (CONT'D)
Then get rid of him Sergei and
clean up.
          (A beat)
I'm going home, I don't want to look
at gore and shit today, I've had
enough.

He turned and walked a few steps, then paused,
glancing around at Sergei.

                    ANDREI LEBOV (CONT'D)
               (Thoughtfully)
He was quite a man you know Sergei,
back then. I met him out at Nerpiche,
a squalid corner of Russia where the
air stank of sewerage and families,
when they had a room, lived six or
seven to it, sleeping in shifts on
rattan mats and subsisting off little
more than rice and dal.
          (A beat)
They called him Uddam Sidarov in those
days, Uddam the Lion, which sounded
very impressive until you realized
that half the fucking country was
called Sidarov.

Andrei thrust his hands in his pockets as
another muted scream came through the plastic.

                    ANDREI LEBOV (CONT'D)
Uddam had come from the dirt-poor
province of Blihar, penniless with
nothing more than his own diligence,
a modicum of loyalty and a penchant
for slitting throats.

Together we rose to become kingpins of Moscow's trade in narcotics, prostitution, and a few other delectable activities.

Sergei had heard some of this before, but was tolerant and forgiving towards his boss, to whom he owed everything.

> ANDREI LEBOV (CONT'D)
> We met, aptly enough, in a street known locally as Cut-Throat Alley. A foul-smelling passage of flophouses and hovels, where indolent dogs roamed in packs and itinerant cows grazed on the bounty of an open rubbish tip.
> (A beat)
> It was all a long time ago Sergei. Now here we are in London dressed in three-piece suits, and now that fucker, my old partner, in there is Adam Stevens, the betrayer of his old friends, his partner, and his mentor.
> (A beat, resigned)
> Enough! Finish it Sergei! Take him down.

Andrei walked wearily towards the escalator.

Sergei watched him go, a troubled look on his handsome face. Then he turned and walked resolutely through the plastic curtain, letting it fall behind him.

FADE TO BLACK

EXT. LE CINQ RESTAURANT. MAYFAIR. LONDON. DAY

Andrei Lebov exited his limo outside the Le Cinq Restaurant in Mayfair. He nodded imperiously to the uniformed doorman and entered the reception area, immediately turning right, he stepped onto soft carpeting, into a broad space of high ceilings, gilt, shades of taupe, biscuit and 'fuck you' colours. The Le Cinq Restaurant is designed for people for whom feelings of guilt are unfamiliar, and who don't expect menus to display prices.

Andrei paused, glanced around the half-filled room, raised a finger, and was immediately approached by an earnest waiter, he conferred, and was led to a table in a semi-private alcove. Andrei sat where the chair was proffered, but then got up and sat in another seat facing the main room with his back to the wall. After a beat an iced Perrier with lime was placed before him. Andrei sipped, leaned back, his hooded eyes sweeping the room.

From the side of the room, an elderly dark suited man appeared, urbane and self-assured. He moved smoothly between the tables and slid into a seat facing Andrei. They exchanged a formal nod and a perfunctory handshake. The two men appraised each other briefly, Andrei leaned in slightly.

>   ANDREI LEBOV
>   (Quietly)
>   I am told the flaky brioche is
>   compelling Emanuel, with salted
>   butter, Irish of course.

EMANUEL DEGERE
(Faint smile)
I hope the things we will discuss
today will not take away your appetite
my dear friend.

ANDREI LEBOV
(Shrugging)
The last time I was here I was less
than impressed anyway. The stickiness
of the scallop mush made my lips
purse like a cat's arse that brushed
against nettles.

Emanuel Degere allowed himself a vague smile
as the waiter appeared. They ordered a light
lunch of eye-wateringly expensive titbits and
wine from a list that included bottles at £1500.

Neither man inquired about prices.

ANDREI LEBOV (CONT'D)
(Hands flat to the tabletop)
So, Emanuel, I imagine that you are
the bearer of news?

Emanuel paused, his eyes searching his companions
earnestly.

EMANUEL DEGERE
Perhaps my friend, we should eat first,
then discuss our business afterwards.

ANDREI LEBOV
Ah... as bad as that Emanuel. I
suspected as much.
(A beat)

No, I think we should not feel
restricted in our conversations, or
our appetite.
          (A beat)
Be frank and forthright and to hell
with the consequences Emanuel. Let us
eat, drink and be merry, for tomorrow
we die.

Emanuel Degere glanced around the restaurant,
shifted in his seat, eyes on Andrei, both hands
flat to the tabletop.

                    EMANUEL DEGERE
     Stage 3 my friend. I am so sorry. It
     is not yet in the lymph nodes, but
     soon maybe.

Andrei acknowledged the comment with an arched
brow, his vaguely amused gaze sweeping several
'older man - younger women' tables in the room
behind Emanuel.

                    ANDREI LEBOV
     So.. there it is then.
          (A beat)
     How long do I have?

Degere was uncomfortable, taking off his glasses
to polish them.

                    EMANUEL DEGERE
          (Clearing his throat)
     Well... I don't really...
          (A beat)
     Andrei, our task is to slow things
     down you know, exert some controls
     here and there, and remove a little
     heat from this situation.

ANDREI LEBOV
(Flatly)
How fucking long Emanuel?

EMANUEL DEGERE
(Uncertain)
6 months maybe, after that you will
not be moving around much.

Andrei held his companion's gaze for a beat,
considering, then he tasted his wine with a
grimace, placed his glass carefully down and
dabbed his lips as the waiter arrived with food.
Andrei gazed critically at his plate; the waiter
hovered. Eventually Andrei pointed disdainfully
downwards at his plate.

ANDREI LEBOV
What pray, is this green stuff?

The waiter leaned over to look, then straightened.

WAITER
It is frozen parsley powder Sir. Its
very nice.

Andrei delicately tasted it, then fixed the
waiter with a glare.

ANDREI LEBOV
(Sharply)
No, it isn't nice at all. It tastes of
grass clippings. Its one of the worst
things I have ever eaten.
(A beat)
In fact, this entire dish reminds me
of a fucking crime scene.
(Leaning back, gesturing)
Take it away.

Emanuel Degere winced at the exchange, then leaned back and pushed his own plate away. The chastened waiter apologized profusely, Andrei waved him away irritably, then turned back to Degere.

                    ANDREI LEBOV (CONT'D)
          Thank you for being so frank Dr
          Degere, and for meeting me away from
          your consulting rooms. I prefer to
          receive bad news directly, and alone
          with the bearer, and in a place of
          my own choosing.
                    (Smiling bitterly)
          I have a horror of bad news in written
          form. When someone tells you to your
          face, you hear it once, and that's
          it, done.

          When it is written, each time you read
          it you get the news again and again.

Emanuel Degere dabbed his lips and rose fluidly to his feet, his hand outstretched. Andrei took it, rising slightly. The two men locked eyes.

                    EMANUEL DEGERE
          Thank you for the lunch, Mr Lebov,
          again, I am very sorry Sir.

Dr Degere unobtrusively left the restaurant.

Andrei dropped back into his chair and watched him go. He raised his finger for the bill, the waiter spotted the signal immediately from across the room and moved smoothly towards Andrei through the tables, flicking through his notepad with a sad expression.

                                        FADE OUT

EXT. MAYFAIR. LONDON. 14 HALF MOON ST. NIGHT

14 Half Moon St has six above ground storeys of opulent luxury with a 3rd floor balcony looking over the street as well as a vast basement.

There was no kerb parking, so the driver pulled the limo to a soundless stop in the middle of the street and quickly got out to open the rear door before Andrei was able to stop him. The two men exchanged a curt nod, and Andrei walked to his front door, touching the fingerprint security button. The Bentley slid silently away, turning left along Curzon St.

The kitchen was dimly lit and spotless. Andrei glanced in, then went on up the stairs towards low volume music in the lounge on the 1st floor.

Ekaterina Lebov (30), former model, his wife of 7 years, rose fluidly from the low settee and enveloped him in Chanel No5 and a soft feminine embrace. She kissed him three times, on both cheeks then his mouth, her breath lightly in his face, then with her hands cupping both sides of his face, drew back and regarded him with concern, her beautiful eyes wide, questioning.

> EKATERINA LEBOV
> Have you spoken to Dr Degere yet Andrei?

Andrei's eyes dropped momentarily, and Ekaterina stiffened, her eyes filling with tears. She searched his eyes.

                    EKATERINA LEBOV (CONT'D)
          You have.
                    (A beat)
          And...

Andrei steered her gently towards the settee,
both sitting, knees together, her hands holding
both of his.

                    ANDREI LEBOV
          We have some time my love, it's not
          so bad...

Ekaterina drew back, her eyes flashing with
passion, her hand clenched tightly into a fist,
biting it, looking towards the dark window.

Andrei held still, waiting. In a blinding flash
of numbing violence, she hit him hard across
the face with a flat hand. As he reeled back
in shock, she rose to her feet with a heart-
breaking cry of anguish and pain

                    EKATERINA LEBOV
                    (Broken voice)
          This is where we blame people Andrei,
          the ones we think are somehow
          responsible, but there's no-one, is
          there. It's just you and me here.
                    (A beat)
          Just us Andrei.

Ekaterina drew away, facing him for a beat,
then shook her head and ran out of the room.
Somewhere a door slammed, and then the house
was quiet.

Andrei sat unmoving for a long time, alone in
the palatial silence. Then he rose and poured

3 fingers of fine vodka. He walked over to the window and gazed along the street to where the Third Church of Christ Scientist sat regally in upward orange light 300M away, its windows black and sightless like a skull.

FADE OUT

INT. 408 NELSON ROAD. PARA HILLS. ADELAIDE, SOUTH AUSTRALIA. MID-MORNING.

Endless roads of brick veneer homes, 4 beds and 2 bath, carports and pool with paved BBQ areas coated the rolling low wooded hills with a mosaic of muted colours, here and there a sports oval. The smells of roasting beef burnt grass and lawn cuttings drifting on the wind.

The high decibel drone of the motor-mower calling the faithful to worship the virtues of domesticity, conformity, consumerism and sex, drugs, and ABBA.

The Australian suburbs, pushing firmly out against the red-brown wilderness and momentarily winning. The suburban male stereotype busy polishing Holden estates, taking beers with the boys, marital sex on Saturday nights, furtive gropes, adulteries here and there, the occasional gambles on horses and lotteries and the worship ritual of the Sports Channel. Here and there flickering shadows in lounges of cops, robbers, car chases and advert jingles.

Suburbia, easy to denigrate and dismiss, nonetheless a hotbed of cultural diversity and intellectual energy, here and there merging with and celebrating the rich frontiers of ancient Australian philosophy and spirituality.

John Cantrell turned off the Main Northeast Road on the Para Hill ramp and rolled along Kesters Road at the speed limit. He pulled into the small parade of shops, left the engine and air-con running and dialled.

> JOHN
> It's me. In at Kesters shops. Anything?
>   (Listening)
> OK, be with you in twenty.

Cresting the hill on Kesters gave him a view of the house. All the traffic turning onto Nelson Rd had the same view through his dining room window. So much so that he had painted a huge multi-coloured target on the wall opposite the window. He looked at it now every time he came towards the junction, he imagined lots of drivers did.

He bumped the wheel marker in the carport and carried bits of shopping through into the kitchen, dumping them and walking immediately to the double door fridge. Sarah eyed him as she chopped salad ingredients.

> SARAH
> I remember when you'd kiss me before getting yourself a beer John Cantrell.

John dropped into a low chair, legs splayed, and drank.

                    JOHN
    Ah, you know I loves you baby. Want
    me to light the barbie?

He carried his drink and two steaks out to
the BBQ and performed the sacrificial ritual
of Australian suburbia, slapping them onto two
plates as Sarah arrived with salad and sauce.
They sat, chewing silently, then...

                 JOHN (CONT'D)
    That was weird you know, the
    other day...

                    SARAH
    Weird?

                    JOHN
    While you were in with the Jeweller
    sorting the bracelet. An ABBO feller
    hugging a massive side of raw meat
    tried to get in the car with me.
        (A beat)
    He must have pinched it from the
    Abattoir back up the road, then
    thought I was his getaway car.

Sarah chewed thoughtfully, regarded him.

                    SARAH
    Meat? Raw, you say? You never said
    anything at the time?

                    JOHN
    I know, it was hot, I was pretty damn
    fed up.
        (A beat)

Fucking massive chunk of meat though, covered his whole chest under his coat. Blood everywhere.
(A beat)
When he saw I wasn't his man he buggered off sharpish. A Chinaman chased him, but he was long gone I reckon.

                    SARAH
(Concerned)
It's rough down that area of town. Is there any blood in the car John?
(A beat, grimace)
Urgh...

                    JOHN
Don't think so, I'll have a look and sort it later babe. He wasn't in the car more'n a few seconds.

LATER; CAR PORT.

John opened the passenger side door and looked in the seat, then knelt, looking underneath. Something was under the seat, he crouched, reaching in, puffing, couldn't reach. Clicked the seat adjuster slide and the seat suddenly lurched back, skinning his knuckles.

He sat back, cursing, blowing on them. He got down again, reached under and managed to grab a bloody chunk of raw meat, obviously left there from the street incident. He looked distastefully at it, dropped it on the paving, sat looking ruefully at his blooded hand. He went to get some Dettol spray and cleaning equipment and a plaster for his bloody knuckles. Sara was ironing in the kitchen when he rummaged irritably under the sink.

                    SARAH
        What's up baby, you OK.

                    JOHN
        Skinned my fucking knuckles under
        the car seat.
                (Holding up his injured hand)
        Look...

She glanced briefly at his proffered hand, continued ironing, folding.

                    SARAH
        God, you are such a wimp John, I
        can't see anything.

He sat back on the kitchen floor looking astonished at his hand, flexing his fingers. The broken skin was gone. He could feel a slight fizzing sensation where the injury had been, then that was gone, but it was healed, as if it had never happened.

                    JOHN
                (Totally perplexed)
        Fuck me...

John looked from Sarah and back to his knuckles, eyes wide.

                    JOHN (CONT'D)
        I swear...

                    SARAH
        Oh John. Bloody men, you are all
        soft. Was there any blood in the car?

                    JOHN
     Yes, a small chunk of raw meat was
     under the seat. I'll sort it.

                    SARAH
     Wrap it in foil before you chuck it
     in the bin John. I don't want rats
     around here.

John went back to the carport. The car door
stood open. Next door's cat sat a meter away
looking at the piece of raw meat, then back at
him, its eyes luminous and hostile.

He knelt, picked up the meat and tossed it
towards the cat.

                    JOHN
     Hello Genghis. Here you are mate.

The animal recoiled, snarling, its back arched,
then ran off. John stared after it, surprised.
He wrapped the piece of meat in foil and threw
it in the bin, then bent back to the task of
cleaning up the car.

Above him, as he worked, Genghis the cat paced
silently along the roof of the carport, its
hackles raised, eyes alert and watchful. It sat,
tail swishing, looking down the row of dustbins,
particularly one of them. A low primordial yowl
coming from the back of its throat.

                                FADE TO BLACK

INT. NEWS MEDIA ARTICLE.

CHANNEL 9 NEWS UPDATE:

'BUNYIP' SIGHTING (Headline across screen)

> CHANNEL 9 REPORTER
> (Excited, gesturing to headline
> behind him)

FIRST DOCUMENTED BY THE ABORIGINAL PEOPLE IN STORIES OF THE DREAM-TIME TENS OF THOUSANDS OF YEARS AGO, 'SIGHTINGS' OF THE BUNYIP WERE ALSO RECORDED BY ENGLISH SETTLERS IN THE 1800S.

OVER TIME, DESCRIPTIONS OF THE LEGENDARY BUNYIP HAVE TAKEN MANY FORMS, FROM A MYTHICAL DESERT BEAST TO A FEROCIOUS NOCTURNAL AMPHIBIAN THAT LURKS IN SWAMPS, BILLABONGS AND RIVERBEDS.

> (A beat, more serious)

TODAY, CHANNEL 9 CAN REPORT UNCORROBORATED BREAKING NEWS FROM THE BROKEN HILL REGION OF SOUTH AUSTRALIA, NOT ONLY HAS A BUNYIP BEEN SIGHTED BY SEVERAL PEOPLE ON THE WAGADOO CATTLE STATION, WE HAVE UNCONFIRMED REPORTS THAT IT WAS SHOT BY A STOCKMAN AFTER IT SAVAGED SEVERAL LONGHORN CATTLE.

CHANNEL NINE NEWS ARTICLE.

NEWSREEL FOOTAGE

Newsreel footage of altercations between new media teams, photographers, reporters scrumming with several scary looking armed men standing across the main gateway to Cordillo Downs Cattle Station preventing all entry. Police presence can be seen with flashing blue lights, but the police officers are standing back from the media circus.

A tall man in cowboy clothing and sweat stained Stetson stood aloof in the shade of a veranda. He was smoking, watching the activity with distaste, one hand in his pocket.

> CHANNEL 9 REPORTER
> (Shouting to him)
> You Sir, can we speak to you please? Do you know anything about this creature? Did you shoot it?

The reporter and crew are jostled back by uniformed police, the screen showing scuffling, people protesting.

> CHANNEL 9 ON-SITE REPORTER
> (Excited)
> We are unable to show verified footage of this creature or speak to any actual witnesses at this time, because our reporters are unable to gain access to the farm property.
> (A beat)
> We will continue to pursue this Breaking News article, watch this space.

BACK TO STUDIO

> CHANNEL 9 STUDIO REPORTER
> According to Australian Aboriginal religion and mythology, the word

'Bunyip,' was originated by the Wemba-Wemba tribespeople of northern Victoria, and is roughly translated to 'scary monster' or an 'evil spirit.' According to their legend the bush-dwelling creature is allegedly a monster that feasts on humans, whose cries can be heard in the Outback come nightfall.

The Reporter turns to two other people sitting by his desk.

CHANNEL 9 REPORTER
We have Professor Bruce Reynolds, anthropologist from the University of NSW with us, and also, Birani Pemba from the Dangali Tribe whose indigenous land is close to where the sighting took place.
(A beat, consulting notes)
Professor, can I come to you first. What do you make of all this? Can this incredible story have any truth in it?

PROFESSOR BRUCE REYNOLDS
(Portentous, full of self-importance)
Good day to you.
(A beat, clearing throat)
Nowadays, we scientists and researchers believe that it's possible the Bunyip could be related back in the Jurassic period to the now-extinct giant wombat known as the 'DIPROTODON' that lurked in the inland waters 20,000 years ago, and maybe the haunting sounds that have often been heard,

perhaps come from bittern marsh birds when that region is in flood during wet seasons.

I think this situation may simply be a case of mistaken identity.
        (Smiling indulgently)
Look, there's nothing really new about this sort of thing, sightings etc, back in the day, early European settlers thought kangaroos were giant rabbits, and quite mystical in their own right.
        (Shrugging)
So, in this particular case I think...

                CHANNEL 9 REPORTER
        (Flatly)
So, I take it Professor, from your tone, that you are very sceptical of this sighting?

                PROFESSOR BRUCE REYNOLDS
Well, I didn't exactly say...

                CHANNEL 9 REPORTER
        (Turning away)
Thank you, Professor, can I turn to you Birani Pemba. As a politician and representative for the Native Australian community, what is your take on this breaking story?

                BIRANI PEMBA
        (Slow, thoughtful)
Well, we are not surprised by this, why would we be? But we are very sad for a variety of reasons.
        (A beat)

We are very concerned that it seems that a Bunyip has been shot.
> (Leaning direct to camera, very serious)

It is very important that the body of the Bunyip must be returned to us immediately and must not be interfered with or dissected in any way. That could potentially create a very dangerous situation.

CHANNEL 9 REPORTER

Wow, so Mr Pemba, you have no doubts at all that this news is credible? And more, you are asking that the body of the alleged creature must be 'returned' to you intact. I assume by that you mean returned to your Tribe.
> (Sideways smirk into camera)

Why should the Bunyip be returned to you? And furthermore, why returned intact? Because I assume that scientists will want to examine the remains of this creature in some detail...

BIRANI PEMBA

> (Shrugging, defensive)

The Bunyip is part of our cultural heritage. It exists for us in the same way that you have cats and dogs and other creatures.
> (A beat, vaguely bored)

But the Bunyip does not exist in your timeframe as you recognize it.

It is timeless, and it's shape and form can be many.

The camera cuts to the faces of the newscaster and the academic, both are having some difficulty keeping straight faces.

                    BIRANI PEMBA (CONT'D)
Whatever shape it had when and if it was killed, will be very significant, and could possibly be extremely dangerous to anyone in contact with its remains, in particular its flesh and blood.

                    CHANNEL 9 REPORTER
OK, dangerous you say Mr Pemba? How can a dead body of this alleged creature, or any other dead creature for that matter, be dangerous to humans?

                    BIRANI PEMBA
                    (Patiently)
Well, the Bunyip has poisonous fangs, but I am referring more to the Bunyip's spirit, and its blood and its flesh. They have powers and effects that are beyond the understanding of non-indigenous people.

                    CHANNEL 9 REPORTER
                    (Mock serious look to camera)
Effects? Beyond our understanding?

By 'our' I assume you mean non-Aboriginal people? And what do you mean by power? Do you mean healing power?

BIRANI PEMBA
(Becoming more defensive)
Hmm, yes possibly, but other immense
and uncontrollable powers.
(A beat)
There is a spiritual harmony, an ebb
and flow to the affairs of man and
beast. They are all connected.

Hundreds of years ago your westernized
science took a wrong turn and has
proceeded along that path ever since.
Your established perspectives leave
you lost and without direction, and
now, in hopeless convulsions of
self-protection, you pour scorn on
anything that you don't understand
and doesn't fit with your pathetic
infantile models.

Birani Pemba moved more upright in his seat,
his eyes flashing dangerously at the Newscaster
and the Academic.

BIRANI PEMBA (CONT'D)
You are both glaring examples of this
sublime ignorance, and you have my
pity.
(A beat)
The return of the Bunyip to our people
immediately, and intact, is vital to
the continued peace and existence of
all Australians.

Its body must be purified by us and
made safe immediately.
(a beat, losing interest)
Otherwise, I cannot predict what
might happen.

                    CHANNEL 9 REPORTER
           (Smirking conspiratorially to
           camera)
      Well folks, there we have it.

      Channel 9, as always, brings you the
      latest and the best in Australia's
      breaking news.
           (Full face to camera)
      While the increasingly vexed Bunyip
      debate rages on, the mystery of the
      creature from Australia's dark past
      has become a central part of today's
      news. More on this developing story
      later.

INT. 408 NELSON ROAD. PARA HILLS. LOUNGE. NIGHT.

Sara and John sat comfortably, feet up. John
dozed while Sarah gazed fascinated at the TV,
willing him to wake up.

INT. 14 HALF MOON STREET. MAYFAIR LONDON. LOUNGE. NIGHT.

Ekaterina Lebov watched her husband sleep, his
head lolling to one side. The room was mainly
dark, the only light coming from the silent TV.
She noticed a syndicated NEWS article playing
from Channel 9 Australia. She reached for the
remote, flicking on the sound, but was too late.
A flicker of annoyance crossed her face.

EXT. CORDILLO DOWNS HOMESTEAD. SIMPSON DESERT. VERANDA. NIGHT.

Billy Bob Mason rocked back cracked a cold beer and drank deeply. His boots crossed in front of a portable TV. For a moment there he had seen himself on it, cool and aloof standing under this same veranda.

Over the handrail of his veranda, he could see the lights and hear the media encampment buzzing with unabated activity and excitement two hundred meters away outside his fence.

To his right, separated from the media camp, a smaller and quieter encampment of police cars and panel vans. From time to time the wind bringing snatches of radio communications.

By his gate, two quietly serious men in dark suits leaned, sharing cigarettes. Their faces illuminated briefly as a match flared.

They were both looking at him.

EXT. 408 NELSON ROAD. PARA HILLS. ADELAIDE. NIGHT.

The house was dark, flickering TV light showing in the lounge window.

On the roof of the carport, Genghis the cat sat staring at the dustbins with huge luminous eyes, claws slowly and rhythmically kneading the bitumen roof, tail out in a straight rigid line.

DISSOLVE TO:

4 HRS LATER. NIGHT.

John awoke, something stellar and alien in his head. The time showed 0251 on the digital clock on his bedside table. He lay there looking at the ceiling, the orange streetlight bathing the room in faint warm light like a summer moon.

He swung his feet from under the cover and sat up. He looked at Sarah's naked back, her hair spread across the pillow. He reached and pulled the blanket up and over her shoulder, got up and padded into the kitchen.

The kitchen was dark except for pilot lights here and there. Blue light spilled across the floor as he opened the fridge reaching for iced water. He took the jar of water, unscrewed the cap and stood there drinking in the brief cold of the open fridge door gazing down Kesters Rd. He stood there a long time. The residential area was quiet, steeped in orange streetlights and a pale moon.

He studied an old Holden FJ Flat bed parked at the kerb 30M away, it didn't belong to anyone he knew in the vicinity. As he looked an ABORIGINAL male got out and leaned, both hands in pockets, looking towards him.

A cold curl of familiarity flickered in his gut as the man met his eyes, but it was too dark, after a beat the man got back in the car, let off the handbrake and coasted silently down Kesters Rd hill towards the shops.

In the distance, the lights of the FJ illuminated, and he heard the faint rumble of a Hemi500 engine as power came on. He watched the lights out of sight. Momentarily red taillights pulsed as the car took the Main NE Rd ramp towards the city.

John realized his hand was numb from the cold glass. On an impulse he leaned across to check his car was still parked in the carport. On the car-port roof, silhouetted against the moonlit sky sat Genghis, next door's ubiquitous tomcat.

He watched the cat thoughtfully for several beats finishing his cold drink, then padded back to the bedroom.

EXT. SIMPSON DESERT OUTBACK. STH AUSTRALIA. NIGHT

Birani Pemba drove north all night towards desolate outback in a Ford pickup truck. City lights dropped incrementally away until it was just his probing headlights out there, and the black bitumen rushing towards him.

Somewhere near the dawn he took a long sweeping right-hander and crossed a dried-out riverbed onto a concrete bridge gleaming white in the moonlight. He pulled the truck to a halt, turned off the lights, shut the door and walked stiffly around in front of the vehicle as the headlights slowly died. He stood leaning against the bull-bar, the cooling engine ticking and creaking. He was unsettled and wasn't sure why.

He pulled his pouch out of a hip pocket, rolled, lit-up and dragged pungent smoke deep as he watched the first streaks of iridescent violet, orange light over a blue reservoir. Beyond, moonlit gleamed on twin lines of railroad track over to the east.

A sudden growing rush of thunderous noise spun him around. A west-bound 27-meter Semi-Truck covered in lights was rolling fast around the long curve towards the bridge. It downshifted and swept over the bridge, the sound changing, then changing back as it hit bitumen again.

The driver saw him and leaned out of his window.

                    DRIVER
          (Shouting)
     Don't jump son, she ain't worth it.

Birani Pemba, rocking back in the side blast wave of hot displaced air, flashed a grin and waved, loving the cross-cultural spontaneity of the moment.

The big overland truck flashed both indicators, wailed its horn, and drew away west into darker skies, its massive noise and illuminated bulk diminishing into the ground as if it was never there.

Birani Pemba stood there smoking in the sudden silence and waited for the earth to turn, bringing dawn. He seethed in the cusp of his spiritual aboriginal culture, and his emerging westernized identity, and he loved them both intensely.

After a while, he realized his dark mood had lifted, he flicked his stub away, streaking red over the rail and down into the riverbed below, exploding in a shower of red sparks. He took a long breath and climbed back in the pickup and drove north towards Cordillo Downs, violet sky turning to deep orange over his left shoulder.

FADE OUT

TV. CHANNEL 9 BREAKFAST SHOW. MORNING

CHANNEL 9 PRESENTER
G'Day Ozzie's!

This is Channel 9 bringing South Australians gently into a new day. We are heading for a 39c high later today, the temperature right now is a balmy 22c with 18% humidity. We have a range of exciting guests dropping in all morning, but before that we go to our newsroom for a morning News Update.

Shifting icons, music, and flashes of news footage, cutting to a serious faced newscaster shuffling paper, looking offscreen, then realizing he is live.

C9 NEWSCASTER
Good morning, this is C9's World at 0700am.
(A beat, intense stare into screen)
Whatever the Australian voters' political hue, Tory blue, Labour red or Lib-Dem orange, these days it always ends up green-tinged.

All the parties in their different ways have and are using their positions to argue that everyone must go further

and faster towards achieving NET CARBON ZERO as the planet heats up and weather patterns become increasingly unstable.
(A beat, consulting notes)
These views are not shared by everyone.

Others believe that westernized governments are creating massive economic damage in trying to solve a climate change problem that is not man-made at all, and we are simply experiencing natural planetary cycles of warming and cooling that have taken place since the dawn of time.

When you add that 71% of the planet is covered with water, and humans occupy a tiny 9% of the remaining 29% of land above water, then they may indeed have a point.
(A beat)
Around the fringes of this heated, and I use the word advisedly, discussion, the environmentalist bogeymen, various scientific experts, and Green Campaigners vie with each other to befuddle the public with acronyms, jargon, fear, and even worse, statistics. Trying in their various ways, to over-ride democratic legislature and coordinate an increasingly wide range of alternative global actions and protests.
(A beat)
Against this frenetic clamour it is no wonder that a story rooted in Australia's primal history, some would

use the words Australia's Dreamtime,
has captured the World's attention.

The screen cuts to a high circling drone shot of
a remote ranch in flat brown scrubland. Outside
the perimeter fence are dozens of 4*4 vehicles,
panel vans, blue flashing police cars laying
siege across the long double gates.

VOICE OVER

>   C9 NEWSCASTER (CONT'D)
> This is the Cordillo Downs Cattle
> Station in the southern Simpson
> desert 100 miles shy of Birdsville
> at the hot end of South Australia.
>   (A beat)
> 3 days ago, a Cattleman, William
> Robert Mason, known locally as Billy-
> Bob, investigated the mysterious
> death of seven of his cattle near a
> remote waterhole, known locally as
> the MIKIRI waterhole.
>   (A beat)
> It seems that in the course of his
> investigations, Mr Mason disturbed
> a strange creature, which he
> subsequently shot dead.

Screen returns to studio Newscaster head shot.

>   C9 NEWSCASTER (CONT'D)
>   (Leaning into camera)
> We have not been able to see the
> creature, verify its remains or
> formally identify its origins.

> Neither have we yet been able to
> secure an interview with Billy-Bob

Mason yet, but some people believe that the dead creature is in fact a BUNYIP.

A mythical creature from the primal swirling mists of the Native Australian Dreamtime.

VOICE OVER

The screen cuts to a mix of cave drawings, and graphics showing a range weird creature from swamp reptiles to bear-like animals.

The Bunyip, like the Yeti, the Sasquatch and Bigfoot exists in folklore and mythology, and could be described as a 'hybrid' of several creatures.

Sightings of the Bunyip have been reported in the Southern Simpson Desert region since records began, and even before.

Drawings of the Bunyip in caves in the region have been carbon dated at several thousand years old.

Screen cuts back to C9 Presenter.

(A beat)
There are many opinions coming to bear on this incredible story.

Some dismiss it out of hand, others hold back for a scientific explanation, and yet others are already 'googling'

and researching for themselves while they speculate that the BUNYIP's flesh could have unprecedented healing and curative properties that could transcend 2000 years of medical science's history and development.
(A beat)
We tried earlier to speak to Billy Bob Mason, owner of Cordillo Downs Ranch, and the man who reportedly shot the creature.

The screen cuts to a jostling camera where a reporter climbs a rung of a fence and shouts to a tall man leaning nonchalantly smoking on a veranda 30m away.

ONSITE C9 REPORTER
Mr Mason, Billy Bob, can you come over and speak to us please. Can you confirm that it was you who shot the Bunyip?

The slightly jostling camera showed Billy Bob Mason looking in the direction of the Reporter, drawing on his smoke, looking around and appearing to consider the request for several beats, then he squared his Stetson and stepped down from the veranda, grinding out his cigarette, and walked laconically towards the camera.

As he approached the fence, he was interrupted by two burly men in dark suits, who jostled the C9 Onsite Reporter backwards and away, effectively barring any further conversation.

ONSITE C9 REPORTER (CONT'D)
(To the plain clothed
official - Angry)
Excuse me Sir, we want to speak to
Mr Mason... who are you guys? Are you
Police? What the hell is going on here?

The Reporter and Camera Crew are expertly man-
handled away from the fence. Billy Bob Mason,
still framed in the moving camera shot, stood
there for several beats, then stepped back away
to his veranda, leaning and lighting up another
cigarette.

ONSITE C9 REPORTER (CONT'D)
(To Camera)
Well, as you can see, feelings are
running pretty high here. Not only
is news in the public interest being
shut down, but our camera crew have
also been assaulted and man-handled
in a way that resembles working in
a warzone.
(Looking wildly off-camera)
What the hell is going on here? Who
are these people who are blocking us
from reporting here?
(Taking instruction off-camera,
then turning back to camera)
OK, we are now returning you back
to the News Commentary studio from
Cordillo Downs Cattle Station.

The screen returns to a flustered looking C9
Presenter.

C9 NEWSCASTER
Well, thanks to our onsite crew up
there in the Simpson Desert.

We will of course bring you more on
this developing situation later.
        (A beat, shuffling papers)
Meanwhile...

The screen switches to a circling drone shot of
Adelaide cityscape.

VOICE OVER

        C9 NEWSCASTER (CONT'D)
This is the industrial area south
of downtown Adelaide. It is believed
that the BUNYIP's remains have been
brought here to a laboratory to be
examined. We are hoping for more
information as the day proceeds.

The screen returns to the unsettled Newscaster
as he looks offscreen to his right, touching his
earpiece, expression changing.

        C9 NEWSCASTER (CONT'D)
        (Back to camera)
I'm getting some breaking news here.

It seems that part of the Bunyip's
remains has been stolen from the
Adelaide laboratory in the last few
hours. Police are now involved in
this investigation.
        (A beat)
We will stay with this and bring you
more on this developing story later.
Back to main studio.

                            FADE OUT

EXT. 408 NELSON ROAD. PARA HILLS. ADELAIDE, STH AUSTRALIA. MORNING

Para Hills, vast residential area on rolling hills dotted with clumps of eucalyptus, 8 miles north of downtown Adelaide, is bathed in mid-morning sunlight. Light traffic purrs after the frenetic school runs. No: 408 sits on a tee junction with lounge windows looking down-hill along Kesters Rd.

John Cantrell, in the carport, rummaged in the trunk of the Holden looking for something. He paused, listening.

                    SARAH
          (Shouting from inside house)
     John, are you there?

John straightened, grimacing.

                    JOHN
     What...I'm here.

He looks to his right as Sarah appears at the back door.

                    SARAH
     What did you do with that chunk of
     meat you took out of the car John?

                    JOHN
     The fuck... what did you say?

Sarah comes decisively out of the house, confronting him.

                    SARAH
The piece of fucking meat John, you
know what I'm talking about...from
under the seat. The Meat, yeh?

                    JOHN
Oh, that meat...yeah OK, I gave it to
the cat, Genghis.

Sarah is astounded and angry.

                    SARAH
What, you did what,
        (A beat, horrified)
I don't believe it...you gave that
fucking meat to the cat.

Oh my God...

                    JOHN
        (Defensive)
Why wouldn't I? That's what people
do with waste meat don't they, they
give it to cats, or fucking dogs, or
bloody fucking passing donkeys, or
whatever.
        (A beat, incredulous)
For fuck's sake...Are you going out of
your tiny mind or what Sarah?

Sarah paces, tearful, angry, and frustrated.

                    SARAH
John, you are a fuckwit, This is
beyond belief!

How could you do that? You stupid
useless piece of shit, of all the
idiotic...

                    JOHN
              (Shouting)
          Sarah, enough already!

John walked towards Sarah, taking her shoulders
in his hands, looking down into her tearful
angry face.

                JOHN (CONT'D)
          What the hell is wrong with you? What
          is going on here? Why are you losing
          it like this over a piece of rotten
          bloody meat?

                    SARAH

          Get off me!

She shook herself violently free of his hands
and marched into the house, he followed her.

                    JOHN
          I mean it! What is it with you? As
          it turns out, Genghis wouldn't touch
          it. He ran off as if I was trying to
          poison him.
              (A beat, shaking his head)
          Bloody weird cat that Genghis anyway.
          The bloody pair of you are weird.

Sarah turned, breathless, searching his face,
taking a ragged breath.

                    SARAH
              (Articulating slowly)
          So, what did you do with the meat
          John? Where is it now?

John stared at her, completely mystified.

                         JOHN
     Well, assuming the bins haven't been
     emptied...or the contents of our bin
     been stolen, or taken to the fucking
     CIA headquarters for analysis, I
     guess it's... it's in the bin.

     I wrapped it up and chucked it in the
     bin. Its wrapped it up tight in some
     foil, you know, so the rats wouldn't
     get a whiff of it. Its in...

Sarah ran past him in a billow of skirts and
Chanel perfume, he followed her. She ran to the
row of different coloured bins at the back of
the carport. She stood wildly looking at them.

                         SARAH
          (Breathless)
     Which one?

John came tentatively up behind her.

                         JOHN
          (Indicating vaguely)
     That one, there.

He watched, shocked, as she sprang at the bin,
tipping it onto its side, spilling out foul smelling
rubbish across the carport floor. She threw herself
down into the mess, sorting, searching, pulling
clumps congealing rubbish apart.

Finally in triumph, she sat, covered in gore,
her hair askew, holding up a tightly rolled pace
of foil.

                         SARAH
     Is this it?

John looked down her, totally astonished. He could only nod mutely. Sarah, covered in old gravy stains, peelings and random rubbish, bounded to her feet clutching the foil package, she laughed and threw her arms around him, kissing him hard on the mouth.

                    SARAH (CONT'D)
          John, my darling, you are wonderful!
          Thank you, baby.

She ran into the house clutching the foil package, leaving John standing in the mess of rubbish, dishevelled and flabbergasted, looking after her.

2 HOURS LATER

John and Sarah, freshly showered, sat at the kitchen table facing each other. On the table between them is the foil package recovered from the rubbish bin.

                    JOHN
          It was on the TV you say.

                    SARAH
          The Morning Show, yes.

John stares from the foil package to his wife's face, an uncertain grin forming.

                    JOHN
          Let me get this straight. You think
          this piece of meat is from a Bunyip?
               (A beat, grin widening)
          You are being serious? A fucking
          Bunyip...Sarah, look I...

Sarah takes a long breath, he tailed off.

> SARAH
>
> Look John, this was stolen the same
> day we were parked in south Adelaide.
> They just showed the actual street,
> where we were on the News. That black
> guy got in our car with the meat...
> remember?

> JOHN
> (Impatient)
> Yes, I know all that. It's still a
> long shot to where you seem to be
> right now babe, you know, like in the
> Dream time...
> (Shaking his head)
> A fucking Bunyip... Bunyip's don't
> even fucking exist Sarah!

Sarah looks pityingly at him, smiling gently.

> SARAH
> (Patiently)
> John, I just watched it, I did, on
> Channel 9.
> (A beat)
> The creature, the Bunyip, killed some
> cattle up north somewhere, and a
> cattleman shot it.
>
> Then they brought it, the Bunyip body,
> back south to Adelaide to check it
> out. Some bastard stole some of it,
> got in our car by mistake.
> (A beat, shrugging)
> It all makes plenty of sense to me.

John stared at her, incredulous.

SARAH (CONT'D)
John, don't you even remember? You
cut your hand?

She reached for his hand, holding it flat down
next the foil package, her fingers on his scarred
knuckles.

SARAH (CONT'D)
Look, you forget... you cut this hand,
and then it immediately healed as you
watched. It happened John, you know
it did - is that normal? Is it? No,
it's not normal.
        (A beat)
I think it was the meat that did
that. Bunyip meat. You said yourself
that you could feel it, you said it
felt like the cut was fizzing...then
it was healed. It proves it John,
doesn't it?
        (A beat, leaning back)
Everyone is going mad about this
John.

This is going big mate. We could get
rich, or at least maybe pay off a few
outstanding bills. Do you think we
should go to the papers? - they might
pay us something?

JOHN
        (Forcefully)
No, we should not!
        (A beat, hard look)
I mean it Sarah, no! You hear?

                         SARAH
OK, don't get your knickers in a
twist then, I won't. But it is not
going in the bin John, def, It's going
into the deep freeze.
          (Knowing look)
You never know...

John looked at Sarah, slightly mollified, but
still disbelieving.

                         JOHN
Sarah, I'm trying to deal with a
new experience here. I never, in
our nine years of marriage, saw my
beautiful, perfectly made-up wife
dive enthusiastically into a bin-full
of filthy rubbish before.

This is all very new Sarah.
          (A beat, grinning)
Hmm, now that I've seen it, I quite
like you stinking of peelings and
last week's gravy... dead sexy babe...

Sarah swiped him, smiling broadly. He got up
to get more coffee. Her eyes rested on the foil
package, her smile fading, her beautiful face
becoming harder and vaguely grotesque.

She picked the package up, weighing it in her
hand, then headed to the freezer.

                         FADE TO BLACK

INT. 'ALTERN' HEADQUARTERS. 46-52 EDINBURGH ST. CANBERRA. PRIVATE OFFICE. DAY

The HQ of the Australian Long-Term Ecological Research Network (ALTERN)is housed in air-conditioned smoked glass, concrete and steel splendour on a street of identical high-rise buildings populated by cool, business suited, quietly spoken people who gaze earnestly into screens, drive mostly hybrid cars and regularly tantalize their taste buds in the Central Business District's fine dining restaurants over extended lunches.

Jeff Uteri, 54, divorced bachelor, Deputy Director of ALTERN for the past 6 years, closed his Mac Power-book and touched the screen of his iPhone.

                    JEFF UTERI
          Mish, its me, can we meet?

He listened, smiling vaguely, nodded.

                    JEFF UTERI (CONT'D)
          OK, yes, why not. Blu Ginger in thirty?

30 MINUTES LATER

INT. BLU GINGER RESTAURANT. GENE ST. CANBERRA. DAY

Jeff rose slightly out of his seat as Michelle Rogan 37 sashayed between tables and slid smoothly into her seat opposite. She acknowledged his courtesy with a faint curve of her perfectly formed dark red lips.

She glanced around, ignoring the wave of sexual energy she had generated, sat back, red nails touching her throat and regarded him with a self-assured gaze.

                    JEFF UTERI
          Thank you for this Mish, short notice,
          I know.
                    (Glancing around)
          Been here before?

                    MISH ROGAN
                    (Non-committal)
          I assume you are recommending.

                    JEFF UTERI
                    (Consulting menu)
          Well, after careful consideration,
          the Railway Canteen Goat with basmati
          and garlic naan?
                    (A beat, smiling)
          Providing of course you have no
          romantic assignations this afternoon?

Mish smiled, leaning back as a waiter arrived with iced water.

                    MISH ROGAN
          Er no, none today, Jeff, and yes, the
          goat curry will be fine, thank you.
                    (A beat, waiting)
          Something up?

Jeff Uteri glanced around the sparsely populated tables, placed his iPhone down flat to the tabletop, touched it, and spun it so she could see the screen. She leaned and read, leaned back.

MISH ROGAN (CONT'D)
Why would ALTERN be interested in
garbage like this Jeff?

The sighting of a non-existent
mythical creature? It doesn't exactly
merit a lunch at short notice.

Hot flat bread arrived with hummus. Jeff tore off a
piece, scooped hummus and chewed thoughtfully.

JEFF UTERI
A mate of mine is a Doctor in Papua
New Guinea, Mt Hagen. It's remote
highland jungle.

A while back a tribesman brought his
family's pig to his surgery. Pigs
are pretty damned important currency
in PNG. Told my friend that his
neighbour had raped his pig, fucked
it several times apparently, he was
rightly outraged.

Furthermore, it was now most likely
carrying a human/pig child.

MISH ROGAN
Oh Jeff, for god's sake...where are you
going with this?

JEFF UTERI
Hear me out Mish.
        (A beat)
My friend had less choices than you
might think. Choice 1; Sending the
man on his way could result in someone
dying needlessly with a stone axe in
his brain.

(A beat)
Choice 2; Ask the man to wait. Knock the pig out, cut its belly and then stitch it up again. Tell the man the human/pig foetus has now been removed. The man goes away happy. Job done. Get on with your life.

Mish chewed, thinking about it.

MISH ROGAN
Your point?

JEFF UTERI
My point beautiful lady, is that sometimes, regardless of the accepted science, accepting that a human/pig child might be real, satisfies a political and business expedient.
(A beat)
You are our media contact Mish. Sooner or later, they will come down from the pinnacle of excitement about this fucking Bunyip sighting, and some of the more sober and thoughtful pundits are bound to ask ALTERN to comment.

They will ask what we, as the Government's formal opinion on these matters, make of it all.
(A beat, shrugging)
Whether they ask us directly or not, we will definitely need to issue a Press Release and a Statement setting out our position.

MISH ROGAN
Jeff, are you being serious? Does ALTERN even have 'a position...

(A beat)
The sightings of mythical creatures is an example of daytime TV at its lowest possible denominator. Why pray, would we, as a Govt funded professional organization employing some of the best scientific brains in the World, even begin to acknowledge that this story is even credible?

Food arrives. They taste.

                    JEFF UTERI
Mm, this is good.
          (A beat, chewing. 'Mansplaining')
Michelle, we have a number of delicate operations around the country. Some of these in the Simpson Desert. We are currently facing huge challenges with the Government's Climate Change agenda.

Expanding populations, major pressure on water supplies and land area, and from the Left lobby, protection of endangered species and other natural resources, not to mention the fucking Aboriginal's so-called 5000 years spiritual ownership of land that may or may not have potential rare earth metals mining possibilities.

                    MISH ROGAN
          (Low whistle)
Bloody hell Jeff, go on.

                    JEFF UTERI
It gets worse Mish.
          (A beat)

In one of our sites in the southern Simpson Desert, in fact, not far from where this Bunyip sighting is based...

We have inadvertently, because we weren't looking for it, found massive deposits of rare earth metals that could have major world-wide consequences on the Green Agenda and the Lithium/Cobalt battery production.
(A beat)
You might recall from some of our internal meetings, that are not for public consumption, that OZ will run out of essential rare earth metals in less than two years from now.

The hard reality is, that the world needs to increase production by 800% if we are all gonna drive an electric vehicle (EV)by 2030.

Mish was spellbound, her food forgotten.

MISH ROGAN
I hear you Jeff, I really do, but where is all this going?

What has it got to do with some hill billies shooting a unicorn.
(A beat, taking a bite)
Great food, but why am I here? I haven't got there yet.

Jeff held her gaze, his hands flat to the tabletop.

JEFF UTERI
Mish, I want ALTERN to neither confirm nor deny the possibility that this

creature, that has reportedly been shot, whatever it is, it may or may not, be a Bunyip.

It doesn't matter.

For the time being, we do not declare either way.
        (A beat)
That will be our formal position at this time.
        (A beat)
I repeat, ALTERN can neither confirm, nor deny that the creature is a Bunyip.
        (A beat)
Got that?

Mish is astounded, uncomfortable, buying time, she looks around the restaurant for a beat, places her fork carefully on her plate, takes a breath.

                MISH ROGAN
But Jeff, if we do that, we may as well confirm that a fucking Bunyip actually exists.

That it is real.
        (A beat)
That's the way our position will be interpreted, by everyone, like you know, everyone Jeff.

Jeff picked up his fork again, pointing it at her.

                JEFF UTERI
I know.
        (A beat)

Fact 1; The whole Bunyip thing is shite, yeh. We both know that.

Fact 2; The rare earth mining deposits exist, they could change the World's geo-political landscape in Australia's, and thereby ALTERN's favour.

Fact 3; ALTERN's tacit acknowledgement of the Bunyip's existence, even though we neither confirm nor deny it, puts the Aboriginal lobby on our side, because a Bunyip is like a fucking house-pet for them.

A fight with militant ABORIGINALS could close us down.

Fact 4; The rare earth deposits are not on Government land. The fucking land belongs to Billy Bob Mason, the 'Hill-Billy' who shot the Bunyip and started all this. Apparently, he is a local 'Crocodile Dundee' type popular in the Birdsville bars, they call him Billy Bob.

Jeff leaned back exhaling, staring directly at Michelle.

                    JEFF UTERI (CONT'D)
So, are you traveling the distance here with me yet Babe?

There is one more fact I should mention... ALTERN's funding could be withdrawn, yes, they are talking about it - we could be shut down

as the national imperatives relating the Green Agenda reshape the funding landscape.
          (A beat)
So, Mish, right now, we formally refuse to discredit the Bunyip.

The existence of the Bunyip links three powerful LOBBIES, the LEFT and the RIGHT, and the ABORIGINALS, and we baby - ALTERN, are in the middle for now, the vital link.

Mish leaned back, exhaling in a whoosh of air.

                    MISH ROGAN
So OK, no Government is going to close ALTERN down for the foreseeable future. They couldn't...it would be seen as a cover-up to discredit Bunyip existence.

Wow!

Mish leaned back and held his gaze for several beats as she processed, then slowly nodded.

                MISH ROGAN (CONT'D)
Fuck me!

                    JEFF UTERI
          (Broad grin)
Well, now that you mention it Michelle...

                              FADE TO BLACK

INT. 14 HALF MOON STREET. MAYFAIR LONDON. LOUNGE. NIGHT.

Ekaterina sat up in bed, her hand instinctively feeling the cold sheet on his side of the bed. She listened; the house was silent. She glanced over at the dressing table; his watch and bracelet were gone.

She clawed for her iPhone handset and sank back, deleting the night's spam, there were no messages. She thought for a beat, then searched, touched the screen, the phone rang.

> EKATERINA LEBOV
> Hello. My name is Ekaterina Lebov, may I speak to Dr Degere please.

She waited, her eyes tracing a discoloration in the ceiling.

> RECEPTION
> Dr Degere is with someone at the moment madam do you...

> EKATERINA LEBOV
> I will wait, thank you.

5 MINUTES LATER

> EMANUEL DEGERE
> Ms Lebov, this is Dr Degere, my apologies Madam, can you bear with me a moment, I will close the door.
> (A beat, movement)
> OK, I assume you have spoken to Andrei?

                    EKATERINA LEBOV
We have spoken briefly last night
Doctor, I had hoped we would continue
our conversation this morning over
breakfast, but he must have left the
house very early.
          (A beat)
This is a very delicate matter,
Doctor, I'm sure you will not want to
discuss details over the telephone,
so I will simply ask you a question,
you will answer in any way that you
are able to, and I will interpret
your response in any way that I am
able to.

There was an uncomfortable silence for several
beats.

                    EMANUEL DEGERE
     Ms Lebov, I...

                    EKATERINA LEBOV
          (Succinctly)
     Dr Degere, do we have a year?

Ekaterina could hear faint movements and
breathing in her ear. She waited several beats,
then clearing her throat, her voice charged
with emotion.

               EKATERINA LEBOV (CONT'D)
     Thank you for your time Doctor Degere,
          (A beat)
     I think we understand each other.

She cut the call, her eyes blurring, looking
back up at the faint stain in the ceiling,
tracing it to the wall, where it turned into a

tiny settlement crack. She pushed a fist down into the hard knot of tension in her gut, adjusted the pillows and reached for the TV remote, flicking the channels.

TV TALK SHOW

> TV HOST
> .... now is not the time to take possible solutions off the table.
>
> Specifically, nuclear power holds a powerful argument against digging up of rare earth metals where vast amounts of materials must be processed to extract relatively minuscule amounts of the refined materials.
>
> And, in the process laying waste to thousands of square miles of land for the foreseeable future. It cannot be used for anything. Birds don't even fly over it.
> (A beat, despairing)
> We simply don't have enough Lithium and Cobalt to produce the batteries now, never mind in 10 years.

The Talk Show Host shuffled papers, turning to a panel of three other guests.

> TV HOST (CONT'D)
> Right, can we lighten the discussion here somewhat. You have all had an opportunity to trawl today's newspapers, is there anything jumping out at anyone?

The table is covered with the day's newspapers.

                    TALK SHOW GUEST 1
I've got a superb one here Jeremy.
        (A beat)
Apparently, in South Australia, they
have their own version of the Loch
Ness Monster.

It called a Bunyip.
        (Smiling around)
Well, apparently one has been shot,
and the story is going viral at an
alarming rate.

                    TV HOST
A Bunyip? What the hell is a Bunyip?

                    TALK SHOW GUEST 1
        (Reading)
It's a mythical creature that goes back
into Australia's primeval history.

It says here that its flesh has magical
healing powers that the Aboriginals,
and many other alternative opinions,
believe can ERADICATE MAJOR ILLNESSES
that are still beating medical
science, LIKE CANCER FOR EXAMPLE.

Ekatarina's attention focused, sitting upright
in her bed. She increased the TV volume.

                    TALK SHOW GUEST 2
OK, don't anyone laugh yet...
        (Shuffling papers)
I have another article here that
gives another interesting perspective
on this story.
        (A beat)

Yesterday, under some pressure I guess, the Australian Long-Term Ecological Research Network **(ALTERN)** gave a press conference and have issued a formal statement.
(A beat, reading)
Well now, this is most interesting...

TV HOST
Oh Mags, for God's sake, don't keep us in suspense.
(Smiling around)
She's such a diva, loves to milk her moments doesn't she...

TALK SHOW GUEST 2
It seems that everyone was expecting ALTERN, who are the Australian Government, for Pete's sake, to totally poo-hoo the Bunyip story.
(A beat, triumphant smile around)
Well, they didn't!

Everyone reacts in surprise.

TALK SHOW GUEST 2 (CONT'D)
(A beat, reading)
Michelle Rogan, their Media Spokeswoman, REFUSED TO EITHER CONFIRM, OR DENY, the existence of the Bunyip.

It has caused a Media storm that is reverberating around the globe.

                    TALK SHOW GUEST 1
     Wow! That's pretty well the same as
     CONFIRMING that this creature is
     credible. What...?

                    TV HOST
          (To camera)
     Wouldn't that be astounding if this
     Bunyip creature's flesh could cure
     cancer, and/or all sorts of other
     diseases.

     OK guys, can we move on to...

Ekaterina killed the TV, new energy coursing
through her.

She sat on the side of the bed, feet flat to
the floor staring through her window at London's
roof-scape until her vision blurred.

                                    FADE OUT

**EXT. MCKENZIE RD. WEST LONDON. LARGE
HOUSE. DAY.**

Treadstone House was a collection of buildings
set back from Putney's McKenzie Road with
massive, rusted iron gates. It was a compound
of sorts with a main residence, a huge multi-
car garage, and a decaying garden pavilion with
several outbuildings.

The grounds were unkempt and overgrown, but
still retaining a vague 'Constable' style
elegance, with drooping trees into green water
and dim pathways leading into dark tangled
leafy grottos. It belonged to Andrei Lebov, who

presented himself to the World as an upstanding citizen and international businessman.

Midday on a foggy, raining Thursday. A dozen large late model cars, bespeaking power, and privilege, were parked along McKenzie Rd outside the gates. Several 'Rolex-ed and Ray-Banned' suited thugs leaned and smoked, arrogantly eyeing the solitary police cruiser double-parked 200m away.

The meeting in the austere drawing room was cool and professional, giving no notion or impression of the rolling miasmic fog of bloodletting, slayings and mayhem that had preceded today's event.

The two Partners, Lebov and The Lion, their friendship now a battleground of distant memory, had torn each other asunder like two mythical Norse Gods in a welter of corpse-strewn murderous executions as each one strove for dominance and succession over their criminal empire.

Sergei Narratova, Lebov's man, lounged by the huge rosewood table idly watching business suited colleagues assembling, pouring ice water, hunching over flaring lighters and billowing cigar smoke. For all their sartorial elegance, the meeting's occupants shared the same basic philosophy, that all money in another person's pocket, really belonged to them.

Their business plan was simple, work out how to take it from the sucker's pocket and get it into their own.

The murmur gradually stilled, and the men sat waiting quietly, a haze of blue cigar smoke swirling, chairs angled slightly towards the two empty chairs at the top of the table. Some with hooded eyes downwards to phone screens, others looking towards the door behind Sergei.

Andrei Lebov entered. Perfectly groomed and self-assured, a picture of Hollywood elegance and restrained power. He looked impassively around the room's occupants, ignoring vague smiles and nods, checked his watch and placed his iPhone by his right hand. Leaning slightly forward, he looked deeply into the eyes of each person around the table, holding their gaze until the other showed discomfort, moving his body so he faced each man directly.

The silence was total, the concentration electric. As he gazed at the last person, he suddenly spun his chair and placed an elegant shoe against the seat of the empty chair next to him.

His foot shot out explosively, and the chair launched violently across the room on its castors, smashing into the panelled wall, splintering, and falling on its side. Broken fragments of varnished wood sliding to a stop on the polished oak, a castor spinning away, a haze of brown dust hanging in the air.

The room was rigid with shock. Even Sergei was taken by surprise. Men looked at the wreckage of the chair and back to Andrei's blazing eyes, immediately dropping their gaze, getting the powerful message.

Andrei faced them again, allowed the silence to build.

Finally, he leaned and poured ice water into a crystal glass, the glass and liquid sounds accentuated in the silent room. He sipped minutely and put down his glass. He spoke, still facing everyone.

ANDREI LEBOV
Sergei, do we have an agenda?

Sergei slid a typed paper across the rosewood. Andrei glanced briefly at it, then slid it away into the centre of the table distastefully.

ANDREI LEBOV (CONT'D)
(Slow and succinct)
In less than one year from now, I will be dead, and our entire business will be 100% legal and legitimate.
(A beat)
We have a very short time to eradicate even the slightest reason for the establishment's continued interest in our activity.
(A beat, eyes to crestfallen faces)
I require from each of you here, one week from now, a plan to achieve this objective. The cost, financially or human resource terms, is of no importance.

The outcomes are unequivocal and incontrovertible and will be faced head-on.

Andrei moved slightly in his seat, nodding to the wrecked chair that once belonged to his partner.

ANDREI LEBOV (CONT'D)
I have already started this process.

Andrei stood, shot his cuffs, picked up his iPhone, and stalked from the room. A moment later, Sergei Narratova followed him.

No-one else moved for a long time.

FADE OUT

EXT. MAIN NORTH EAST ROAD. ADELAIDE. LATE AFTERNOON

John Cantrell drove home west against low sun in shades with the visor down. The first couple of miles out of the city were quick and efficient, but as John approached the Gepps Cross five-way junction red brake lights began flickering on.

John flexed his hand, glancing again down at his scarred knuckles. Traffic gradually stopped, the junction a glittering 500m ahead of gleaming pitiless metal and glass distorting and twisting in the heat mirage.

He was in the nearside lane. Over the low fence was a dilapidated scrub desert trailer park campground. A dirty-white low-pitched canvas tent flapped. Near it a dry-stacked blackened pile of bricks forming a rough BBQ with a crude wooden table.

An Aboriginal woman sat listlessly on a stool in front of the tent, a dirty child playing in the dust by her feet. Behind them, hanging from a straggly tree, a child's swing moved gently in a swirl of heat. As he looked, the woman looked up suddenly, as if she had been prodded.

Her eyes caught his, pale where they should have been deep brown, they followed him as the traffic drifted in fits and starts towards the junction. John didn't like the intensity of her attention; he shuddered and broke the eye contact.

A row of small wooden scrappy buildings, then a sign: ANDY'S GARAGE - GAS-CAMPING. Shiny tin signs advertising tires, spark plugs, and Coke and other paraphernalia were nailed to the side of garage facing the road. The flat-bed FJ pick-up in front of John's Holden pulled out of the traffic and stopped next the Gas Pump.

John moved up, closing the gap to the next car. A grizzled one-legged man hobbled out of the black opening of the rickety garage, wiping his hands on a greasy rag. He walked easily on a peg belted tight to his upper leg. He greeted the FJ driver with loose grin of blackened teeth. The driver got out, and John did a double-take and froze. It was the Aboriginal man who had got into his car with the slab of raw meat.

The traffic lurched forward again, and John's Holden was now 30M away. The Mechanic shouted above the traffic noise.

                    PEG-LEG MECHANIC
                  (To the FJ Driver)
Warm day out on the highway today mister, it'll get hotter, its only January yet. Another week, it'll be hotter than a pistol around here.

The Mechanic engaged the pump. The driver leaned on the hood facing towards the traffic as the old gas pump whirred and clanked.

The surreal laughter of a child caught John's attention, he looked to his right. The child from the campsite had broken away, her chubby legs taking her along the hard shoulder and towards the highway, the pale eyed woman chasing her.

John reacted without processing the thought. He lunged out of his seat towards the running child, meeting both the FJ driver and the woman as they all reached the child together in a miasma of orange dust and diesel fumes.

They sprawled, the child scrabbling towards her mother's protective arms. The peg-legged mechanic was slower, but the alarm in his eyes was real, his hands outstretched to the pale eyed woman clutching her child to her bosom.

John got to his feet, brushing himself down. The woman backed away from John, her eyes wide with fear as if threatened by him. John backed away slightly, his hands up, placating, palms outwards.

The Flat-bed driver spoke to the woman in soothing manner and she scuttled off with the child. John looked after her, then back at the FJ driver, questioning. The peg-leg mechanic spat wetly, shaking his head, muttering something, then went back to his wheezing gas pump. John, the realization still dawning, eyed the FJ Flat-Bed driver.

JOHN
You, it was you. You were outside my
house the other night. You were the
man with the meat.
(A beat, outward breath)
Fuck...

Behind them the glittering metal traffic strained
forward, horns blipped as traffic moved inexorably
on. Drivers shouted and gesticulated at John to
return to his car.

FLAT-BED DRIVER
You better get back to your car mate.

The Flat-bed driver turned away towards his
vehicle, then looking back with a slow grin
widening...

FLAT-BED DRIVER (CONT'D)
I'll be seeing you Mister, we have
business.

2 HOURS LATER AT 408 NELSON RD.

John nosed the Holden into the carport, then
still tense, sat looking into the mirror and
onwards down Kesters Road. No one had followed.
He felt surreal and somehow out of himself -
not even sure what that meant.

He got out, stretched, looking along Nelson Rd.
Next door at 406 a white van with TYRE SERVICES
parked. A man with overalls too short for his
long legs was crouched bolting a wheel back in
place to a jacked-up Toyota. His neighbour stood
watching.

As he looked, a Ford Falcon Police Car pulled up next the Toyota, the driver leaning out.

A brief exchange and the neighbour nodded towards him. The Falcon coasted silently along the kerb to park at the end of John's car port. Two uniforms got out, stretching and putting on hats.

> UNIFORM 1
> Mr. John Cantrell, is it?

John nodded.

> UNIFORM 1 (CONT'D)
> Can we have a word please Mr Cantrell.

The neighbour and the Tyre Fitter were both watching curiously. Sarah appeared at the end of the carport, lips parted, slightly white, questioning look at John.

> JOHN
> (To the policemen)
> Better come on in then.

They all filed inside, John and Sarah exchanging cool glances. Sarah poured tumblers of iced water and they sat around the kitchen table, the officers consulting notepads.

> UNIFORM 1
> Thanks for the drinks, Ma'am, its hot out there. I assume you will be Mrs Sarah Cantrell?
> (A beat, to John)
> Right, first things first guys, may I ask what your purpose was to be

parked along Adelaide's Commercial Street 5 nights back.

John looked at Sarah questioning, she shook her head minutely.

> JOHN
> (Shrugging)
> I took Sarah to get a silver bracelet altered, while she was in the shop, I waited on the street.
>
> I couldn't get in the shade, so it was a hard wait.

The policemen both looked at Sarah. She held up her wrist.

> SARAH
> This one. New links and fastener.

> UNIFORM 1
> (Leaning to look)
> That's it?

Sarah and John answered 'yes' together nervously, then grinned at each other self-consciously.

> UNIFORM 1 (CONT'D)
> Nothing to add to that then? Sorted the bracelet then came home, eh?

> JOHN
> Pretty well, yes, I guess that's it.

The two policemen were silent, both reading notepads. Then the second officer spoke for the first time.

UNIFORM 2
(Clearing throat)
You 'guess' Mr Cantrell?
(A beat, patiently)
At this point I am going to ask
you both again, did anything else
happen that day that was unusual, or
strange, and that you feel we need
to discuss here today.
(A beat)
I need to warn you at this point, that
we have other sources of information
that we are pursuing.

John and Sarah both looked downwards avoiding
each other's gaze. There was a silence for
several beats.

SARAH
(Tentative)
John, do you want to...

JOHN
(To the officers)
Is this something to do with that
story on the TV, the Bunyip thing?

The two policemen were silent and watchful,
pencils poised over notepads.

JOHN (CONT'D)
(Defensive)
Look, there was this guy, he ran down
the pavement behind me, got in my
car. He had a huge chunk of raw meat
clutched to his chest.

I'd never seen him before. He just...

UNIFORM 2

So, he came from behind you Mr Cantrell, you saw him coming in your mirror.

JOHN

Yes, he just opened the door, got in, then I guess he realized he didn't know me, got out again and ran along Commercial St, then turned left into an alley.

A Chinese guy chased him, but I never saw either of them after that.

UNIFORM 2
(Patiently)
So, you think he mistook you for a getaway car. Would you be able to describe him?

JOHN

Yes, I could, well-built ABORIGINAL man, thirties maybe.

SARAH

Then I came back to the car later, I never saw him at all, but John told me everything.

The two officers exchanged glances.

UNIFORM 1

We have all of this on CCTV Mr Cantrell.

Have you seen this man again since the incident on Commercial St?

                    JOHN
              (Uncomfortable)
No, nothing. It was an isolated
incident, I guess.
              (A beat)
Was the blood from that Bunyip? The
creature they are talking about on
the news.

Both officers closed their notepads.

                  UNIFORM 1
Can we have a quick look at your car
Mr Cantrell?

                    JOHN
Oh, yes, OK. In the carport.

They all trooped out to the carport, and they
looked into the car. Getting down to shine a
torch under the seat.

                  UNIFORM 2
We would like you to lock the car
Mr Cantrell, and we will take the
keys with us today. They will be
returned to you after a forensic team
have examined your vehicle in detail.
They will get this done as soon as
possible.
              (A beat)
I have to tell you Mr and Mrs Cantrell,
your car may be impounded for further
investigation, depending on the
results of the initial forensic.

John was angry, bright color showing in cheeks.

                    JOHN
          (Petulantly)
So, how do I manage getting to and
from my work then? That bloody car
is essential to us. We can't even get
to the shops.

                  UNIFORM 2
          (Eye contact, firmly)
Mr Cantrell, I suspect that if we
had not pushed you today, you would
have with-held some vital information
from us.

For that reason, I suggest strongly
that you work around the inconvenience
in the best way that you can and get
on with your life. We will conduct
our business as fast as we can.
          (A beat)
OK then?

The policemen walked stiffly out through the
carport, paused to take cell phone photographs
of the car and house, then drove off. The
neighbour and the Tyre fitter were still there
radiating curiosity, leaning against their van
with coffees apiece.

Back in the kitchen, John dropped into his seat,
Sarah looked at him knowingly.

                   SARAH
You've seen that fucking meat thief
again, haven't you? Those two cops
saw right through you.
          (A beat, shaking her head)

It was so incredibly obvious, you dipstick. They will be back here hassling us again.
        (A beat)
Look, I'm gonna go to the media with this. If we don't, we'll lose the initiative for levering any cash out of it.

                JOHN
Sarah, no, I mean it babe, NO!
        (A beat, slower, focusing)
I'm just thinking, we never told them about that piece of actual meat, did we? We just said there was blood...

                SARAH
        (Pitying)
Fuck you, John!

                                FADE OUT.

EXT. CHANNEL 9 HQ. CENTRAL ADELAIDE. DAY.

Sarah crossed the wide pavement in crushing heat, then went through the smoked glass doors into blessed cool to a long dazzling white reception desk. A perfectly made-up vogue model look-alike glanced imperiously up at her and brought an obviously private telephone conversation to an end.

A faint receptionist's false smile, eyebrows raised.

                SARAH
I'd like to speak to someone about the Bunyip story please.

The vogue model shook her head minutely, and consulted a screen, looked up.

                    RECEPTIONIST
     Your name?

                       SARAH
     Sarah Cantrell

The vogue model searched her screen, made a short call, then looked at a point somewhere above Sarah's head.

                    RECEPTIONIST
     You have no appointment madam.

Sarah took a breath, glancing around the wide reception area.

                       SARAH
          (Evenly)
     Channel 9 is my first choice. If you
     guys are not interested, I'll go to
     one of the other media. I'm not going
     to spar with you lady.
          (A beat)
     I'd make another call if I were you
     kiddo, receptionists like you are ten
     a penny.

The exchange was overheard by a perma-tanned suit coming out of the bottom of the wide stairway.

He looked curiously at Sarah, came over, a right-hand palm outward to the vogue model.

> CALVIN JENSEN
> Hi, I'm Cal Jensen, can I help you
> at all?

> SARAH
> Maybe... I want to speak to someone
> about the Bunyip story. I have some
> information you might find interesting.

Cal smiled disarmingly at Sarah, touching her
elbow lightly.

> CALVIN JENSEN
> Let's sit over here, shall we.

**INT. 14 HALF MOON STREET. MAYFAIR LONDON.
LOUNGE. NI...**

Andrei sat on the edge of the chair and waited
for the dull pain to subside in his lower back.
Across the room Ekaterina watched the silent
TV, glancing surreptitiously at him from time
to time, neither of them commenting on the
obvious.

He took a ragged breath, angry with himself
and the way his body was letting him down. He
reached and lit a cigar, leaned back into the
chair, and watched the match burn right down
to his fingers, then blew it out with his first
outgoing smoke.

> ANDREI LEBOV
> Baby can we talk?

She looked across at him surrounded by swirling
blue smoke, it seemed from a great distance.

                    ANDREI LEBOV (CONT'D)
                (Slowly)
            I know that you are not a woman to be
            set aside and ignored. I know that.
            Its not you.
                (A beat)
            It's me, I'm trying to come to terms
            with this. I'm going to...

Sergei entered the room silently from the stairs.
They both looked at him. He stood looking at
them both, considering, his fingers flexing. He
turned to go.

                    ANDREI LEBOV (CONT'D)
            Sergei, stay. It's OK. You can hear
            this.

Sergei sat on the edge of a settee, coiled, he
was long legged, long armed and muscled. He
looked capable of fighting his way out of a sack
of wildcats.

Ekaterina looked at the two men she loved more
than life. She rose in a fluid motion, pouring
frozen Beluga Noble vodka into three glasses, so
cold they were opaque. The liquid was viscous,
pouring like oil.

She placed a glass carefully in front of each
man, then sat with her own, raising it in
perfect symmetry with them, the three glasses
all held at a high point for a millisecond, then
they all tossed the iced fire into the back of
their throats, their eyes locked on each other.

                    ANDREI LEBOV (CONT'D)
            I have decided, when I know more,
            that I will set a date.

> You, Sergei, will shoot me in the
> head on that date.

Ekaterina jumped visibly but stayed silent, her eyes glittering.

Sergei didn't react, but his jaw tightened, and a pulse throbbed in his temple. His dark eyes strayed across to the silent TV, but not seeing.

> ANDREI LEBOV (CONT'D)
> I cannot and will not go down gradually
> to the point where I lose control of
> my faculties. That is not an option
> that is acceptable to me.
> (A beat)
> I fully realize what I am asking
> of both of you, but the only other
> choice is that I do the thing by my
> own hand.
> (A beat, bitterly)
> It may yet come to that.

There was silence in the room for five minutes.

Andrei blew smoke in a perfect ring and regarded the glowing end of his cigar, his composure resolute.

> ANDREI LEBOV (CONT'D)
> I am going to bed now, please
> excuse me.

Andrei stood with some effort looking at Sergei and Ekaterina for several moments. Not a hint of softness broke the blunt hard craggy lines of his face.

                    ANDREI LEBOV (CONT'D)
        I know about things...
                (A beat, softer)
        I have known from the beginning. How
        could I not, both of you live in my
        soul.

Ekaterina and Sergei both reacted, their faces
pale with growing shock.

                    ANDREI LEBOV (CONT'D)
        All actions have consequences that
        must be paid for.
                (A beat)
        In another time and place I would
        have destroyed you both, like you
        never existed.

        I would have then destroyed every
        member of both of your families and
        eradicated any trace of you from
        history.
                (A beat, gentle smile)
        Life changes my loved ones, nothing
        stays the same, I think it was 'Mr
        Spock' that said that.

Both looked uncomprehendingly at him.

                    ANDREI LEBOV (CONT'D)
        Star Trek.

Andrei bent gracefully, ground out his cigar
and left the room, his back rigid and straight,
a swirl of blue smoke where he had stood.

Ekaterina, her vision blurring, looked across at
Sergei, he was now crying openly, tears cursing

down his high cheekbones and along his hard jawline.

He poured another vodka, spilling onto the rosewood table. He held the bottle poised, looking at her, she shook her head minutely.

                    SERGEI
        How could he have known? All this
        time...

He blew a whistling breath, shaking his head, then tossed the second vodka with closed eyes. Ekaterina brought herself under control with a shuddering effort.

                EKATERINA LEBOV
        Well, now we are all here, our tears
        cannot wash out the tracks we have
        made on the way. Somehow, maybe
        it's strange, but I feel a sense of
        vindication.
            (Long outward breath)
        Sergei, there's something I want you
        to see.

She touched buttons on a handset control and the TV flickered, screen changing to a talk show set, two people in chairs facing each other. She switched on the sound.

            EKATERINA LEBOV (CONT'D)
        Look at this Sergei. It's a recording
        from Channel 9 in Australia.

ON TV.

The screen shows the start of a studio news show. Tanned, boyish handsome, 40s, pinstripe, square jaw to camera.

>   CALVIN JENSEN
> Good evening, my name is Calvin
> Jensen speaking to you from Adelaide
> in South Australia. This program is
> syndicated to ITV in United Kingdom
> and the HBO in USA and Canada.

Cal turned to his guest, a striking woman in her 30's, self-assured with a clear gaze.

>   CALVIN JENSEN (CONT'D)
> My guest tonight is Mrs Sarah Cantrell
> of Para Hills, Adelaide.
>
> Before we discuss anything, I will
> replay some contextual news footage
> from the past few days.

The screen cuts to circling drone footage of an outback desert cattle station, Cordillo Downs Ranch. Cuts to jostling media scrum footage trying to speak to an unresponsive tall man in western clothes on his veranda - Billy Bob Mason.

Snippets of interviews with Birani Pemba, a Native Australian politician, and various other expert opinions both given and refuted.

Back to Calvin Jensen in a headshot.

CALVIN JENSEN (CONT'D)
The past few days have been
hectic and frustrating as we have
unsuccessfully tried to investigate
the alleged shooting of a Bunyip, a
mythical creature existing in the
same historic belief systems that
have kept the YETI, the ABOMINABLE
SNOWMAN and the LOCH NESS MONSTER in
the public's awareness for millennia.
        (A beat)
We have been effectively prevented
from interviewing Billy Bob Mason,
the alleged BUNYIP shooter, by police,
and by representatives and agents of
ALTERN, that is Australia's Long-Term
Ecological Research Network.

For some reason, this investigation
has hit a series of brick walls and
setbacks, except for two specific
breakthroughs which we will discuss
here today.

The screen cuts to a turbulent press conference
showing an elegant ice queen in her 30s (Michelle
Rogan) coolly fencing with red-faced reporters
and media pundits while she delivered, and
then stuck resolutely, to a prepared ALTERN
statement.

CALVIN JENSEN (CONT'D)
The first breakthrough was ALTERN's
press conference and subsequent Press
Release, where the representative,
Michelle Rogan, REFUSED to either
confirm, or deny the existence of the
BUNYIP, and the vexed possibility that
its flesh could hold unprecedented

curative powers beyond anything yet discovered or devised by hundreds of years of medical scientific research.
(A beat, full face to camera)
ALTERN represents the Australian Government. The unprecedented position they have taken is extraordinary.

Mythical creature sightings are periodically reported and crushed pitilessly by these people.
(A beat)
This time they didn't, and we do not know why.
(A beat)
So, unpacking ALTERN's position, we are left with this unmistakable conclusion.

On the one hand they are knowingly giving credibility and legs to this story, and on the other, they are preventing access to our investigations.
(Raising eyes to camera)
Some would interpret this as giving even more credibility to the existence of the BUNYIP.

Ekaterina and Sergei watch the screen, she is aware that Sergei is losing interest and wants to go. She pauses the recording, the presenter's face freezing on-screen.

                    EKATERINA LEBOV
            (Earnest eyes to Sergei)
Stay, please Sergei, please. It's important.

He nods, settling reluctantly back in his seat.
She presses 'Play'

ON TV

                    CALVIN JENSEN
        Of course, the native Australian
        Aboriginal Community have what they
        describe as a spiritual ownership of
        the BUNYIP since the dawn of time, or
        in their parlance - The Dreamtime.
            (A beat)
        They have no doubts whatsoever
        as to its existence, and also the
        extraordinary claims about its flesh
        and its blood's curative powers, which
        they say, curiously I must add, that
        this power must be strictly controlled
        by them, and by them alone.

        To allow it free rein would be, and
        I quote, 'extremely dangerous'.

Calvin turns to Mrs Sarah Cantrell, who waits
her turn, composed and patient. The shot cuts
to a wider angle showing both parties.

                    CALVIN JENSEN (CONT'D)
        The next breakthrough in the
        extraordinary story is from this
        lady, Mrs Sarah Cantrell.
            (To her)
        Sarah, in a few words, can you tell
        us why you are here today.

Sarah Cantrell sat slightly more upright, her
hands flat to her thighs, eye contact with
Calvin, jaw set.

                    SARAH
Hello Calvin, yes.
         (Deep breath)
Several days ago, a man stole a chunk
of raw bloody meat from a laboratory
in Adelaide. He ran with it, clutching
it to his chest. He must have been
confused, or maybe panicked, because
he got into my husband's car with the
meat, we think, in error.

This was while he waited for me
outside a jewellers in Commercial St.
         (A beat)
The man immediately realized that he
had made a mistake, he got our car
and ran off, leaving blood on our car
seat and on the floor.

Later when we tried to clean some of
the blood from our car, my husband
injured his hand quite badly. The
seat slid on its runners unexpectedly
while he was reaching underneath it
to clean up the blood.

The cut would have probably needed
stitching.

Sarah Cantrell looked from Calvin's face directly
into the camera, her eyes clear and focused.

                SARAH (CONT'D)
This is specifically why I am here
tonight.

We have watched the news reports
and speculation as this story has

unfolded, particularly the healing issues.
(A beat)
My husband came in the house with a bad gash that would have needed stitching at the ER. His hand was covered with blood, his own, but crucially, also blood from the floor of the car that had been left behind by the meat thief.
(A beat, succinctly)
Calvin, on my life, we both watched, as the gash in his hand healed in a few seconds.

The skin pulling itself together, cells repairing themselves right in front of our eyes. He said that it felt like his wound was fizzing.
(A beat)
In less than two minutes, the wound had healed perfectly to scar tissue.
(A beat, seriously)
It happened Calvin, it's the truth.

CALVIN JENSEN
(Intoning carefully and clearly)
And you believe Sarah, that

(A): this raw meat was BUNYIP meat, and...

(B): that it healed your husband's hand in front of both your very eyes.

SARAH
Yes, to both A and B.
(A beat)

It was on the news that night, that someone had stolen some of the BUNYIP meat from the Laboratory on Commercial St.

(A beat)

We have also had the police round at our house, saying they have clear footage of that theft taking place on CCTV, including the thief getting in our car in error.

They have impounded our car for forensic investigation. No doubt they will find traces of BUNYIP blood, I'm sure of it.

Calvin turning to camera.

CALVIN JENSEN

This unfolding story is a vexed issue. Powerful political lobbies are watching this story as it develops.

(A beat)

We are sure that ALTERN's intervention has significant elements yet to be unpacked.

What is becoming more and more certain by the day is that whatever your view of mythical creatures in the past, that view may be forced to change as the BUNYIP mystery intensifies.

(To Sarah)

Thank you for bringing your story to C9 and syndicates today, Sarah Cantrell.

(Back to camera)

We hope to bring you an interview with BUNYIP shooter Billy Bob Mason

over the next few days, and also more from Birani Pemba, a representative from the Aboriginal Community who are stating their spiritual ownership of the BUNYIP and demanding the return of its remains.
            (A beat)
      This is Calvin Jensen signing off for Channel 9 in Adelaide.

Ekaterina killed the TV recording, took a long breath, eyes fixing Sergei. She knelt in front of him in a rush of silk, her hands clasping his, tears running down her beautiful cheeks.

                    EKATERINA LEBOV
            (Broken voice)
      I love both of you Sergei. You and I, we have to save him my darling. This may be our one chance.

      Everyone else has given up on him.

Sergei held her gaze, grief stricken and shaken.

                    SERGEI
      I'll do whatever it takes Ekaterina, you know I will.

Ekaterina leaned in, putting her face next to Sergei's, their tears mingling.

In the darkness of the stairwell, Andrei sat, one hand holding his lower back, his face grim and drawn. A single tear rolling down his hard jawline, falling silently onto the carpet.

                              FADE TO BLACK

EXT. SIMPSON DESERT OUTBACK ROAD. STH AUSTRALIA. DAY

Birani Pemba hit the corrugations in the dust road on a long sweeping right hander 20 miles south of Cordillo Downs. He had travelled the last 50 miles at 75mph plus on a recently graded road. The sudden thunderous roar of the change to ungraded road conditions, along with the shuddering steering column, made him drift in a sideways slew off the road in a cloud of dust.

He sat there for a beat, sweat in his eyes, swearing, heart thumping, then gathered himself and pulled laboriously back onto the road.

Two hours later at a sedate 30mph he was thoroughly fed-up, but in the distance could see the glittering media circus spread out on both sides of the main gates to the Cordillo Downs ranch. He stopped, sudden heat and dust closing in, rummaged and found binoculars. He swept the array of randomly parked vans and trucks, aerials spiking upwards here and there. The front gate was a no-go.

He decided to go off-road, circle the ranch, and come in from behind, out of the line of sight of the cameras and probing microphones.

An hour later he hit the dingo fence and bumped along it, trying not to raise attention with a dust cloud. He came to a double gate where four dingoes were ripping something apart in a scrabble of orange dust. They stopped as he pulled up, hostile opaque eyes on him, blinking.

He blew the horn, shouted out of the window. Three of them slunk away and sat 40m away. One, more wolf than dingo, stayed and snarled at him.

He rummaged under the seat, came up with a tire lever. Considered for a beat, then got carefully out of the car. The dingo didn't hesitate. It ran at him, and he tried to retreat rapidly back into the pick-up, dropping the tire lever. The crazed animal sank its teeth into his boot, dropping its haunches and almost pulling him out of the truck with the power of its backward thrust. He kicked and hung on to the steering wheel as the animal went berserk, ripping, snarling, and shaking its head from side to side.

A shaggy dog came running from the main ranch house, barking furiously, running up and down on the other side of the fence. Any chance of a silent entry to Cordillo Downs Ranch was now a distant memory.

There was a piercing whistle from somewhere. The dingo jumped back, then Birani heard the simultaneous sounds of a rush of air, the dead thud of a bullet strike, then the receding sound of a rifle shot.

The dingo was catapulted 3 meters away from him by the impact. It kicked and scrabbled, then was still, orange dust hanging in the air. The barking dog behind the fence dropped down, nose between its paws, silent, watchful.

Birani, shaken, slid down the vehicle door, squatting down in the dust as Billy Bob Mason strode up, jacking another round into a Marlin lever action rifle.

                    BILLY BOB MASON
                 (Calm and precise)
          Be still now Birani, might be some
          life left in that fucker yet.

There was another shot and the dingo flipped
over, dust flying. Billy Bob opened the gate and
walked over to look at the dingo, nudging it
with a high-heeled boot. A putrid odour hung in
the super-heated air.

Billy Bob grinned and looked across at Birani.

             BILLY BOB MASON (CONT'D)
          Thought you'd come in the back way then
          eh mate? Looks like there's vermin at
          both my fucking gates right now.
                 (A beat, grin fading)
          Dingoes are easier to deal with I
          reckon.

Billy Bob stepped over, reached down, Birani took
his hand and he came up into a male embrace.

                    BIRANI PEMBA
          Good to see you Bill. Thanks mate.

Billy Bob indicated the hood of Birani's pick-up.

                    BILLY BOB MASON
          Sit up there old mate, lets have a
          quick look at you. If that bastard
          has drawn blood on you... well, you
          know what that means.

Birani sat on the hot metal hood pulling up his
jeans above his boot tops. There was a trickle
of blood, and he felt his chest constrict. Billy
Bob bent to look close.

                    BILLY BOB MASON (CONT'D)
             Not yours mate, you are good.

Billy Bob went to the back of Birani's pick-up,
took a steel can of gasoline, stepped over
and poured it on the body of the dingo. Then,
walking backwards, he poured a trail of the
gasoline for 5 meters.

He set down the gas can well away, walked
over and struck a match on the sole of a boot,
dropping it onto the gasoline trail. The low
fire travelled rapidly along the ground to the
dead dingo, where it burst into a whoosh of
sizzling flames.

He came back to Birani, pulled two smokes from
his breast pocket, lit both, handed one to
Birani, and they both smoked and watched the
fire for several minutes.

                    BILLY BOB MASON (CONT'D)
                    (Squinting at Birani)
             There's a common saying along the
             Stuart Highway old mate. They say a
             man with only one mattress on the
             back of his Ute is a poor man.

Billy Bob glanced at the bed of Birani's pick-up
soberly, leaned and spat.

                    BILLY BOB MASON (CONT'D)
                    (Laconically)
             You are traveling light Mr Pemba.
             Fucking light.
                    (A beat, blowing blue smoke)
             What's up Birani?

Birani Pemba pulled a last drag from his own cigarette and stubbed it on his boot heel.

                    BIRANI PEMBA
          (Quietly)
     I need to ask you something Billy Bob...
          (A beat)
     Did you touch it my friend?

     After you shot it, I mean? I just
     wanted to know, direct from you, not
     from anyone else.

Billy Bob squinted over towards the media scrum on the other side of the ranch. He ground out his own smoke.

                    BILLY BOB MASON
     We better go mate; they will have
     heard them shots.

Birani reached, gripping the iron bicep of his friend.

                    BIRANI PEMBA
     Did you Bill? I have to know.

Billy Bob spat dryly into the orange dust. A few meters away the falling light seemed to make the dingo fire even brighter.

                    BILLY BOB MASON
     Don't you be worrying about old Billy
     Bob Mr Birani Pemba.

     I ain't got no fucking blue eggs
     growing in me.
          (A beat, full eye contact)
     You hear me, none... Fucking NONE!

Birani waited a beat, holding Billy Bob's gaze, feeling the tension in his gut lurch downwards and subside.

Billy Bob opened the gate and Birani drove the pick-up on through. Then got in and the dog jumped on the truck bed. They headed for the ranch-house.

Behind them the thin line of smoke from the burning dingo arced into the blue, orange sky as deep purple streaks gathered low on the eastern horizon.

FADE OUT

INT. HEATHROW DEPARTURES. LONDON. EARLY MORNING

Heathrow Airport.

A vague grey mist hung over vast tarmac, costly objects of technological beauty loom indistinctly, and the bitter tang of kerosene drifts in the cold air. A Qantas Boeing 777 glides past, silent behind triple glazing, the massive GE90 engine pods swinging lightly off its composite wings. Inexplicable tannoid messages echo amid intermittent wafts of fresh croissants and coffee smells.

Sergei Narratova and two suits sprawl on uncomfortable plastic seats at Gate 26. Flight AD-LHR461a is full but not yet boarded. Everyone gazing into phone screens or dozing.

No-one relishing the 31hrs and 15 min flight duration, stopping at Zurich and Singapore en-route.

Sergei texts.

TEXT EXCHANGE.

> SERGEI
> Have you told him yet?

> EKATERINA LEBOV
> Yes, over coffee this morning. He's gone back to bed in disgust. It's OK my darling. Travel safe. X

> SERGEI
> We are at the gate now, boarding in 15. Stay close Kat.

> I love you. We will sort this.

FADE OUT

INT. 14 HALF MOON STREET. MAYFAIR LONDON. BEDROOM. MORNING

Andrei leaned into blissful pillows and willed the dull ache in his lower back to stop, it gradually subsided.

He touched the TV remote and a list of Ekaterina's programs appeared on a rising screen. He clicked to the top one and watched Calvin Jensen's interview with Sarah Cantrell. In spite of his conjured-up visions of shamans, charlatans and crackpots, he found Sarah Cantrell's story of her husband's healing from alleged contact with the BUNYIP flesh strangely compelling, and even believable.

What the hell, he thought, he might as well go with the flow because there were certainly no mainstream medical options left open for him. He would still stay with his overall plan to have Sergei shoot him anyway.

At some point he drifted and slept.

Ekaterina came in with a cup of coffee in both hands, she paused, looking from the sleeping Andrei to the TV still playing the recorded BUNYIP story.

A wan smile passed across her face as she touched the remote, killing the TV screen.

                                        FADE OUT

EXT. 408 NELSON ROAD. PARA HILLS. ADELAIDE. NIGHT

During the day, Nelson Rd and Kesters had filled up with a glittering array of media traffic bristling with aerials, pulsating with electronics, the ground covered with thick snakes of squirming power cables.

Alien tripods with cameras focused on doors and windows. The house land line was off the hook, his cell phone muted, John Cantrell existed in a half-life of fear and tension, vaguely rehearsed soundbites endlessly looping through his brain.

Sarah, on the other hand, was bright, buzzing with excitement and finely tuned into her own carefully rehearsed performances. She glanced across at John lurking fearfully to the side of their lounge window.

                    SARAH
     They are just doing their jobs you
     know John.

                    JOHN
                 (Miserable)
     These fuckers defy the theory of
     bloody evolution you know.

     They are the new great unwashed.
     They live in buses and vans, eating
     junk, no sleep, no showers, no family
     routines, living on adrenaline and
     the promise of that next news scoop,
     or some shitty paparazzi photographs
     to wreck someone's life.
                 (A beat, groaning)
     This is awful.

At the edges of the media scrum, sightseers, and rubber neckers were napping, some cooking on BBQs, some even climbing trees to get a better view. Everywhere people, commotion and excitement.

                    SARAH
                 (Brightly)
     John, Channel 9 paid us $5k for that
     interview the other night. I was only
     there an hour. A couple more like
     that and maybe we can clear some
     debt.

John looked at her, she was clearly enjoying their new celebrity status and being the centre of attention. Something occurred to him...

                    JOHN
          (Wondering)
     Have we still got that piece of meat
     recovered from under the seat?
          (Realization dawning)
     You have never actually told anyone
     about the piece of meat, have you? We
     have just said there was blood.

                    SARAH
          (Triumphantly)
     I know John.
          (A beat)
     It's in the fridge. It's safe and I'm
     keeping it mate.

     That, my love, could turn out to be
     our insurance policy.

Overnight, the news-crews intensified their attack, tapping on windows and doors, calling their names, initially good-natured, but as time wore on, the atmosphere changing to hostility and frustration as the house defences refused to yield.

Sometime after 0600 in the morning police arrived following several calls from John. By this time there were scuffles promising the descent into violent exchanges.

Watching quietly to one side from a clump of eucalyptus trees was a small encampment of Aboriginals. They didn't join in the melee or attempt to speak to anyone, they waited with patience and deadly resolve.

FADE OUT

INT. 'ALTERN' HQ. 46-52 EDINBURGH. CANBERRA. CONFERENCE ROOM. MORNING.

Jeff Uteri was unsettled. The call from the Minister's office had been brief and terse.

The Rt Hon Arthur McCloud MP, Minister for Industry, Energy and Emissions was at a nearby meeting, and would like to fit in an unscheduled late-morning meeting with himself, and include if possible, Michelle Rogan.

Jeff had asked immediately, 'What is the agenda?' He was told unceremoniously that an agenda would be agreed in the meeting.

His worst nightmare, not able to prepare.

Michelle arrived in an intoxicating cloud of Chanel No5 and perfectly presented female executive persona. She pulled back a chair, eyebrows raised.

                    JEFF UTERI
            (Shaking head, hands spread)
        Mish, I have no idea. They said an
        agenda would be agreed in the meeting.

                    MISH ROGAN
                (Flatly)
        It will be the fucking BUNYIP Jeff...
        you know it!

Arthur McCloud arrived, handsome 50s, vigorous, self-assured, pinstripes, direct gaze. He dismissed his two aides with an imperious wave and sat at the end of the long conference table. Jeff and Michelle moved to sit along one side near him. The Minister nodded to them both, flattened his hands to the rosewood, paused.

> ARTHUR MCCLOUD MP
> (Precisely, looking down)
> Consider this sentence: 'I didn't say you were beautiful'.
> (A beat)
> There are only six words. But, by placing hard emphasis on each of the six words in turn, six completely different subtle meanings can be derived.

Arthur McCloud leaned back regarding them both.

> ARTHUR MCCLOUD MP (CONT'D)
> If inflection, tone, facial expression and body language is added into the delivery mix of this six-word sentence, matters get immediately murkier and even more complex.
>
> You could, in fact, do a fucking PhD on it.
> (A beat, rising anger)
> Your Press Release Statement on the BUNYIP was 400 words in length. It was a masterclass in non committality, yet it has served as the global, indeed the planetary, confirmation by the Australian Government that 200 years of previous denials of the existence of mythical creatures

were all lies, Miss-speaks, or cover-
ups, or fake news, or even worse,
conspiracy theories.
          (A beat, outward breath)
God, how I hate that expression.

Jeff and Michelle are mute, white faced, awaiting
execution.

                    ARTHUR MCCLOUD MP (CONT'D)
          Why...?
                    (A beat, barely controlled)
          For fuck's sake Jeff, why?

Jeff and Michelle both moved in their seats
simultaneously, leaning forward, earnest eyes
on their superior. Jeff cleared his throat.

                    JEFF UTERI
          Er, Minister, er, as we speak,
          Australia has two mines producing
          rare metals.

          By far, the biggest being Mt. Weld in
          Western Australia, owned by the Lynas
          Corporation.

The Minister held his gaze, unblinking, straight
back, hands flat.

                    JEFF UTERI (CONT'D)
          ALTERN has several projects running
          in the Simpson. They are all ECO
          based, looking at water distribution,
          possible new food systems, all
          supporting research elements into
          the achievement of an OZ NET ZERO in
          ten years or so.
                    (A beat)

Our teams are still working out there
as we speak.

The Minster drummed his fingers slightly, took
a breath, glanced at Michelle Rogan, shifted in
his seat minutely.

>   JEFF UTERI (CONT'D)
> Hear me out Sir, please.
>   (A beat)
> In world terms, Australia has around
> the 6th largest, rare earth metal
> reserves.

The Minster slammed both hands hard down on the
table. Jeff and Michelle jumped visibly.

>   ARTHUR MCCLOUD MP
>   (Taking moral high ground)
> I don't want to listen to these
> bollocks right now Jeff, we, and I
> mean our Government, are being made
> to look a laughing stock on the
> World stage right now, the fucking TV
> programs are being syndicated around
> the globe, and you sit there and
> recite bloody statistics at me...

Jeff looked helplessly at Michelle, she avoided
his look, her eyes becoming moist, her usual
rigid body language control faltering.

>   JEFF UTERI
>   (Hoarsely, too loud)
> Minister, ALTERN's scientific research
> teams in the Simpson have discovered,
> by chance, because we were focused
> on other things, rare earth metal
> reserves, that will dwarf the entire

planet's supply for the foreseeable next 20 decades.
            (A   beat,   explosive   outward
            breath)
Minister,   the   fucking   Simpson,
Australia, is going to be the next
Middle East.

There was silence in the room. Both Jeff and Michelle sagged in their seats.

The Minister sat rigidly upright, his tanned face becoming pale, his eyes fiercely fixed on Jeff Uteri's face. After several beats, he looked around the room.

            ARTHUR MCCLOUD MP
Have we got cameras in here?

            JEFF UTERI
No Sir, we are secure.

            ARTHUR MCCLOUD MP
            (Low voice)
Run that by me again Jeff, please.

            JEFF UTERI
            (Slowly, clearly)
Sir, the Simpson is going to make
the last 30 years of oil boom in
the Middle East look like the childlike, infantile, pubescent tinkering
of a fucking badly managed playschool
kindergarten in a sandpit.

Silence again in the room. Michelle sniffed into a tissue. Minutes ticked by. The Minister paced, sat down, paced again, rounded on Jeff, legs apart.

                    ARTHUR MCCLOUD MP
         Who else knows about this?

                      JEFF UTERI
                  (Shrug)
         Our teams out there in the Simpson,
         that's it, no one else.

The Minister sat down again, both hands pressing
his face into a grotesque mask, then leaning
back, exhausted.

                    ARTHUR MCCLOUD MP
         So... let me try to understand this...
                  (A beat, musing)
         You let the BUNYIP story run, you
         purposely gave it legs, even though
         you knew it was total bollocks, to
         buy us some time.

         To bury the news until we are ready
         for a big reveal.
                  (A beat, face clearing)
         And...
                  (Sudden grin)
         To put ALTERN into a driving position
         uniting the two main political lobbies
         with the Native Australian lobby.
                  (A beat, widening grin)
         My God guys, that is fucking
         totally fucking unbelievably fucking
         brilliant!

The Minister came out of his seat, his tie
askew, pulling both Michelle and Jeff into an
extended group hug that became an awkward
skipping dance across the conference room floor.

At that moment, the glass door opened, and the Minister's two Aides entered the room, stopping open-mouthed in astonishment at the tableau of dancing professionals.

The two groups gaped at each other agog.

FADE OUT

EXT. ADELAIDE INTERNATIONAL AIRPORT. STH AUSTRALIA. DAY.

Flight AD-LHR461a circled wide over West Beach, shafts of impossibly bright sunlight gyrating around the cabin. The 747 lined up on runway 1 for a perfect landing.

A puff of white smoke from the wheels, a lurch as the Auto-Point corrected the slight leftward pitch, a bump as the nosewheel dropped on the tarmac, then the rushing reverse thrust pushing tired passengers forward hard against their seatbelts.

The whining systems shut down and the barely controlled mayhem of de-boarding began. Cabin bags hefted, phones connecting and blipping with new emails as unwashed bodies file past dazzling fake smiles, down steel steps and into the unrelenting wall of 35c heat, the smell of kerosene mixed with the burnt tang of dry grass, then through passport control, luggage collection and finally through the smoked glass, out of the aircon and into the glittering superheated frenetic taxi rank.

Sergei and his two companions, Dmitri and Igor, entered South Australia seamlessly on a 90-day visa as international businessmen, taking an ice-cold taxi to the 5* Beach House Hotel on Glenelg waterfront.

They checked in, went to their rooms, fell onto taut bedspreads, and slept for six hours straight.

                                    FADE OUT

EXT. MAIN NE ROAD. NORTH ADELAIDE. DAY

Birani Pemba was two 12-hour days south on the Prince's Highway from Cordillo Downs to Adelaide. The Port Augusta ramp beckoned, but he had ignored it, deciding to get nearer before he stopped again. At Winninowie he could no longer ignore the gas needle flickering at less than quarter of a tank.

He looped down and under the highway to a rubbish dump masquerading as a filling station in the shade of the overpass.

He pulled in next to a battered row of gas pumps, a shiny black Mercedes crouched aggressively feral on the other side of his pump.

A big man in a white shirt and black felt hat was leaning on the trunk. He was almost as wide as he was tall and was sweating profusely. He had an unlit cigarette in the corner of his mouth. Birani eyed him as he got stiffly out of his pick-up, cigarettes and gas pumps spell IDIOT, big-time.

A female pump-jockey, 20s, jeans, skimpy top, tattoos, cowboy boots, sashayed up, looked at them both, nodded to Birani.

                    PUMP JOCKEY
          Birani.

Need gas guys? Who's first?

                    BLACK FELT HAT MAN
          That'd be me I reckon. Why else do
          think I stopped here.

The pump jockey slammed her way metallically through the well-worn gas-up routine, ignoring his comment. She eyed the unlit cigarette warily. The man looked across balefully at Birani, leaned and spat.

                    BLACK FELT HAT MAN (CONT'D)
                 (To no-one in particular)
          Fucking stinks around here, somebody
          run over a dingo?

Birani turned away. The pump-jockey eyed them both as she worked the hose.

                    PUMP JOCKEY
                 (To the Black Hat)
          How much do you want?

                    BLACK FELT HAT MAN
          How much is it?

The pump-jockey nodded awards a huge neon sign by the highway. He looked at it, spat again.

                    BLACK FELT HAT MAN (CONT'D)
Your prices are too high I reckon,
but I guess being out here on the
Highway, you guys have no problems
suckering honest folks out of their
money.

The pump-jockey glanced at him, resigned,
her shoulders tense. She stopped pumping gas
and looked into the man's eyes. Birani moved
slightly away from his vehicle, heart rate
rising, getting his balance.

                    PUMP JOCKEY
What exactly do you mean 'suckering?
Explain...

                    BLACK FELT HAT MAN
You know exactly what I mean sister,
you got us where you want us...

                    PUMP JOCKEY
          (Temper flaring)
I'm not your sister, and I don't have
to take your fucking insults, you
cocksucker.

You saw the price. Why don't you
head off down the road and try to find
someone else to insult.

She clanged the pump hose back on the hook and
stepped over to Birani Pemba.

                    PUMP JOCKEY (CONT'D)
          (To Black Hat)
Just piss off mate!
          (To Birani)
Fill her up Birani?

Birani nodded, watchful and alert.

Black Hat watched her begin gassing Birani's pick-up in disbelief.

                    BLACK FELT HAT MAN
                    (Outraged)
          What the fuck are you doing lady?
          Get back over here bitch, do your
          fucking job.

Birani reached his limit. He moved between the Pump Jockey and the man.

                    BIRANI PEMBA
                    (Evenly, eye contact)
          You saw the sign big man, like she
          said. It's time to move along I reckon.

          This lady works here, she makes
          nothing on the gas sales.

The big man snorted and launched off the trunk of the Mercedes. Birani stepped in close, dropped his shoulder and hit him hard on the bridge of his nose before he had his balance. His boot heels shot forward and he sat down hard on the base of his spine, his nose flattened, snorting blood like a bulldog.

Birani wrung his hand, blowing ruefully on his skinned knuckles. The man sat on the oily concrete holding his face. The pump jockey coolly finished filling up Birani's tank and hooked up the hose. She nodded at him.

                    PUMP JOCKEY
          Pay over there at the cabin Birani.

Birani stepped over to pay.

When he returned to his vehicle, the big man was still sitting there by his car, holding his face. At the next pump a battered estate car with three adults and four children had pulled up. The children, stood all in a line from tallest to smallest, looked curiously at the big man sitting on the floor holding his face.

A old man in overalls, a straw hat, with white stubble whiskers walked over from the yawning blackness of the garage door. A thin smile on his lips, he indicated the Pump-Jockey working on another gas-up

                    STRAW HAT MAN
          She's a good'un, that one Birani.
               (A beat, squinting at him)
          Saw you on the Telly the other night
          I reckon, How's my old mate Billy Bob?

                    BIRANI PEMBA
          Aw yeh, Billy Bob is good mate. He's
          a bit busy lately.

The old man considered that, nodding. Turned to watch the big man at the rear of the Mercedes as he struggled to his feet, drooling blood, and snot. His audience of solemn children still standing in a row, watching silently. The old man grinned at Birani with blackened teeth.

                    STRAW HAT MAN
          Yeh, I heard that.
               (A beat)
          You might need something sometime
          Mister Pemba. Come on back here if
          y'all do, y'hear me now.

Birani slid into his pick-up, raised a finger and took the long loop upwards into the afternoon sun and onto the Prince's Highway, barrelling south.

The old man pivoted slowly on his heel, watching him out of sight.

FADE OUT

EXT. 408 NELSON ROAD. PARA HILLS. ADELAIDE, STH AUST...

The media circus had come down from its frenetic high over the past two days, not quite giving up on John and Sarah, but reverting now to publishing a fall-back series of semi-fictional stories and low-level trailer-park dramatic reports, each more extreme than the previous.

Editors were now beginning to pull reporters off the Bunyip story in favour of digging up various soap opera D list celebrity love life scandals.

John was by the lounge window, he shouted to Sarah.

                    JOHN
        Police coming.

Loud knock on front door.

                JOHN (CONT'D)
        Coming.

A burly policemen stood dangling keys.

                    POLICEMAN 3
     We are done Mr Cantrell. Your keys.

                      JOHN
     So, you find anything? Was it Bunyip
     blood?

The policemen gave him a look, ignored his
question, produced a form, holding it in front
of John with a pen poised. John looked at it,
perplexed.

                    POLICEMAN 3
     You need to sign, here.

                      JOHN
          (Exasperated)
     You not going to tell us shite are
     you? After all our cooperation and
     your assurances etc.

The policeman spoke to the mike on his shoulder,
all the while looking hard at John.

                    POLICEMAN 3
     He's not going to sign Sarge. Do I
     bring it back?

John reacted, blowing air in disgust, reached
for the pen, initialling the form. The policeman
passed over the keys with an arrogant flourish
and left without another word.

John shut the door in the faces of several
converging reporters, microphones extended. He
went over to the lounge window, watched the
police car head down Kesters Rd towards the
shops.

He was aware that the media circus was wasting away gradually. The TV outside broadcast vans were packing up. An air of decay and disinterest hung over the litter strewn site. John moved over to the other side of the window, his eyes drawn to a quiet group of Aboriginals camped in a stand of Eucalyptus, two hundred meters away, separate from everyone else. A thin line of campfire smoke rose through the branches.

As he watched, a white pick-up truck covered in red dust, came up Kesters Rd, bumped over the kerb, and made its way over to the encampment. A tall Aboriginal man got out and stretched his back.

Several people congregated around him with greetings. The man shaded his eyes and looked over at No 408. John watched him, there was something vaguely familiar about him.

Sarah came up behind him, she was depressed.

>   SARAH
> Looks like they are losing interest
> in us now Jonno. I guess that's it. We
> are not going to make any more money
> out of it now.
>   (A beat)
> What are you looking at?

John went to the sideboard, getting binoculars.

>   JOHN
> Not sure. A guy over there looks
> familiar. A black guy in a white
> pick-up, he's just arrived.

Sarah looked; interest piqued.

                    SARAH
         Can I look John, please.

He handed the binoculars to her, and she focused
for several beats, handing them back to him.

                    SARAH (CONT'D)
               (Brightening)
         Hmm, the game may not be over yet...

John looked at her, eyes questioning.

                    SARAH (CONT'D)
         That black feller over there is
         Birani Pemba. He's the one they have
         interviewed several times on the TV.
         He's the Leader of the Aboriginal
         political lobby.
               (A beat)
         The one who said the Bunyip remains
         belongs to them.

John took the binoculars back and focused on
the Aboriginal encampment, the handsome face
of Birani Pemba jumping into crystal focus as
he looked directly into the binoculars.

John recoiled involuntarily, then realized that
Pemba could not see him. He then swept his
glasses along the tree line on the open ground
opposite the house. The image in his binoculars
caught a flash of sunlight and he swept back,
re-focusing.

A black Range Rover was parked, its image moving
in the heat distortion, it was half covered in
the pale brown grass. A curl of white smoke came
from the exhaust - the engine was running to
keep the aircon working.

The sun was on the windscreen so nothing could be seen, but unbidden, John's stomach coiled with a cold twist of fear.

FADE OUT

EXT. SIMPSON DESERT OUTBACK. STH AUSTRALIA. DAY

Billy Bob took off his pack, sat in hot sand with it in his lap, leaned on it and swept binoculars over the scrub desert below him. His hat was pulled down over the binoculars to exclude extraneous light as he studied the baked terracotta floodplain. He had seen a flash of sunlight off a surface somewhere in front of him, and his curiosity was alerted.

He was interested in a slight ridge where the ground dipped, probably just under a mile away. Something moved in the landscape over to the right, he turned, focused. A Big Red Female Roo with a wallaby was strained upright, she was looking towards the dip, highly alert, both ears locked forward. He swung back, saw nothing, decided to get closer.

He worked his way diagonally down a scree, moving slow to keep the dust down. When he got to the bottom, he looked for the Roo. She was gone, but a low haze of pale orange dust hung where she had been. She had taken off; something had spooked her. Whatever was in the dip was below his sight line, but it had now become his entire reason for existing on the planet.

He worked his way to the crest of a ridge, stayed below it, and traversed, the effort blackening his shirt with sweat. At the end of the ridge was a rockfall, sprouts of brush and cat-claw thrusting between rounded boulders. He sat in the rocks with his elbows on his knees and looked down at tire tracks curving down into a small canyon. He took out his Sat-phone and noted the Map-Ref, pressing SAVE.

A hundred meters on, and he saw two yellow Pick-Up trucks. Glassing them, he read ALTERN on the doors in black capitals, with a logo. He rose, face clearing, stretched, hefted his rifle and shoulder bag, and walked purposely along the tire tracks like a man at ease with himself.

The two trucks were nosed together as if mating. Three men and a woman in hard hats pored over maps and graphs spread over a hood.

Billy Bob switched his sat-phone handset to RECORD and walked on up. They all looked up in surprise.

> BILLY BOB MASON
> G'Day folks, looks like another hot one.

All of them were shocked at his sudden appearance in this remote place. The woman reacted first.

> DR ASTRID KARLSEN
> Hello, good morning...
> (A beat, glancing at colleagues)
> Er, please excuse me, this is a research site, may we ask Sir, that you cannot hunt here.

Billy Bob looked critically at them, memorizing faces. He took out his handset, switched it to

PHOTO, and took several still high-def photos of them and their trucks, then returned the handset to MOVIE RECORD.

                    DR ASTRID KARLSEN (CONT'D)
          Hey, excuse me, what are you doing?

The three men came from behind the vehicles. One of them middle aged, red in the face, walking forward, hand out.

                    DR HANS ABELMAN
          Give me that phone, you cannot photograph here.

          This is an Australian Government research project, and it is top-secret. We are scientists, we do not seek trouble with you Sir, but you must surrender your phone to delete those photographs.
                    (A beat, hand out)
          Please.

Billy Bob spat dryly, he glanced all around, taking his time. Turned and looked behind him, tucked his phone handset away in a pocket.

                    BILLY BOB MASON
          I'd like y'all to stand away from the vehicles a bit if you wouldn't mind.
                    (A beat)
          If that would be OK.

                    DR ASTRID KARLSEN
                    (Becoming angry)
          What the hell are you talking about?

Billy Bob unslung his rifle, and in a continuous motion while walking about, shot out two tires on each of the vehicles. Four shots, close together, the echoes rolling along the ridge, repeating. Dust hanging in the still superheated air.

The four scientists recoiled from him, grouping together protectively, their white faces registering fright. They watched him alertly, shocked into silence.

> BILLY BOB MASON
> (Evenly)
> My name is Billy Bob Mason. You people are conducting illegal research on my land. I have disabled your vehicles.
> (A beat)
> ALTERN have not obtained my permission to conduct operations on this map-ref, so you have no right to be here.
>
> Your registered sites are 40 miles south of here. You have not wandered over a hidden or an obscure border, because there is not a border, or a line fence within 80 miles of where we are standing.
>
> I am certain that you are all aware of these facts because I can see the detailed maps and graphs that you were all busily consulting when I walked up.
> (A beat)
> So, I will ask you please, lady and gentlemen, do not insult my intelligence with a stream of blustering denials.
> (A beat)

To be clear, I have disabled your
vehicles, but I will not take away
your Sat-phones, or harm you in any
way, and I have recorded the entirety
of this encounter on my own handset.
(A beat, grin)
Just to remove any future ambiguities
that may arise, you understand.
(A beat)
I'm pretty sure that ALTERN will
rescue you and your equipment well
before you become distressed.

The four scientists remained white-faced and
silent but moved slightly apart from their
previous frightened huddle.

BILLY BOB MASON (CONT'D)
I'm not going to engage with you as to
what exactly you guys are researching,
but I am assuming, that its possibly
a bit outside your normal remit,
maybe...?

DR HANS ABELMAN
(Face clearing, to colleagues)
This is the fucking hilly billy
that is supposed to have shot that
imaginary creature, the BUNYIP!

The other scientists looked curiously at Billy
Bob, registering a mix of guilt and outrage.

DR HANS ABELMAN (CONT'D)
(Scornfully)
I thought you would have been busy
raking in the money from Channel 9
and the fucking news media for your
fake 'creature feature' story, not

skulking around in the bloody desert spying on genuine scientists who are trying to do their job and save the planet.

Billy Bob scanned the sky, spinning slightly on a heel.

                    BILLY BOB MASON
          If I was you, I'd be making your rescue
          calls pretty damn quick. Otherwise,
          you might have an uncomfortable night
          out here in the donga. It gets bloody
          cool once the sun goes down.
                    (A beat, nodding to the west)
          Oh yes...
                    (A beat, as if suddenly
                    remembering)
          A few miles over there, are what's
          left of some of seven of my Texas
          Longhorn steers. Whatever it was that
          ripped them apart might be sniffing
          the air right now, locating their
          next prey.
                    (A beat)
          I'd stay in the cabs of your vehicles
          tonight, if by any chance ALTERN don't
          come get you by nightfall.
                    (A beat)
          Just saying...

Billy Bob walked to the two ALTERN pickup trucks and looked at the various paraphernalia in the flatbeds, he poked around, picking up some rock samples and stuffed them into his pack.

He hefted his rifle and shoulder pack and walked back along the tire tracks to the ridge. He turned to look back from a high point. The four scientists were all sitting inside the cabs of their pick-up trucks, windows up, anxious faces looking out.

                                        FADE OUT

INT. 'ALTERN' HQ. 46-52 EDINBURGH ST. CANBERRA. DAY

Jeff Uteri leaned, touched his handset screen.

ON PHONE.

                    JEFF UTERI
          Get me the Minister. Tell him its
          sort of urgent.

He waited drumming his fingers.

                    ARTHUR MCCLOUD MP
          McCloud. What's up?

                    JEFF UTERI
          Minister, we have an issue. William
          Robert Mason, that is, Billy Bob, the
          alleged BUNYIP shooter, ran into one
          of our research teams - on his own
          land I might add.

There was silence while Arthur McCloud MP processed the information.

                    ARTHUR MCCLOUD MP
          'Ran into'
                    (A beat)
          What the hell does that mean Jeff. We
          have full contracted permission for
          our research projects.

                    JEFF UTERI
    Er, well, No, not exactly Minister.
    They were a bit 'off piste'

                 ARTHUR MCCLOUD MP
    Jeff, I really do not have the fucking
    time to extract this from you bit by
    bit like a demented dentist. Give it
    to me in a single sentence please!

                    JEFF UTERI
    He found them where they shouldn't
    have been Minister.

    Shot out their fucking tires and
    guessed that they were researching
    stuff outside ALTERN's contracted
    remit.
         (A beat)
    They sat freezing in their cabs
    all night scared shitless in case a
    fucking BUNYIP attacked them.

                 ARTHUR MCCLOUD MP
    You are being serious, right?

In spite of himself, Arthur McCloud exploded
into gales of uncontrolled laughter, Jeff joining
in, until it subsided.

              ARTHUR MCCLOUD MP (CONT'D)
             (A beat, strangled voice)
    He shot out their tires, and they
    locked themselves into the vehicles
    in case a BUNYIP got them?

He roared with another paroxysm of laughter,
calmed himself with some effort.

ARTHUR MCCLOUD MP (CONT'D)
This is a movie? Right? This isn't real.

Jeff's laughter subsided into uncertainty.

JEFF UTERI
Its real Minister. I'm sorry. We managed to get them out today. They are all pretty shaken up. They don't want to go back out there again, because...

ARTHUR MCCLOUD MP
Oh please, not because of the BUNYIP? They are scared of the fucking BUNYIP?
        (A beat)
Jeff, the BUNYIP story is total absolute bollocks! Its bloody fucking BOLLOCKS! What the hell is this...

JEFF UTERI
        (Resigned)
I know Minister. I know.
        (A beat)
So, what do you think we should do about this Hill Billy, Billy Bob Mason?

He could cause us all sorts of problems, particularly with permissions for mining rights etc.

ARTHUR MCCLOUD MP
        (Coldly, patiently)
Jeff, we are the Government. First option is offer him money, a lot of it, 2nd option is compulsory purchase, 3rd option, we **'accident'** him.

(A beat)
Why do you even ask me?

The phone call went dead in Jeff's hands. He sat there like a man who had come to the end of something, his world somehow darker, the laughter a memory.

FADE OUT

EXT. WASTE GROUND OPPOSITE 408 NELSON RD. PARA HILLS. DAY

Sergei, Dmitri and Igor sat in aircon with the engine of the Range Rover running. From time-to-time Sergei watched the house with binoculars.

SERGEI
The media are pulling out I think, must be losing interest.
(A beat, glancing around)
We will go in late tonight.

CUT TO:

EXT. WASTE GROUND OPPOSITE 408 NELSON RD. PARA HILLS. AFTERNOON

Birani Pemba accepted the coffee, leaned, and sipped. It was awful, but he kept a straight face, wondering if they purposely made it bad to check if he was losing his cultural identity. All around lay the detritus of a large camp. Vehicles were pulling away, some quickly, glad to be on the move to new things, some slower, reluctant to let go of something. He looked across at the house, they had not ventured out, even though their car, an old Holden, had been returned to them by the police. He looked across at his companions, held their gaze and nodded.

                    BIRANI PEMBA
          Soon, we will go soon.

                              CUT TO:

INT. 408 NELSON ROAD. PARA HILLS. ADELAIDE, STH AUST...

Sarah stood back and surveyed the kitchen cupboards with distaste. The fridge was a similar story.

                    SARAH
          Jonno, we have to do it today.

John is in his usual place by the window. He is miserable.

                    JOHN
          I know. I'll make a run for it. I
          won't go the shops on Kesters, I'll
          go to the Tea Tree Gully centre.

He scanned the litter strewn street and the open ground opposite the house. The media had finally deserted them and moved on, but he was unsettled. He focused binoculars, as he had done countless times, on the aboriginal group under the stand of eucalyptus. There was nothing to see that wasn't there before. The same lazy line of campfire smoke, a few pick-up trucks and other beat-up vehicles. People moving around listlessly.

He swung the glasses to the Range Rover. Still there with engine running. It had briefly left a few times, always returning to the same place. He reached a decision, stood, grabbed bags, shades, and hat.

>   JOHN (CONT'D)
>   (Brief grin)
>   OK, give me that list babe. I'm gone.
>   Keep your phone handy.

Sarah handed him an extensive shopping list, he glanced at it, shaking his head ruefully.

>   JOHN (CONT'D)
>   You've got no chance with all this.
>   I'll get what I can.

He reversed the Holden onto Nelson Road and took off. Sarah watched, her spirits lifting.

>   CUT TO:

INT. RANGE ROVER ON WASTE GROUND. PARA HILLS. DAY

Dmitri sat upright, alert, nudged Sergei. They watched the Holden head off along Nelson. Sergei focused binoculars.

>   SERGEI
>   She's still there, I can see her in
>   the window.

The three men exchanged glances.

>   CUT TO:

EXT. ABORIGINAL CAMP. WASTE GROUND OPPOSITE 408 NELSON RD. PARA HILLS. DAY.

Birani sat bolt upright with seven others watching the Holden out of sight. He nodded to the others.

> BIRANI PEMBA
> Shopping trip I reckon lads, he'll be back directly. He's alone.

> CUT TO:

EXT. MODBURY NE RD. TEA TREE GULLY. ADELAIDE. DAY

John cruised the Holden, enjoying the sense of freedom after being holed up for three days. He resisted the impulse to put his head out of the window and let the hot wind massage his scalp.

Traffic was light in the residential area until he crossed the bridge over the deep gully, the high tower of the shopping Centre ahead on the skyline. He joined the main road and slam-dunked into a gridlock of late afternoon home-comers heading into the shops to forage for the night's supper. He hit the brakes, leaned back, and lit a cigarette flowing with the traffic, feeling OK with it, glad to be out of the house.

Now and then it loosened as streams of vehicles turned off into the different carparks, he grinned, picked up speed, then swung the big car into a parking area with too many choices.

He picked one, then sped on to another, nearer the supermarket entrance, then saw another appear as a Falcon pulled out. He switched off, grinning broadly, feeling like he had won something, opened his door, then suddenly felt the air pressure change in the car.

Deja Vu hit as the big aboriginal man slid into the passenger seat next to him. The box cutter knife touched his thigh.

John froze, staring at a familiar face.

                    JANDAMARRA
        We have to stop meeting like this
        mate.
                (A beat)
        Sit tight you fucker, or I'll cut your
        leg, face forward - now relax...
                (A beat)
        That's it. Good boy.

                    JOHN
                (Realization dawning)
        I know you, don't I? The meat thief.
        FJ Holden flatbed. You were outside my
        house as well.

The two men sat, facing forward as shoppers moved around them loading bags, shooing children, reversing, bumping doors onto pock-marked wings, making calls, consulting lists.

An attendant with a coiling snake of connected shopping trolleys negotiated parked cars expertly, sliding perfectly into position in the covered trolley park. He turned and did a mock bow to John, gesturing to the mass of galvanized steel as if it was a conjuring trick.

The man next to John waved and grinned, acknowledging the skill. John sat there mute with shock, inexplicably his nose itched. He raised his hand to rub it, the knife point sank into his thigh, blood ran, his hand dropped immediately.

                    JANDAMARRA
     Be cool Jonno, be very still.
          (A beat)
     Listen to me real close and we can
     all be OK here. Do something stupid
     and I will cut you inside your thigh.

     You will bleed out in 20 minutes or
     so. After 10 you will most likely be
     brain dead. We don't want that, do
     we mate?

It was hot and airless in the car with the windows up. Both men sweated freely.

                    JANDAMARRA (CONT'D)
     My name is Jandamarra, they call
     me Jandi. I have the slab of Bunyip
     meat, and I'm in a bad place mate, I
     need your help.
          (A beat)
     I'm an aboriginal man and boy. I stole
     the Bunyip because at the minute, I
     thought it was the right thing.

     I saw these science boys take it into
     the laboratory, and they left the
     fucking door of their truck open.
     Next thing I'm getting into your car...

Jandi shook his head in disbelief.

JANDAMARRA (CONT'D)
Anyway, I ran. They never got me. I
hid the Bunyip, then watched the TV
News go totally bloody crazy mate.

Tracked you down from your car reg.
Saw your missis do her stuff on the TV.
        (Nodding)
Impressive.

                JOHN
What do you want? We can't help
you, how?

                JANDAMARRA
I'm fucked every which way from Sunday
mate. Everybody is gonna kill me. My
own people, and yours.

I took the Bunyip but now I know I
can't give it to anybody, and my own
KANYINI won't let me free whatever
I do.

                JOHN
KAN... what? What the fuck is that?

                JANDAMARRA
Hard to explain, it's intuitive
awareness, I guess. But it's much
more for me. I don't want to get into
that with you, that would be a waste
of fucking time.
        (A beat)
Here's the deal Jonny boy...
        (A beat)
I want you and your missis to negotiate
the BUNYIP for me.

I'll get the flesh to you; you do the
rest. Make whatever money you can
out of it, I don't care. I want free
of it. Pay me whatever you can, then
after that I'll go bush.
          (A beat)
Your missis is dead smart, she seems
to be well connected to these big TV
people.

If I stick my head above the parapet,
then I am fucked big time and
immediate - gone forever mate. And
any family I have are gone too.

John watched Jandi's mouth move but was having
difficulty staying aware. He kept losing the
sound as it rose and fell. He knew he was going
to pass out.

                    JANDAMARRA (CONT'D)
               (Loud, outraged)
          Are you even bloody listening to
          me man?

The tip of the knife went deeper into John's
thigh, and he snapped back into reality. He
focused with massive effort.

                    JOHN
          Yes, yes, we will do that. Take the
          knife off me for fuck's sake. What do
          want us to do?

Jandi took his knife away but held it close.

                    JANDAMARRA
          Well, first we gonna go back to your
          place - over that back fence. Talk to

your missis. Then we gonna get the
Bunyip.
        (A beat, sideways grin)
Simple eh.

An elaborately decorated bus pulled up in the
next parking bay, the sound system playing
'No Woman, No Cry' full blast. The driver
was a Rasta. He looked across at John, nodded
seriously and raised a finger. John nodded mutely
back.

Across the carpark was a shop named 'McIntyre's
Electronics'. He focused on the sign, trying not
to pass out.

                JANDAMARRA (CONT'D)
        OK, John, now we's gonna drive man.
        You up for that?
                (A beat)
        I'll be right here, next to you old
        mate.

John pulled himself together with massive effort
and drove. He loathed the man next to him with
a white-hot intensity that blazed like molten
steel in his brain. The man next to him looked
across at him and nodded.

                JANDAMARRA (CONT'D)
        I know man. Believe me, I do know.

                                FADE OUT

EXT. WASTE GROUND OPPOSITE 408 NELSON RD. PARA HILLS. EVENING

Dmitri stirred, something moved somewhere in his awareness. He glanced around the darkened Range Rover; both of his companions were asleep.

He pulled himself more upright and looked towards the house lit orange in the streetlights. The carport was still empty, so John Cantrell had not yet returned. The media encampment was now deserted, the detritus of their occupation showing as litter strewn flecks of white catching the vague moonlight and street lighting.

This time the movement was easy to spot. Several dark figures were converging on the house from the aboriginal encampment. They moved quickly and efficiently, but simply walked to the house, some disappearing around the back, two others to the front door.

A slab of interior hall light fell onto the pavement briefly as the door opened and closed.

> DMITRI OLVO
> (Prodding)
> Sergei, Igor, you need to see this.
> Comon guys.

The other two sat up, disorientated initially, then focusing.

> SERGEI
> What the fuck?
> (Rubbing his eyes)
> Did they just go inside? Guys from that ABBO camp?

                    DMITRI OLVO
          Yep, the others went around the back.
          Smooth operation I'd say.

Sergei hit the steering wheel and swore
continuously for several beats, then calmed
himself.

                    SERGEI
          OK, we watch and wait. Check your
          weapons, let's see what happens.

                    DMITRI OLVO
          Whoa boys, look at this...

John Cantrell's Holden had just swung into the
carport from moving fast along Nelson Rd. Two
men got out, glanced around, then walked to
front door. The brief slab of hall light fell
onto the pavement, then they were in.

                    SERGEI
          Well, now this is now very weird.
          One of those guys was John Cantrell,
          right?

                    DMITRI OLVO
          Yes, didn't know the other, he looked
          like a black feller.

                    SERGEI
          OK, let's be cool here, we are on
          this. These boys have the Bunyip
          stashed somewhere

                                        CUT TO:

INT. 408 NELSON ROAD. PARA HILLS. ADELAIDE. NIGHT.

John stepped into his hall, behind him, Jandi closed the door, slipping on the lock.

> JOHN
> Sarah, you there?

There was no reply and John pushed open the door into the lounge. It was crowded with seven people. Sarah sat in her usual armchair, ashen faced and tense. John, shocked, staggered against the door frame as Jandi stepped in behind him.

> JOHN (CONT'D)
> Who...what the...

> BIRANI PEMBA
> (Smoothly)
> Hello Mr Cantrell, John.
>
> Do not be alarmed please. No one needs to be harmed here. I realize that it looks very threatening, but let's take the heat down a bit if we can.

John looked around the room, then back to Sarah.

> JOHN
> Are you OK? Have these fuckers hurt you?

Sarah shook her head mutely, tears on her cheeks.

> BIRANI PEMBA
> She has not been hurt John. But I accept she is frightened, for that I am truly sorry.

                    (To a henchman)
          Get Mr Cantrell a seat.

John sat, and for the first time, Birani Pemba
acknowledged the presence of Jandamarra. He
nodded to him.

                    BIRANI PEMBA (CONT'D)
               (Vague smile, gesturing around)
          John, my name is Birani Pemba, these
          people are my tribal associates.

          Collectively our mission is to recover
          the remains of the BUNYIP. That's it.

          We knew, from what Sarah said on TV,
          that you must have at least some of
          the flesh in your possession, or at
          least been in contact with blood. So
          that's our start point.

Birani broke off, smiling around. Turning his
attention to Jandi.

                    BIRANI PEMBA (CONT'D)
          Hello Jandi. We got lucky tonight
          with you turning up.

          We guessed it was you all along. But
          you hid well.
               (A beat, leaning back)
          Well, as they say in England, here we
          all are then, why don't you come on
          in and join the tea set.

                                        FADE OUT

EXT. 14 HALF MOON STREET. MAYFAIR LONDON. NIGHT

Ekaterina leaned on the 3rd floor balcony and looked down and along the street bathed in pools of orange light. Several cars cruised on sidelights, then she saw the familiar shape of Andrei's limo sliding to a stop beneath her.

The doors stayed closed for several beats, then the driver got out and opened the back door.

She watched, tears springing, as Andrei's hands came out, clasping the burly driver's shoulders. It took several minutes of painful manoeuvring to get Andrei standing upright next to the car, holding on.

The driver stood back, letting his boss get his balance. He lit a cigarette, blowing smoke, passed it to Andrei, Andrei inhaled deep looking around and upwards. Ekaterina ducked backwards. The next time she looked down, the car was sliding silently away, and she felt the air pressure in the house change as the front door opened and closed.

Ekaterina went down a floor, meeting Andrei at the top of the stairs. He greeted her with a kiss, and she looked pointedly at his glowing cigarette.

> ANDREI LEBOV
> (Faint smile)
> I know, sorry darling.

He sat down, grinding out the cigarette. She put a vodka beside him and sat down facing him in a flourish of silk and lace.

151

                    EKATERINA LEBOV
          How have you been today my love?

                     ANDREI LEBOV
          Today has been a good day Ekaterina.
          I have been well thank you.

He tossed the vodka, eyes raising to hers,
questioning.

                    EKATERINA LEBOV
          They have located the people with the
          Bunyip flesh in Adelaide. It's just a
          matter of time Andrei.

She watched a faint flicker of disappointment
before the mask of inscrutability set again. He
leaned back, his eyes closing.

The streetlights reflecting in the corners of
the windows were all that lit the silent room.

Andrei slept, while Ekaterina lay awake studying
his profile in the semi darkness. She gradually
relaxed, the anxious knot in her stomach easing,
her fingers touching her iPhone, switched to
silent and vibrate.

                                        FADE OUT

EXT. DESERT ROAD.SOUTH AUSTRALIA. NIGHT

John and Jandi sat crammed together in the
jump seat of a double cab in a convoy of three
vehicles.

Bit by bit the city fell away to single story
'scrub' shops and workshops, used car yards, open

overgrown plots, hoardings, junkyards, sudden crossroads opening and closing, a John Deere tractor up on blocks, the occasional oncoming vehicle, then fleeting stands of eucalyptus set away from the road.

A run of loose fencing, looping rhythmically, and then no lights at all, just dark scrub desert rolling past. From time-to-time plastic bottles of warm flat water, tasting of copper, were passed around.

Between the seats John could see Birani Pemba's strong hand and wrist as he held the wheel. Beyond that, headlights flaring away, the road rushing at them. Beside him, Jandi stared away out of the other window. He had slumped into a smaller version of himself, facing death and possibly worse, spiritual destruction at the hands of his own cultural tribesmen.

For ten miles they sat behind a road train as it rolled north, smells of arid dust, diesel and sweat and dry baked earth. The road train was too long to pass, and the old pickup didn't have the legs.

Iridescent dawn streaks turned to flares of deep purple and orange on John's shoulder and at some point, Jandi spoke, his voice low and defeated.

                    JANDAMARRA
        Here, take the left.

Birani grunted and indicated for the others to follow. He spun the wheel and turned onto gravel and into the lightening sky, the relative quiet of bitumen changing to a a low roar as they hit the bulldust. Birani grinned back at John, his teeth flashing white.

                    BIRANI PEMBA
          At least we are in front mate. The
          others are eating our dust back there.

Full day arrived, then the harsh monotonous sunlight, dead grass on either side of the track, scorched wind, worn rock formations flitting past. John spat grit, cleared his throat.

                    JOHN
          Are we nearly there?

Birani roared with laughter, even Jandi raised a haunted smile, and slapped John's knee lightly.

                    JANDAMARRA
          (Bitterly)
          Won't be long son, hang in. Do you
          want an ice lolly? I've got one here
          somewhere.

Everyone but John in the car laughed.

                                        CUT TO:

EXT. SIMPSON DESERT OUTBACK. DAY

The black Range Rover floated north in a wind-rushing silence along the Prince's Highway. Inside with the aircon on full, it was cool and luxurious behind the tint, low music playing. The refrigerated glove box held several litres of cold water, the three dark suited men adjusted their Ray-Rans and relaxed into the easy chase, glancing from time to time at the massive sat-nav screen in the centre of the console. Outside, the white-hot scrub desert south of Port Augusta, sped past, muted through smoked glass.

The three pickups were 200 meters in front, cruising at 65 on the sparsely populated six-lane. Sergei felt OK about things.

> DMITRI OLVO
> Do you have a plan boss?

> SERGEI
> Well, I don't right now, but on the face of it, these guys don't present too much difficulty to me.
> (A beat)
> I'm guessing that at least one of these guys has stashed the Bunyip in a remote place. That's now where we are all heading. There is obviously some conflict going on between them, but we don't care about that.

Dmitri grinned wolfishly.

> DMITRI OLVO
> (Leaning back with iced water)
> Kill them all and let The Man upstairs sort it out, yeah?

They all laughed.

> DISSOLVE TO:

THREE HOURS LATER

Sergei, increasingly fed-up, kept looking at the fuel gauge, knowing in the depths of his soul that he had fucked up. Eventually, Dmitri saw it as well.

> DMITRI OLVO
> (Alarmed)
> Sergei, what the hell... have you seen the bloody fuel gauge?

> SERGEI
> (Flatly)
> I know!

The three men exchanged glances.

> SERGEI (CONT'D)
> Is there any fuel in the back?

> DMITRI OLVO
> If we stop now, those fuckers could turn off somewhere. We have to keep them in sight, or we are buggered.

> SERGEI
> (Suppressed anger)
> I fucking know that Dmitri. Climb over the seat and see what's in the back.

With much huffing and swearing Dmitri reported that the back of the Rover did not contain any fuel. He climbed back, slumping dejected into the passenger seat. Everyone stared forward, silent, tense.

> FADE OUT

EXT. DESERT NORTH OF PORT AUGUSTA. SOUTH AUSTRALIA. DAY.

The desert was bone dry, singed brown, flat and barren, only the odd brittle bush broke up the emptiness. The three vehicles were spread apart, doing less than 30 mph on corrugations, the occupants' tension taut as bowstrings.

> JOHN
> Guys, I can't take much more of this, we have to stop.

> JANDAMARRA
> (Raising a hand, pointing)
> We are here, look.

A small stand of straggling eucalyptus, remnants of an overgrown fence. A rusted-out Chevrolet, no wheels, sitting on its belly, skeletons of a few farm implements, then the abandoned buildings standing, bone dry, the same colour as the desert. A power line ran away over the horizon on drunken poles.

> BIRANI PEMBA
> (Surprised)
> Power, out here?

> JANDAMARRA
> Yes, I guess someone forgot to turn it off.

The three vehicles parked haphazardly, everyone getting out, stiff and cramped, stamping, stretching. John went to Sarah, taking her hand, looking earnestly at her.

                    SARAH
         I'm OK, just glad to be standing up.
              (A beat, eyes searching his)
         What's going to happen now?

Jandi led them inside, they followed, glad to get
into shade. Bits of furniture, chairs, a table,
a rusted machine of some sort with a lopsided
pulley in the ceiling, blown sand drifted into
corners. Jandi looked around warily.

                  JANDAMARRA
         Stand dead still guys. Could be
         snakes.

He cast around the building with a stick, poking
here and there.

              JANDAMARRA (CONT'D)
         It seems to OK. Keep an eye out
         though.

Someone came in with a 5-gallon drum of tepid
water, setting it on the rickety table with tin
cups. It had a tap, they all drank.

              JANDAMARRA (CONT'D)
         There's a well out the back, still OK.

Birani flicked a switch on the wall, looking
across at Jandi.

                  BIRANI PEMBA
         No power.

Jandi was shocked, he tried another switch. He
went into another room, came back, face blank.

JANDAMARRA
It was fine when I was here last. I
don't know how long it's been off.
(A beat, indicating a door)
There's a fridge in there.

He slumped down against a wall, his legs out
straight. Birani disappeared for several beats,
came back hit the wall with a fist, then wringing
his hand...

BIRANI PEMBA
Its rotten, stinking. looks like the
power has been off a couple of days.
(A beat)
Fuck! Fuck! Fuck!

The other aboriginals went outside silently,
their eyes dead. John and Sarah looked at each
other blankly.

SARAH
The Bunyip meat, looks like it's gone
rotten? The power's been cut...

Birani looked at her, shaking his head.

SARAH (CONT'D)
So, all this was for nothing then.
That's it?

Jandi looked at her and smiled sadly, hugging
himself.

JANDAMARRA
I wish that it was Mrs Cantrell, I
really wish it was...

FADE OUT

INT. CORDILLERA DOWNS STATION. SIMPSON DESERT. 0500AM.

Billy Bob sat in the dark kitchen with a coffee and the ALTERN rock samples spread on his table. He turned them over a few times but could see nothing special about them. He thought for a while, then got his laptop.

LAPTOP SEARCH:

> BILLY BOB MASON
> What is the most precious thing found in rock samples?

> LAPTOP
> *15 of the most expensive gemstones in the World*

He thought about that, shook his head. Nope! Re-typed...

> BILLY BOB MASON
> What are Australia's critical sought after minerals?

> LAPTOP
> *Australia has the World's largest resources of titanium, zirconium and tantalum.*
> (Next line:)
> *Australia's most precious resources of critical minerals like antimony,* **cobalt, lithium,** *manganese ore, niobium, tungsten and vanadium rank in the top 5 globally...*

He sat back a long time thinking, then…

                    BILLY BOB MASON
What metals do we need most for the
GREEN ENERGY?

                       LAPTOP
Cobalt   and   Lithium.   *Others   are:*
Copper; Silicon; Silver and Zinc.

                    BILLY BOB MASON
What are the RAREST of rare earth
metals NOW?

                       LAPTOP
Cobalt and Lithium.

                    BILLY BOB MASON
Are Cobalt and Lithium magnetic?

                       LAPTOP
Lithium is not magnetic. Cobalt is
ferromagnetic metal, as such is highly
magnetic.

Billy Bob sat back considering. He got up and
looked around his kitchen. Saw a huge cast
iron grill pan hanging above the cooking
stove. He brought it over the the table.
Before he could sit down, some of the rock
samples galvanized off the table and clanged
onto the grill pan with such force that it
startled him. He tried to prize them off but
had great difficulty.

Some of the other samples stayed inert. He
grinned.

BILLY BOB MASON
(To himself)
So, Mr and Mrs ALTERN. Maybe you have found Cobalt and Lithium on old Billy Bob's land, eh?
(A beat, musing)
I wonder if you were gonna tell me...

Billy Bob made coffee and went outside onto the veranda. The media encampment had long gone and he was grateful for that.

He sat with boots on the rail and rocked back with a well-practiced movement until his hat touched the wall. He rolled and lit up, blowing out the match with the smoke from his first drag.

Suddenly, he sat upright and ground out the cigarette with a boot. He sat there thinking with his hands on his thighs and both feet flat to the boards. He got up and went back to the laptop.

LAPTOP SEARCH

BILLY BOB MASON
Over time, would exposure to COBALT mutate wildlife and/or humans?

LAPTOP
Exposure to COBALT can have dangerous, and in some cases, dire effects on human and animal well-being.
(Next line)
Mutation is caused by exposure over time to high energy sources such as radiation, chemicals, and also high levels of magnetism in the environment.

He closed the laptop and sat with both hands on it, deep in thought, then he stood up like a man who had an urgent job to do.

Billy Bob packed his desert gear, rifle, spare ammunition, binoculars and first aid, water, fuel, and survival rations and went out to his four*four.

He got into the driving seat, then thought for a moment, got out again, went in the house, coming back out with the cast iron grill pan, tossing it into the flatbed.

He pulled down his hat brim and drove off on a cloud of dust.

FOUR HOURS LATER: RAW DESERT.

The gigantic bulk of the grotesque rock formations rose out of the skyline like enormous, fossilized eggs. Two huge, rounded rocks more than 30 meters high off the desert floor lay in drifted sand. They were surrounded by other smaller, but still significant rocks as if scattered by a playful giant.

Billy Bob brought his 4*4 to a stop, put his rifle across his knees and sat there for 20 minutes studying the weird softly distorting landscape. Nothing, that he could see alive, moved in the mid-morning heat. He got out, hefting his pack, his rifle held easy, ready to fire, safety on.

Walking up the steepening incline from his vehicle to the first of the rocks was a full body workout, his feet sinking calf deep with each step. By the time he staggered out of the soft sand onto hard rock, his shirt was dark with sweat.

He stood for minutes, getting his balance then moved carefully through clusters of rocks, stepping softly through dazzling light and deep shade, always keeping his orientation by the sun's position and his watch. He walked around for two hours, then suddenly the smell hit him. He stood still, head up, remembering it. He turned in a complete circle, his rifle still on safety.

The sun a blood-red disk floating in a reef of unexpected cloud.

On the massive rock in front him he saw the faded drawings. Old as time, muted colours showing painted creatures and figures from the Australian Dream time. Chalked faces, snakes, and various indiscriminate creatures that he could not identify.

He imagined the people back then passing the rocks in a curving line like some huge serpent across the desert, bristling with spears and boomerangs, spread out across the landscape with their animals and their naked children, the women suckling babies at their breast as they walked, the low chant of their traveling songs rising and falling, lost in the heat haze, and in the fog of history.

Another wave of the raw iron stench snapped him back into the present, he turned and followed it, the sun coppering his face, his hat brim pulled down. He would have missed the cave but for the stench.

He stood at the black opening considering for several beats, calming himself, then stepped into a world of muted darkness, and blessed cool.

A paper-white bleached cattle skull lay to the side, rows of teeth loose in their sockets. He touched it with a boot and golden sand ran out of an eye hole as if it was liquid, perfectly grained like an egg timer. The joints in its cranium were like the ragged welding of bone plate.

The foul iron stench was making it hard to breath, he stepped deeper into the cool, all his senses now on full alert. Coarse black hair was stuck to a promontory on the cave wall, and deeper in the gloom white bones were scattered.

He rummaged in his pack and brought out the cast iron grill pan and approached the cave wall. A foot away, the grill pan wrenched violently out of his hand and stuck itself to the cave wall with a loud clang. He reached to pull it off and couldn't. He put his boot to the wall and pulled hard.

The grill pan came away suddenly and he sat in the cool sand, the pan in his lap. He grinned to himself and nodded, climbing to his feet, his grin widening.

>   BILLY BOB MASON
>   (With wonder)
>   Cobalt... bloody Cobalt. Cobalt made
>   the bloody BUNYIP, well, fuck me to
>   hell and back.

He flung the grill pan away from him and it clanged onto the vertical wall again, as if welded.

                    BILLY BOB MASON (CONT'D)
                (Shouting)
          FUCKING COBALT...

Billy Bob came out of the cool and stood in the white heat, new sweat stinging his eyes. He checked the gun and his surroundings, leaned his back against a warm rock, took out his Sat-phone, pressed FIND, and then SAVE.

                                        FADE OUT

EXT. DERELICT BUILDINGS. DESERT NORTH OF PORT AUGUSTA. DAY.

Birani paced back and forth along the veranda frontage. His aboriginal colleagues leaned and watched him impassively. Jandi sat in the shade in a depressed gloom, staring at nothing. Sarah and John sat together watching everyone, trying to read the mood, like long-haul airline passengers watching the stewardesses in turbulence.

                    SARAH
          Maybe we could just run for it Jonno,
          they are not even watching us.

John gave her a look, didn't bother to reply.

                    SARAH (CONT'D)
          I wish I'd never...

                    JOHN
     You and me both babe, now shut the
     fuck up.

Sarah bit her lip and stared off into the heat
haze. 10M away, Birani posed for a beat, then
stepped over and conferred briefly with his
compadres in low dialect.

John felt his gut constrict; they had decided
something. Birani's demeanour had gradually
changed from western urbane to something more
primitive, threatening and unpredictable. Even
his physiology was different, more hunched and
his movements more animalistic.

John shook his head, deeply worried.

                    SARAH
              (Fearful, clutching)
     John, they are going to do something...

At the other end of the veranda, Jandi got to
his feet, leaning against the house wall, alert,
his eyes wide. Two of the aboriginals came over
and motioned Sarah to stand. She cringed back
from them.

                    JOHN
             (Looking up, holding her)
     What the fuck are you doing. Get
     off her.

Birani came over, a feral grin curving his lips.

                 BIRANI PEMBA
     Mrs Cantrell, you need to go with
     these guys for an hour or so.

I guarantee they will not hurt you.
Mr Cantrell is going to help us do
something inside the building.
        (A beat)
It is a cultural thing Sarah. A woman
cannot help us do this.

John was staring fearfully up at Birani, trying
to read the situation. Over by the wall, Jandi
had sat down again with his head in his hands
rocking back and forth, making a low moaning
sound. The two men hauled Sarah to her feet and
marched her away to the vehicles. One got in
each side of her and they drove off.

Birani motioned, and two men hauled John to his
feet and marched him into the house, sitting
him in a rickety chair. Someone brought another
chair and Jandi was pushed into it. Both men were
securely bound back-to-back with old electricity
cable from a reel lying in the corner.

Birani squatted where they could both see him,
he spoke slowly and succinctly, his eyes far
away and downcast.

                BIRANI PEMBA (CONT'D)
For the latter part of my life, I
have sought acceptance from both my
native Australian family, and my new
emerging Australian friends, my new
family.

It has been bloody hard, and I have
been pulled both ways and condemned
by both, but whatever words are used
at me it makes no difference, I cannot
deny my condition and my culture. I
am what I am.

(A beat)
In western religion, the eating of
'God-Flesh' is a well-known and fully
accepted tradition of spiritual and
even physical renewal.

More than a third of the entire World
population subscribes to this in
various forms.
(A beat)
Eating God-Flesh, even symbolically,
seems to be the single most powerful
ritual for spiritual renewal.

By consuming it, ordinary humans
believe the can become 'God-Like'.

Birani's eyes rose to meet the frightened eyes
of his captors.

                    BIRANI PEMBA (CONT'D)
          You are, indeed, what you eat.

          This metaphor is the stuff from which
          religious belief is made.

John took a long-ragged breath, his eyes bulging,
straining against his bonds.

                    JOHN
          Aw, gawd, for fuck's sake, you don't
          mean...

His head next to John's, Jandi was making
his singsong moaning sound, it rose and fell,
primitive and unworldly.

                    JOHN (CONT'D)
          (To Jandi)
     Shut the fuck up, you stupid bastard,
     you caused all this.

John struggled violently and Birani motioned to
one of his men to hold him still.

                    BIRANI PEMBA
     Two and a half million years ago
     our ancestors in the Dreamtime ate
     fruit, leaves, seeds, flowers, bark
     and tubers.

     Temperatures rose, forests shrank,
     and the great central grasslands
     grew. The people were forced to find
     new sources of food.
          (A beat)
     Meat, in all its many types, became
     one of the major sustaining forces of
     humanity, and the skills of hunting
     began.

     These skills were later used by humans
     to kill each other.

Birani motioned to one of his men. He got up,
went into the next room, then returned with
a slab of rotten fly-blown meat. It was black,
writhing with maggots, stinking. He slapped the
meat wetly on the table.

                    BIRANI PEMBA (CONT'D)
     The Bunyip was hunting to eat, that
     was its natural instinct.

     Then a man shot it, for what he
     believed were good reasons. The next

natural event in the cycle, is where
we are at now, right at this moment.

Birani rose, business-like, energized.

> BIRANI PEMBA (CONT'D)
> OK, enough already. Hold him.

Two men held John on each side. They forcibly
opened his jaw and held him rigid. His eyes were
bugging and he was hyper venting.

Birani positioned himself in front of John and
dug his hand into the slab of rotten writhing
meat, pulling out a black fistful. Ignoring
John's gagging and flailing, he placed chunks
of the slimy awful mess into his mouth, it ran
down Birani's arm, dripping off his elbow.

They forced John's jaw closed and held his
nose. He spluttered gore everywhere, eyes
staring mutely into Birani's. He was forced
to swallow and ingest several mouthfuls of
the meat, taking huge ragged inward breaths
in between swallows, coughing and retching.
Eventually Birani signaled enough, and John
collapsed with the sheer horror of what was
happening to him.

The men turned their attention to Jandi. With
him it was different. He accepted his situation
and readily swallowed what they put in his
mouth in huge gulps, even though he gagged.
He then crouched down into a stupor. Both men
slumped together, gore running down their chins
and onto their chests.

                    BIRANI PEMBA (CONT'D)
             (Matter of fact)
     If you throw up, we have to do it all
     again guys. Try to keep calm and your
     body will accept the flesh.
             (A beat)
     Its only meat, after all.

The job done, everyone in the room was exhausted.
John and Jandi, still securely bound, sat
quietly, their bodies heaving involuntarily
from time to time.

Birani watched them carefully to ensure they
didn't throw up. When he was satisfied that the
meat had been accepted by their bodies, he
stood like a man who had come to the end of
something.

                    BIRANI PEMBA (CONT'D)
     OK, loosen them off a bit but leave
     them tied. You can bring the woman
     back in now.
             (Gesturing, looking around)
     Clean up that meat, pack it and bring
     it with us.
             (To Jandi and John)
     Guys, we are going to have to leave
     you for a while. You will be OK here,
     there is water from the well behind
     the house. You will not feel like
     eating for a day or two anyway. The
     meat inside you will keep your body
     systems running. Your wife will get
     you free from these ropes.
             (A beat)
     Do not try to walk out of here. Its
     80 miles of raw desert. You definitely
     would not make it.

We will come back for you, in the
meantime, stay here and relax. Sleep,
and don't go out in the sun.

Birani took a water bottle and splashed it on
their faces and chest, washing off the worst of
the gore. He nodded to them, stood back and
surveyed them as if they were prize animals at
auction. The men all trooped out, and minutes
later John and Jandi heard their vehicles start
up, then the sound diminished into the distance.

Sarah entered the tentatively, her face etched
in fear. She stood looking at the two distressed
men, tied together, mute horror in their eyes.
She began to untie them, tears running down
her face.

Finally John was free, he leaned against his
wife's stomach as she held his head. After a
while she stirred and got them water. Both men
drank sparingly, then crawled into a corner,
drew up their knees into a foetal position
and lay, eyes open, now and then convulsing
slightly.

FADE OUT

**EXT. WINNINOWIE GAS STATION. PRINCE'S HIGHWAY.
EVENING.**

The Range Rover circled down into a cluster of
bright lights below the highway, pulling up next
to a battered oil-stained gas pump.

Sergei leaned, his forehead on the wheel in a
foul mood. The female pump jockey approached,
staring at the almost black tinted windows.

The driver's window slid silently down, Sergei
lifted his head and regarded her.

                    PUMP JOCKEY
        Fill her up?

He nodded and sprang the filler cap from the
dashboard. He got out laboriously and stood
next to her, stretching. She glanced at him,
saw a handgun in a leather harness under his
jacket, said nothing.

Dmitri and Igor got out, bizarre in their dark
city suits. They walked over to the toilets and
small shop. Sergei watched the tank filling.

                    SERGEI
        Do you sell spare fuel containers?

The pump jockey indicated stacks of them over
by the shop with a thrust of her chin.

                    SERGEI (CONT'D)
        I'll take two of them, filled.

She continued filling the tank as if she hadn't
heard, then she hung up the hose.

                    PUMP JOCKEY
                (Walking away)
        Pay over there at the cabin.

                    SERGEI
                (Sharply)
        Excuse me lady, did you hear me?
        I said I'll have two of those fuel
        containers from the shop over there,
        filled and put in the back of the car.

The pump jokey stopped, stood, took a breath and cocked her hip.

                    PUMP JOCKEY
          (Patiently)
     Did you hear me? The fuel containers
     are over there, by the shop.
          (A beat)
     I work the pumps. That means, YOU,
     mister... you go get them, then I'll
     fill them.

She sashayed away, Sergei stood fuming. Dmitri and Igor returned, chewing chocolate bars, carrying a plastic bag. Sergei was white with rage, they both looked at him, perplexed.

                    DMITRI OLVO
     What the hell is up with you Sergei?
     We just left you.

                    SERGEI
          (Evenly, barely controlled)
     Go over there and get me two of those
     fuel containers. Place them by this
     pump.

Without another word Igor went over to the shop, returning with two 5-gallon fuel cans. Dmitri shrugged and got back into the car. The pump jockey finished with another car, came back, a wary eye on Sergei.

                    PUMP JOCKEY
     Fill them up?

Sergei took a breath, noticing that she was incredibly beautiful beneath her tattoos, crew cut and uncompromising demeanor. He felt his anger dissipate like pulling the plug on a bath.

                    SERGEI
        Yes Ma-am. Please fill them up.

        I'm sorry to be in such a bad mood.
        Its been a hard day.

The pump jockey filled the two containers, left them by the pump and walked away, ignoring his comment.

                  PUMP JOCKEY
              (Over her shoulder)
        Pay over there.

Sergei, captivated, watched her shapely bottom in the skintight Levis as she leaned over the next vehicle. As she clanged the hose in position, she glanced back at him, her face impassive.

Sergei climbed back in the driving seat. Dmitri handed him a coffee in a paper cup and a Wagon Wheel biscuit. They all ate and drank and thoughtfully watched the pump jockey moving efficiently around the forecourt, her potent sexuality transcending her oily and diesel-stained surroundings.

                  DMITRI OLVO
        So, we know they are somewhere north
        of here.
              (A beat, bitterly)
        So is rest of fucking Australia...

                                    FADE OUT

INT. 'ALTERN' HQ. 46-52 EDINBURGH ST.
CANBERRA. DAY

Michelle Rogan tapped on the open glass door,
then stepped inside at Jeff Uteri's gesture as
he finished a phone call.

She sat, a perfect image of chic female cougar,
remote, beyond reach, her perfectly made-up
eyes impassive and unreadable.

Jeff placed his handset on the empty desk, made
a note on a pad, then smiled enigmatically up
at her.

                    JEFF UTERI
        You are looking fabulous today Mish,
        as always. Can I get you a coffee?

                    MISH ROGAN
        Cut the bullshit Jeff, what's happening?

                    JEFF UTERI
              (Indicating her clothing)
        Have you got any bush gear? We are
        going to...
              (Leaning, glancing at his
              screen)
        Cordillo Downs.

He regarded her triumphantly, a broad grin
spreading across his perma-tan.

                 JEFF UTERI (CONT'D)
        You are going to meet a legend - Mr
        Billy Bob Mason, in his own habitat,
        The Simpson Desert.

Michelle, initially wrong-footed, recovered her composure quickly.

                    MISH ROGAN
        So...the Bunyip Shooter, and
        potentially one of Australia's new
        millionaires.
             (A beat)
        Stage one, eh? Offer him the money...
        Interesting.

She stood, smoothing her pencil skirt to her hips, her hooded eyes on his, seductive.

                MISH ROGAN (CONT'D)
        I'm off to the shops Jeffie baby, wearing
        bush gear is very cool at the moment.

Jeff grinned appreciatively, nodding.

                    JEFF UTERI
        We are driving babe. There are no
        flights from Canberra to Birdsville.
        It's around a 30-hour trip one-way.
             (Grin widening)
        We'll have to overnight...

                                        FADE OUT

INT. DERELICT BUILDINGS. DESERT NORTH OF PORT AUGUSTA. DAY.

It was hot and still in the room. Sarah used a rag to sponge the men's faces. Neither had spoken to her or eaten anything for several hours and she was frantic with worry. Birani Pemba had assured her that the aboriginals would return to get them. He had left fruit and black bread, water they had in abundance.

She leaned down to John, her face next to his.

> SARAH
> John, speak to me please. What did they do to you? Can you tell me baby? Have they hurt you?

John's eyes turned mutely to her, then dropped away. His body convulsed slightly, and he coughed, then was still. Nearby Jandi had his face to the wall. He wasn't sleeping but lay still as death.

EXT. DESERT ROAD.SOUTH AUSTRALIA. LATE AFTERNOON

Sergei stopped the Range Rover on the bitumen, gazing disconsolately along an unidentified gravel road to his right, the heat billowing into the vehicle through the open window. The track led, straight as an arrow, over the horizon. It was not graded, and the gravel lay in rough corrugations and ridges. He slid up the darkened window and the aircon re-established its cool.

> DMITRI OLVO
> What do you reckon?

> SERGEI
> No way of knowing is there. What a fucking awful country.
> (Hitting the steering wheel)
> Fuck!

They sat.

Igor passed around a bottle of cold water. Something moved in the distance. The distorted image of a multi-coloured 4*4 grew upwards out of the heat mirage, gradually formed itself into a sharp image, it was on them, then flashing past. The Rover rocked in the side blast of hot air.

Sergei looked in the mirror as the 4*4's red brake lights pulsed on. It stopped, paused for a beat, then reversing lights on, it came back at them at speed. He slid down his window as the 4*4 drew level.

The young Pump Jockey from the filling station leaned on her open window and Ray-Banned them, her engine rumbling, deep and resonant.

> PUMP JOCKEY
> You guys OK?

Sergei smiled winningly, superheated air in his face.

> SERGEI
> Thank you for asking Ma-am. You are very kind. I guess we are a bit lost here.
> (Gesturing)
> What's along that track? Do you know?

The girl grimaced.

> PUMP JOCKEY
> There's tracks everywhere in the desert mate. Some might lead on to an old ranch, or maybe lead no-where,

they just peter out into a dune.
Dunes move around all the time.
    (A beat)
Driving around a dune to look for
the road again is seriously not
recommended, it kills you.

She moved her vehicle forward slightly, squinting
along the track, then she reversed back again.

                PUMP JOCKEY (CONT'D)
That track hasn't been graded mate, so
I guess its not being used regularly.

                SERGEI
Do you live out here?

                PUMP JOCKEY
        (Nodding ahead, wary)
Along there a bit.

Sergei thought rapidly, he didn't want to scare
off the girl, but had an idea that someone who
knew the area could be useful to them.

                SERGEI
Look, I'm thinking here, maybe you
could help us out...
        (Reacting her expression)
No, honestly. We would not harm you
in any way whatsoever.

In fact, we would pay you handsomely.
We are looking for some friends, they
have come along this way, most likely
turned off somewhere, we need to find
them fairly urgently.

The Pump Jockey regarded him with faint amusement, as it was a proposal from an entertaining child.

                    PUMP JOCKEY
     Best way to find out what's along a
     track, is to drive along it. It might
     kill you, it might not.

     Don't quite see how I can help you
     with that.

Sergei moved in his seat, as if to get out of the car. She reacted minutely, it was enough, he stopped in his tracks.

                    PUMP JOCKEY (CONT'D)
                 (Flatly)
     I have a Remington Pump 12g shotgun
     across my knees, loaded with slugs.
     Its a normal mode of travel for a
     lady around here.
                 (A beat)
     Just saying.

Sergei settled slowly back into his seat; a palm raised.

                    PUMP JOCKEY (CONT'D)
                 (Nodding forward)
     That way...Birdsville.
                 (Nodding backwards)
     That way, Port Augusta. The track, I
     have no idea. 20 miles ahead, the road
     off to your right is Hawker. That's the
     best I can do for you fellers.
                 (Nodding gravely)
     Ill be seeing you.

The 4*4's rear wheels squealed as the 520 Hemi engine revved and the vehicle took off powerfully, a slight tail shift corrected as it merged into the heat mirage in his mirror, soon lost in the haze. Sergei leaned back in his seat, defeated.

> DMITRI OLVO
> Any chance you could put that window back up mate? Getting fucking warm in here.

> FADE OUT

EXT. CORDILLO DOWNS STATION. SIMPSON DESERT. LATE AFTERNOON.

Billy Bob Mason had taken the expected call three days back, so when he saw the hired white Land Cruiser Amazon nose through his ranch gate, he wasn't surprised. The white vehicle was orange with blown sand and distance, the occupants tired, but cool in the aircon and tinted glass.

It rolled quietly to a stop facing his boot soles propped on the veranda rail. The engine stopped, and a fine mist of pale brown dust settled.

The driver's window slid down revealing perma-tan and aviators.

> JEFF UTERI
> Mr Mason, I presume.

> BILLY BOB MASON
> You presume correct mister. Step onto the veranda and I will get you something cold.

Billy Bob disappeared through the mosquito curtain, returning with cold beers as Jeff and Mish stepped wearily onto the veranda. He looked them up and down, indicated seats, and dropped back into his own chair, boots up, rocking impossibly back, serious blue eyes on them.

                    BILLY BOB MASON (CONT'D)
          I am William Robert Mason; this is
          my spread.
                    (A beat)
          Must be important. Most people use
          iPads these days, infinitely preferable
          to 30 hard hours on the road from ACT
          (Australian Capital Territory).

Michelle appraised the tall man with a slight shiver. He was a cowboy lookalike straight from central casting, but there was something totally authentic, even dangerous, in his persona.

He caught her eye and she knew that he knew, what she was thinking. She looked away quickly, unsettled, a city girl way outside her comfort zone.

                    JEFF UTERI
                    (Smooth, urbane)
          Thank you for seeing us Mr Mason.
          Face to face is always better.

                    BILLY BOB MASON
          Its Billy Bob, unless of course I'm
          in some sort of trouble for shooting
          that Bunyip. I imagine that's why you
          folks are here?

          I know you ALTERN people are very
          protective of rare creatures.

(A beat, dryly)
That bugger was killing my cows.

Jeff and Michelle both smiled uncertainly, unsure if he was subjecting them to the outback Australian dry humour they had heard about.

                    JEFF UTERI
I'm Jeff Uteri.
          (Indicating)
My colleague here is Michelle Rogan.
          (A beat)
Mr Mason, er, Billy Bob, yes, the Bunyip story is very interesting, and it has caught the media's attention for sure.

I imagine it has been hectic out here for you. I saw some of the footage on Channel 9.

                    BILLY BOB MASON
Yeah well, hectic is one word I would use maybe.
          (A beat)
Mr Uteri, I'm curious, your scientists took away the Bunyip's remains, its body, back to Adelaide I believe.

Since then, we haven't heard anything. I gather y'all were doing some sort of tests? Do you have conclusions that you can share?

Jeff and Michelle exchanged glances. Jeff nodded. Michelle leaned forward earnestly.

                    MISH ROGAN
Billy Bob, Hello, I'm Michelle.

                    (Dazzling smile)
I can tell you this now that the
media melee has gone down somewhat.

We didn't exactly do any tests. It's
very likely the creature that you
shot was an oversized dingo.
                    (A beat)
You may have seen on the News that
someone stole part of the creature's
remains as it was being taken into
the laboratory. We have no idea why.

Anyway, we all know that Bunyip's
don't actually exist.
                    (A beat)
They are a figment of Australian
folk lore, invented by the native
Australians, the Aboriginals.

Every now and then someone shouts
out that they saw one, a bit like the
YETI sightings.

She leaned back her smile fading to an earnest
expression, her right palm out towards him.

                    MISH ROGAN (CONT'D)
So, I can guarantee that you are
certainly not in any trouble with us
for shooting the creature.

Billy Bob regarded her curiously for a long
moment, then got out his makings and rolled a
cigarette. He lit, blew out the match with blue
smoke, examined the glowing tip critically,
then looked at Jeff.

BILLY BOB MASON
Do you folks want to eat something?

DISSOLVE:

2 HOURS LATER

Back out on the veranda, kicking back.

BILLY BOB MASON (CONT'D)
(To Jeff)
So Jeff, do you share this lady's
opinion about Bunyips?

Jeff glanced at Michelle re-reassuringly, then
grinned at Billy Bob.

JEFF UTERI
(Mansplaining)
It was in ALTERN's interests at that
time to allow the Bunyip story to run
Billy Bob.

That's why we neither confirmed nor
denied it. We were well aware of the
effect of that statement.
(A beat)
You may have heard of the expression
'burying news?' We could have killed
the story off at the time, but for
reasons that we will discuss with
you later, it was a useful media
diversion at that time.
(A beat)
Now, things have moved on, it really
doesn't matter too much.

Billy Bob smoked for several moments, making
them wait for his response, He smoked calmly,

looking out across the deepening colours of the sunset, then he fixed Jeff with a critical eye.

                    BILLY BOB MASON
                  (Slow and succinct)
Now let me get this straight in my mind here Mr and Mrs ALTERN.

You people, your experts, and your scientists and all, y'all don't actually believe that the Bunyip exists, except in the weird imagination of some primitive uneducated people who don't know shite from shinola.
                  (A beat)
You folks think it's a fairy tale creature, maybe like a Unicorn huh?
                  (A beat)
A big fuck-off twisty horn growing out of its forehead huh?

Billy Bob snorted, looked at them both pityingly, shaking his head, then ground out his cigarette on a boot heel in a shower of sparks.

                    BILLY BOB MASON (CONT'D)
                  (Disgustedly)
You come all this way, a 60-hour drive there and back, and sit there and drink my fucking beer, and you tell this old boy that I done shot me a Unicorn.
                  (A beat)
I think now after y'all been fed and watered, that maybe you should finish your beer and drive 30 hours back again to ACT - for damn sure there ain't nothing to see here.

Billy Bob's chair rocked down with a thump, his boots clicked down to the veranda floor, he stood.

Jeff and Michel both winced visibly in their seats.

                    JEFF UTERI
          Billy Bob, Mr Mason, Sir, we are
          not actually here to talk about the
          Unico.. er, I mean the Bunyip...

Jeff and Michelle, unused to being on the defensive, made placating gestures.

                    BILLY BOB MASON
                 (Coldly)
          Look, I knows what I shot mister. It
          was no Unicorn, and no Dingo neither.

          Neither did I touch it, or even
          approach it, or risk getting any of
          its fluid or particles on me.

Jeff and Michelle both looked at Billy Bob frowning.

                    JEFF UTERI
                 (Non-plussed)
          Fluid, particles, I don't understand...

                    MISH ROGAN
                 (Warmly)
          Sorry Billy Bob look, the last thing
          we want is to insult your intelligence
          or antagonize you in any way. We want
          to work with you, not against you.
                 (A beat, curious)

Can you explain please, what do you
mean, about being in contact with any
matter from the Bunyip?
          (A beat)
Are you saying that you believe that
this creature actually does exist?

That it lived?

Billy Bob was silent for several moments,
thinking deeply.

                BILLY BOB MASON
Well, I'm no philosophical expert,
but I guess belief is an acceptance
that something exists, or at least
you think that it's true.

Or maybe even for some, that they
have faith that it's true.
          (A beat)
So, using that definition, what I know
ain't no belief based on faith.

I know it to be true because I shot
that yowling motherfucker. I saw what
it did to my cows. I heard my bullet
strike it, then I shot that bad boy
one more time to make sure it wasn't
gonna get up.

Billy Bob eyed them both sceptically.

                BILLY BOB MASON (CONT'D)
Do you folks know anything about
Texas Longhorns?

                JEFF UTERI
Not really, but...

                    BILLY BOB MASON
They are big motherfuckers. 900kg,
one and half meters high and the same
wide.

Worth around 6000 bucks apiece maybe
full growed. There were seven of them
bad boys around that waterhole. They
were shredded across the landscape
like confetti.

One of them seemed like it was less
ripped apart than the others, turned
out it had the creature inside it.

It burst of that cow's belly in an
unholy explosion of guts, blood, and
gore then it crouched down, dripping,
and stared me down like I was next.

Billy Bob looked at their rapt faces and shook
his head.

               BILLY BOB MASON (CONT'D)
Over the years living out here,
I shot and trapped every damned
creature that you could ever imagine,
everything that walked and crawled,
and then some.

But I swear to you on my life, and I
really do not care whether or not you
people believe me, It don't matter to
me either way, but Mr and Mrs ALTERN,
I never seen nothing before like
that thing that I shot, not before
anywhere, anytime.
          (A beat)

Maybe that thing is the only one, I hope so for damn sure. Me, I don't want to stare down another of those motherfuckers, ever.

It's not an age thing, but I have a daughter, and wouldn't want her to identify me by a tooth or a fingernail if I missed my shot, or had a duff cartridge up the spout. No sir.

Billy Bob looked at their rapt uncertain faces.

BILLY BOB MASON (CONT'D)
I seen the TV debates and the experts all sitting there safe and cool and full of shit, drinking their iced Perrier.

They never looked through rifle sights at something that could turn you into mincemeat if you missed your shot in the millisecond thinking time that you had available.
          (A beat)
The only expert that made any sense to me lately was Mr Birani Pemba, the black feller. So, if him and his people say its theirs, and they want it. Then I say, fucking take it guys, please, fucking take it.

Now, you people have, or maybe had, the means to prove something or other, I don't know. But it seems like you chose to ignore those means.

So now you folks can remain happy in your unproven belief that it's

all bullshit, and that I'm a stupid
illiterate Hillbilly.
          (Yawning, stretching)
And so, here we all are then.
          (A beat)
I guess we all believe something,
then something happens, and then we
believe something else.

I guess it's part of the nature of
being somebody.

                    MISH ROGAN
I'm not following you Billy Bob, what
do you mean?

                    BILLY BOB MASON
Well Ma-am, you think something, then
you take a journey. If you are still
thinking the same thing as when you
started, then you might as well have
stayed home and watched daytime TV.

Billy Bob stood, thrust his hands deep into his
jeans, his eyes distant on the quivering red
disk of the sun as it sank behind the low ridge
of ragged black mountains...

              BILLY BOB MASON (CONT'D)
A long time after my old man died,
and I'm talking a few years, I was
out in the bush.

I'd been out there on my own, a few
days, hunting, looking at stuff, you
know. I hadn't talked or seen another
human for several days, just me, out
there.
          (A beat)

Then one day I saw him, it was after sunset. He was on his donkey. DONK, he called him.

The light was falling fast, and he was carrying a lantern strapped to his saddle, so I saw him coming from a ways off. He came right on towards me and passed me on my left side a few yards away. There was stuff clanking as he rode on by, and I could smell his sweat and donkey shit in the wind as he passed.
    (A beat)
He didn't stop, he just kept right on going by, never even looked at me.

His eyes were fixed on the horizon. I just stood there, you know, with my soul hanging out of me like a loose shirt, and I watched him disappear until there was just a small red glow out there in the mist, then that winked out, and he was gone.

Billy Bob looked at them, Michelle thought she saw a track of moisture on his weathered cheek, and she involuntarily moved, as if to show him affection. His hand came up immediately, palm outwards. She settled back, transfixed.

        BILLY BOB MASON (CONT'D)
Now I know, beyond any doubts, that whenever I get to where I'm going, wherever that will be, that he'll be there a-waiting on me out there in all that vastness, with old DONK standing there patient beside him, and his lantern will be a-glowing

194

to give me direction in the falling
light.
                (Eyes on Michelle)
You see Ma-am, he'd gone on ahead,
so's he could get the camp setup for
me, for when I got there.

Billy Bob held Michelle's gaze until her eyes
dropped away, then he took a long breath and
fell silent. They all sat and watched as the
last rich colours in the west sank down to a
faint pale gray. After a long time, Billy Bob
got and stretched like a cat.

                BILLY BOB MASON (CONT'D)
It's late. You folks must be tuckered
out. We'll talk in the morning.

That's a good time to talk business,
never works late at night. Night's is
for philosophizing.

He caught Jeff's eye and grinned wolfishly, his
teeth flashing white in the light falling from
the window.

                BILLY BOB MASON (CONT'D)
Maybe I'll cook you some beefsteak
for breakfast Mr Uteri. Don't you be
worrying now; I wouldn't be feeding
you nothing that's gonna grow eggs in
your belly.

The two-city people looked at Billy Bob's
departing back with uncertain eyes.

LATER. 0345AM

Michelle Rogan lay naked on top of the covers listening to a clock ticking somewhere. She had gently declined Jeff's tentative invitation to share a bed, and now she stared at the rectangle of starlit sky across the room and vaguely wished that Billy Bob Mason would quietly step inside her door, and just maybe, shake up her world.

She was acutely aware that he had had a profound effect on her in the short few hours she had spent in his company. Her belief system, that she had never questioned in her 37 years, had been challenged logically, and with a primordial passion rooted in their shared origins.

It had not been attacked by bluster or raised voice argument, or been shouted down, or even influenced by civilized debate. It was more by a questioning look, a gesture, and the confident manner and demeanour of possibly the most self-assured male she had ever met.

She resisted the impulse to get off the bed and look out of the window. The irrational fear that something very frightening was lurking out there was somehow made bearable by the fact that Billy Bob Mason was a few feet away somewhere in this quiet dark house, and the knowledge that she would be protected was a feeling she had never felt since she was 12 years old.

Eventually Michelle rose, wrapped herself in a sheet and padded through the dark house to the veranda. She sat in a rocking chair hugging the sheet around her in the strange ethereal light of pre-dawn and looked over the rail at the dim shapes of receding fences and the still dark hulks of barns and parked vehicles.

Used to seeing the sky through the haze and light pollution of the city, she was stunned at the incredible scale of the light show before her. Every few seconds, the flare of a shooting star, movement everywhere in the sky, she was exhilarated.

Over to the east the sky was had lost its deep blackness and she stared towards it. Somewhere in the vast distance a doleful yowl began, low, then rising impossibly, then breaking off, fading away to nothing as if it had never been there. She felt a snake of fear writhe in her gut.

A voice from the other end of the veranda...

BILLY BOB MASON
Dingo... nothing to worry about.

Michelle's shock at not being alone on the veranda was profound and intense. Billy Bob sensed it, stood and walked towards her, effortlessly entering her normally fiercely protected personal space. His muscular arm went tight around her shoulders, and she was both stunned and delighted at his audacity, and at the sheer momentousness of the moment.

Her initial rigidity melted, and she leaned into him with the weirdest feeling that she had just come home. Still trembling, acutely aware that she was naked beneath the sheet, she suddenly, inexplicably, felt safe in the arms of this dangerous, unpredictable, and yet highly sophisticated man.

She stood close to him, feeling shame flood through her for the scorn and derision that she had shown for a preliterate world that was real, and that it existed inside her own country, one that she did not even remotely understand, and in her ignorance, had ridiculed it.

MISH ROGAN
What must you think of us Billy Bob?

Billy Bob, still with his arm encircling her shoulders, moved his face into her hair, breathing it into his memory, his eyes on the iridescent purple streaks growing brighter in the east.

BILLY BOB MASON
Aw hell, I don't think bad stuff of you Miss Michelle Rogan, we all spend our days coming to terms with the consequences of the things that we do.
(A beat)
But you know Ma-am, there is a instant, floating somewhere in that stillness before the new dawn, most likely before we get fixated on something trivial, that it's just us and the planet.

All of us scared creatures coming out of the night, standing there.

Billy Bob stood back from her. He was silhouetted against the shimmering glare that was increasing behind him, his features indistinct, but his voice hypnotic and resonant with an ancient wisdom.

                BILLY BOB MASON (CONT'D)
        You should capture that moment as
        many times as you can Michelle.
                (A beat, then the bombshell)
        When all this stuff is done with, I'll
        come looking for you.

Suddenly she stood alone on the veranda exposed
in the Sun's glare, the fences throwing long
grotesque shadows along the sand, the fly curtain
in the doorway still moving where he had passed
through.

                                        FADE OUT

EXT. DESERT ROAD.SOUTH AUSTRALIA. DAY.

The powerful 4*4 hammered the bitumen north,
then slowed as the Pump Jockey lifted her cowboy
boot off the gas. The dim track came up fast
on her left side and she almost overcooked the
turn in a cloud of dust, the vehicle shuddering
to a stop, stalled.

She sat there for a beat in the settling dust,
frowning in cusp of a decision. Then she checked
the slide on the Remington Shotgun, pulling it
back until she saw the edge of cartridge brass
glinting, put it back across her knees, and then
took off at 30 mph along the corrugated track.

**INT. DERELICT BUILDINGS. DESERT NORTH OF PORT
AUGUSTA. DAY.**

Sarah heard the sound of an engine well before
the vehicle came into view. She went to the
window, her heart rate rising. The dust cloud

appeared first, then the black dot of a single vehicle traveling slow. She looked back at the two comatose men, they were both awake but neither reacted to the sound. She went out onto the veranda.

She didn't recognize the 4*4 and her spirit soared. It stopped 30 meters away, the engine died, and dust slowly settled. After several beats a young girl got out and stood behind the open door, a gun barrel resting on the sill of the window.

PUMP JOCKEY
Y'all OK Ma-am?

SARAH
Oh, thank God. No, we are not OK. Can you help us please. My husband and another man are inside, they are both sick.

The young woman considered, then looked around in all directions, taking her time.

PUMP JOCKEY
You say two men inside Ma-am? What are they sick of? Are they conscious?

SARAH
They are very sick; please can you hurry. They need to get to a hospital.

The young woman considered, then made a decision and stepped away from her vehicle. She carried the gun as if she knew how to use it. She walked towards Sarah.

                    PUMP JOCKEY
        Stand away from the door please Ma-am,
        let me take a look inside.

Sarah moved away to the end of the veranda, and
the young woman stepped up onto the veranda,
poking the gun barrel through the screen
curtain, leaning in.

                PUMP JOCKEY (CONT'D)
        What's happened to them?

                    SARAH
        I think they have been poisoned, I'm
        not sure.

The young woman looked critically at her,
frowning.

                    PUMP JOCKEY
        I seen you, on the TV. The Bunyip
        thing. You said that your man was all
        healed up?

        Has he got sick again? Who's the
        other feller?
            (A beat)
        And Ma-am, what the hell are you
        folks doing out here in the donga
        with no vehicle?

Sarah started to cry, unable to cope any more.
She fell to her knees, sobbing.

                PUMP JOCKEY (CONT'D)
            (Irritated)
        Oh comon lady, sure I'll help you,
        just pull yourself together. I can't
        deal with no blubbing women.

With a supreme effort Sarah got to her feet and went inside with the young woman. They both stood looking down at the two grotesquely comatose men.

> PUMP JOCKEY (CONT'D)
> My name is Louise, but everyone calls me Pump Jockey or PJ, on account of that's what I do. Its sort of stuck.

> SARAH
> (Sniffing)
> I'm Sarah Cantrell, the man down there is my husband, John. That guy over there, I don't really know him, he's called Jandi.

Pump Jockey looked at her curiously.

> PUMP JOCKEY
> Is someone after you Sarah? Are we in some sort of danger here?

Sarah nodded, with tears flowing down her face.

> PUMP JOCKEY (CONT'D)
> Three men in a black Range Rover maybe? Looked like mafiosi?

Sarah looked blankly at her, shaking her head.

> SARAH
> No, I don't know anything about a Range Rover, its three old pick-up trucks. Aboriginal men.
>
> A man called Birani Pemba is in charge of them.

The Pump Jockey looked sharply at her.

> PUMP JOCKEY
> (Reacting)
> Birani Pemba, are you sure Ma-am?
> Birani wouldn't harm no woman. I
> know him.

> SARAH
> I think maybe he would. He's a
> dangerous man.
> (Looking around, anxious)
> Can we hurry please.

With effort they got the two men into the Pump Jockey's 4*4. She dropped into the driver's seat, checked the Remington 12g, pondered for several beats, then drove away from the derelict building into raw desert, away from the road.

> SARAH (CONT'D)
> Why are you going this way? The best
> way is out along that track.

> PUMP JOCKEY
> No Ma-am, it aint!

Particularly if some bad men is heading in along it, maybe coming back here for you folks. Sit back and relax. We'll get y'all to Port Augusta hospital.

> FADE OUT:

EXT. MCKENZIE RD. WEST LONDON. LARGE HOUSE. LATE AFTERNOON.

Andrei stood in the overgrown garden, his hand on a gnarled branch for balance.

The wind had cooled the air, it blew dark clouds across the sky and whistled through the leaves, hinting at worsening weather. Around the ruffled green surface of the lake the hanging trees were more yellow than green and here and there touches of flame and scarlet flared. The air promised rain, but it held off, the scudding clouds revealing brief flashes of watery sunlight.

Andrei shivered and wished he had his coat, but it was lying across the seat of the car where he had tossed it in the heat of his temper.

The man he had just killed sat upright against a tree as if he was resting.

Andrei looked at him dispassionately. No blood was showing yet, but the front of shirt inside his pinstripe suit was punched inwards and torn where the three slugs had hit. As he watched, the man's left foot began twitching, making a tapping sound. After several beats it stopped.

Abruptly, as if a hand had pulled a plug, the rain began. Andrei looked up at the churning black sky, lightning flashed, and a roll of thunder moved across from right to left.

The sound of a car door and Andrei's head snapped around. In the slanting downpour he made out the dim shape of his driver running towards him with a coat spread to envelop him.

Without warning his knees gave way and he sat down on the wet grass, the 1911 Colt Auto going barrel down into the soil.

DRIVER
Comon Boss, lets get you inside.

Andrei kicked weakly but couldn't get up. Another man ran towards them and all three men, now sleek and wet, their clothes plastered to their bodies, made it into a doorway.

ANDREI LEBOV
The gun, its plugged with soil. Sorry.

DRIVER
Boss don't worry about the fucking gun.

The driver and the other man sat him down in a chair, someone else came with a towel and Andrei took it to dry his own face. He looked up at his driver, nodding to the garden.

ANDREI LEBOV
You need to get that bastard out of my garden, cluttering up the fucking place.
(A beat, thinking)
Oh yeah, can you ring Ekaterina, we are supposed to be having people round tonight, I'm going to be late.
(Looking ruefully down)
I'm gonna need another suit.

His phone rang and he retrieved it from an inside pocket. He listened, leaning back, dripping.

ON PHONE

>   ANDREI LEBOV (CONT'D)
>   Oh yes, thank you for returning my call.
>   Sixteen please, yes, red roses. The note?
>   (Thinking)
>   Are you ready? OK, 'To my dearest
>   love who makes all things possible'
>   (Listening)
>   Yes, just sign it 'Andrei'. Thank you
>   very much. Bye.

The driver brought a vodka and Andrei tossed it, winced, and coughed, handed back the glass.

>   ANDREI LEBOV (CONT'D)
>   Can you stop at the off license on
>   Sheen Road on the way back.
>
>   The people coming round tonight are
>   plebs. I don't want to waste good
>   wine on them.

Several men rushed around, busy with various tasks. Andrei sat and watched as the rain drummed on the windows. From where he sat, he could see his former colleague sitting against the tree, the downpour plastering his hair flat and sleek, a trail of watery blood running away from him towards the pond.

He looked at the driver, thrusting his chin towards the garden.

>   DRIVER
>   Yeh, yeh, don't worry Boss, we'll sort
>   it when the rain stops.

>   FADE OUT

EXT. PORT AUGUSTA HOSPITAL EMERGENCY. DAY.

Pump Jockey drove the 4*4 right up to emergency doors, ignoring the parking zones.

Sarah ran inside for help while Pump Jockey opened the rear doors. Several nurses and porters got the two men into the building, Pump Jockey and Sarah stood aside, letting the professionals work.

> SARAH
> You saved us Louise, PJ. Where can I find you after this is all over?

> PUMP JOCKEY
> Winninowie Fuel Station, under the Princes Highway. Anytime.

Pump Jockey, clearly uncomfortable with the situation, touched her temple with a finger, and backed away, then walked quickly to her vehicle. Sarah watched her accelerate away, then turned to meet the questioning eyes of a medic

> SARAH
> (Tears springing)
> I think they have been poisoned. I don't know with what.

> MEDIC
> Drugs? food? snakebite? scorpion?

> SARAH
> I don't know, maybe food. Rotten meat maybe.

The medic rushed away after the two stretchers; spring loaded double doors bouncing back behind him.

A receptionist brought Sarah awful coffee in a paper cup. She sat in the cold anaesthetic smelling aircon with glaring white light all around. Outside she could hear the blaring of a siren getting louder as the next emergency circled down the ramp, heading in.

LATER

The spring-loaded doors slammed open, and the blank faced Medic walked quickly over, serious tired eyes on her.

> MEDIC
> OK Ma-am, we have takcn a look, they are not critical, but both have raised temperature. Vitals are OK. Blood tests are inconclusive yet.
> (A beat)
> A bit puzzling to be honest because both appear to be in some sort of post traumatic shock.
> (Critical look)
> Can you shed any light on that. No apparent bruising, but have they been assaulted in some way.
> (A beat)
> Do we need to check you out as well?

> SARAH
> No, I'm good, just a bit shaken up.

Some aboriginal men attacked us on the road. I was separated from John

and the other guy. Then they just up
and left us.
(A beat)
The lady from the Pump Station saved
us and brought us in here.

The medic didn't buy the story, she knew that,
but he left it as the doors burst open and the
next emergency incident began.

FADE OUT

INT. CORDILLO DOWNS STATION. SIMPSON DESERT.
MORNING

Michelle lay awake in shafts of sunlight watching
a spider abseil from the ceiling. Over at the
window a hornet buzzed and attacked the glass
over and over, never giving up. She contemplated
opening the window, then heard sounds from
somewhere in the house.

She clutched a sheet and sat on the side of the
bed. A stage achieved. Shower next.

KITCHEN.

Billy Bob poured coffee in two mugs as Michelle
came into the room. She sat breathing it to her
face. He took a seat opposite.

BILLY BOB MASON
Gonna be another hot one.

He regarded her curiously, drank and leaned
back.

                    BILLY BOB MASON (CONT'D)
          So, tell me something about Michelle
          Rogan that no-one else in the world
          knows.

She looked at him, a bit shaken, bemused.

                    MISH ROGAN
          Wow! That's a bit heavy, I just got
          up Billy Bob.

                    BILLY BOB MASON
          No better time.

She sipped the coffee a long time, thinking. He
watched, giving her space.

                    MISH ROGAN
               (Slowly)
          Well, this will probably confirm what
          you already think of me anyway.
               (A beat)
          In my last year at UNI, I worked in
          a deli to help with costs. Some other
          students worked there as well.

          At some point, two of us applied for
          the same job in a legal office. I never
          really liked the other girl, but she
          was smarter than me, I just knew that
          she would beat me, I knew it.

Billy Bob topped up the cups, a faint grin
playing.

                    MISH ROGAN (CONT'D)
          Anyway, it was the day before, our
          lunch break. She made the drinks; I

went to the cool display to get two
sandwiches.
          (A beat)
While I was there, I noticed that
somehow a sandwich had fallen out of
the cool area and was wedged down
between the the unit and the wall. It
had probably been there for a couple
of days maybe. I looked around, she
was busy.
          (A beat)
I reached down and hooked that
sandwich out, put lashings of mayo
on it with a napkin and put it on
her plate.

Watched her eat it.

Billy Bob cradled his coffee mug to his face,
breathing in the aroma, his eyes on Michelle.

          MISH ROGAN (CONT'D)
She was sick next day, couldn't attend
the interview.
          (A beat)
I got the job.

Billy Bob nodded, laughed, looking younger.
After a beat, she laughed along with him,
feeling somehow purged.

Jeff came in, looked quizzically at them both,
the dynamic jolted, changed.

          JEFF UTERI
Morning. Coffee smells good. What's
amusing you guys?

Billy Bob topped all three cups. Went to the oven, hauling out a fresh baked loaf. He put it on the table with butter and plates, sat down.

> BILLY BOB MASON
> OK, business...
>> (A beat)
> Shall I go first? I'm assuming, if it's not the Bunyip, it's the COBALT you want to talk about?

Jeff gaped at him, then looked accusingly at Michelle. She shook her head, colour draining.

Billy Bob looked at Jeff pityingly for several beats, nodded as if reaching a decision, then pushed away his plate, looked away, a whistle in his outward breath.

> JEFF UTERI
>> (Recovering)
> Well, er, we may have found some small...

Billy Bob looked from Jeff to Michelle and back, considering.

> BILLY BOB MASON
> So OK, I got that! Its a big deal huh, I thought so, hmm.
>> (Patiently)
> I'm guessing that you are between a rock and a hard place with this.
>> (A beat)
> When a customer you are counting on turns sour on you, your choices are pretty damn limited.

Confrontation ain't gonna work with
me, so Mr Uteri, do you have the
wherewithal, and the permissions, to
make a compromise deal... somehow, I
doubt that. I think maybe you are too
far down the food chain.
(A beat)
So, what are you gonna do Mr ALTERN?
(A beat)
Better still, what is our illustrious
GOVERNMENT gonna do?

Jeff was mute, his confidence drained away at the
sheer speed of his exposure.

Michelle looked at Billy Bob, in spite of herself,
her eyes brimmed in shame, he held her gaze,
then looked away. The silence extended for
several beats.

BILLY BOB MASON (CONT'D)
(Nodding, bitterly)
So, let's cut to the bottom line
shall we.
(A beat)
It's the old, well worn, pathetically
obvious 'ILLUSION OF CHOICE' scam
being hauled out yet again, ain't it?

Your trip up here was ultimately to
make old Billy Bob here believe that
he had more control over his life
than he actually did.
(A beat)
Creating that illusion, Mr fucking
ALTERN, has been the driving force
behind the entire Government
policy for negotiating with Native
Australians for generations, and

now in your arrogance, you haul it out again, and you expect me to be surprised, and even charmed.

Billy Bob stood like a man who had come to the end of something, snorting his disgust.

Jeff scraped back his chair and stood facing Billy Bob, the table between them. Billy Bob leaned forward, his hands flat to the tabletop, his eyes fiercely on Jeff's.

     BILLY BOB MASON (CONT'D)
We can argue through all the various options, but eventually if you can't buy me off, we will hit the bottom line, the big decision.
    (A beat, savage grin)
I stand aside, or the Establishment will kill me. I will disappear.

Like in 'The Godfather', my signature, or my brains will be on the contract.

Billy Bob took a long outward breath, turned away with finality, stepped out onto the veranda, spat in the dust, rolled, and lit up, blew smoke.

Jeff slumped down in his seat, looked downwards for several beats, then up to Michelle.

      JEFF UTERI
   (Low voice, urgent)
Michelle, look, we need to get him on board with...

Michelle, her perception of the World forever changed, looked at Jeff, her lip curling in disgust.

                    MISH ROGAN
              (Suppressed anger)
        Fuck the hell off Jeff. Just fuck off.
              (A beat, succinctly)
        Fuck your arrogance, fuck your
        establishment, fuck your sense of
        entitlement, and most of all Jeff
        Uteri, fuck you.

                                    FADE OUT

INT. PORT AUGUSTA HOSPITAL EMERGENCY. DAY.

Sarah crossed the blistering car-park, the smell
of hot bitumen billowing into her face, through
glass doors and into ice-cold aircon, meeting
the raised eyes of the receptionist's switched
on smile.

                    SARAH
        Cantrell, John.

False smile, computer check, phone, false smile
again.

                    RECEPTIONIST
        Take a seat Mrs Cantrell, the Doctor
        will see you presently.

Sarah sat in the sweet sickly hospital smell,
her body temperature adjusting to the cold,
looking past the newsagent selling crisps, coke,
carnations, and cheap paperbacks, to the swing
doors where the Doctor would appear.

After a while he came.

                    MEDIC
Mrs Cantrell.

                    SARAH
Hello.

                    MEDIC
He's ready to go home. We have kept
him under observation for 24 hours
now. His temperature is still a little
high, but we think he had definitely
eaten something.

He needs to rest a couple of days and
he'll be fine. You must get medical
help if he turns worse.
          (A beat)
Follow me please.

He led off through the swing doors. Sarah
followed in a haze of disinfectant, urine,
random food smells and drains. John was sitting
in a cubicle, dressed with a carrier bag on
his lap. She leaned and kissed him, tasting
toothpaste and something unpleasantly bitter.

                    JOHN
          (Quietly)
Get me the fuck out of here.

He stood, shaky, she took his arm, thinking he
had lost weight. They both watched the Medic's
lips move while he soundlessly delivered a
series of complex instructions, gave them a
package of pills, then they were free.

Through the glass doors, across a white-hot
carpark, and into a superheated car. She started
the engine and took off, enduring the discomfort

until the aircon worked its magic. John leaned
back into the seat, glanced at her, his face
white.

JOHN (CONT'D)
Jandi died in the night.

Sarah's shock almost swerved the car into a
parked vehicle. She pulled up, staring at him.

SARAH
What? He died!

JOHN
He was in the next bed. He seemed OK,
then I heard him making weird noises.

I shouted for them, when they looked at
him, he was blue. They 'De-fibbed' him
a few times, but then they stopped,
stood around looking at each other.
(A beat)
I could see the screen from my bed. He
flat lined. Then they wheeled him out.
(A beat)
Fucking gone, just like that.

Sarah looked at him in horror, blinking tears.

JOHN (CONT'D)
No, I'm OK. Really. They checked me
out. Let's go home babe.

Someone blew a horn behind, Sarah glanced in
the mirror and pulled away, feeling unworldly.

FADE OUT

INT. 408 NELSON ROAD. PARA HILLS.
ADELAIDE. DAY

Sarah Cantrell nosed the Holden into their
carport off Nelson Road. She and John sat there
for a few moments relishing being at home.

She glanced at John, he seemed different,
diminished and somehow frail.

                    SARAH
          How are you doing Babe? We are home
          now. Lots of rest for you.

John nodded wanly. She squeezed his hand. They
went inside.

LATER

John was in bed resting. Sarah wandered the
house, troubled and ill at ease. She checked the
lounge window, suddenly realizing that she was
standing slightly back and behind the curtain.
Each time she heard a vehicle pass she looked
for any sign of the aboriginals' pickup trucks.
From time to time, she checked the stand of
Eucalyptus trees where they had their original
camp, it was deserted.

She watched as several vehicles came uphill
along Kesters, then indicated and turned left
in front of the house on Nelson Road. For a few
seconds, the occupants of every vehicle looked
directly into 408's lounge window. Sarah had
been used to that for all the years they had
lived there, but now it seemed threatening in
a way it had never been before.

At the tail end of a queue of 5 vehicles, a black Range Rover with HIRE plates indicated and turned, following the usual traffic 'rabbit run' to Tea Tree Plaza shopping centre. The windows were heavily tinted, but for a moment, Sarah felt that the huge 4*4 seemed to pause, in a way that other traffic didn't. She strained to get another look at the Range Rover for some inexplicable reason, then it was gone.

An hour later, still troubled, she was making a jug of iced lemon tea and she paused, her mind running wildly back to something Pump Jockey had said to her back at the derelict farmhouse,

'Three men in a black Range Rover maybe'

She sat, her gut twisting with coils of anxiety and apprehension.

FADE OUT

INT. RANGE ROVER. NELSON ROAD. PARA HILLS. ADELAIDE. DAY

Sergei cruised the Range Rover behind several other vehicles towards Tea Tree Plaza shopping centre, a smile of triumph growing.

SERGEI
They are home. The car is in the carport, and I saw her at the window as we passed.

Dmitri hit his knee with a flat hand grinning at Sergei.

                    DMITRI OLVO
          Excellent! Tonight then?

                    SERGEI
               (Nodding)
          Yep, tonight.

                                        FADE OUT

**EXT. DERELICT BUILDINGS. DESERT NORTH OF PORT
AUGUSTA. DAY**

Birani Pemba pulled up in front of the derelict
buildings, killed the engine and sat staring at
the doorway as the dust settled around them.
No-one came to the door, and he exchanged
glances with his passenger.

Waru Iluka, the driver of the pickup behind
got out carrying a baseball bat, walked on
past Birani and stood to one side of the black
doorway, looking back towards him. Birani nodded
and the man quickly disappeared inside. Waru
appeared again almost immediately, shaking his
head.

Birani hit the steering wheel hard with the
heel of his hand.

                    BIRANI PEMBA
          Fuck!

He sat there thinking.

                    BIRANI PEMBA (CONT'D)
          Check around the back. They have
          either tried to walk out, or someone
          else has been here and taken them.

Two other men got out and went behind the house, circling out into the bush. Presently they came back.

                    WARU ILUKA
        Four by four was here boss. Must have
        come along the main track but went
        out across the bush.
                (Gesturing)
        That way.

Birani thought about that.

                    BIRANI PEMBA
        Must be somebody who knows the bush,
        or an idiot maybe. What do you think
        Waru, maybe they are still out there?
        Maybe we should track them, they
        might be in trouble?

Waru Iluka spat dryly, not happy.

                    WARU ILUKA
        We can't go back to our people and
        tell them we lost the eggs Birani.
        We are fucked big-time.

Birani sucked air through his teeth. Made a decision.

                    BIRANI PEMBA
        Waru, you track this vehicle. No idea
        why he would come out here, but I
        guess they must have told him we
        would be back, so he decided not to
        return along the track in case he
        met us.
                (A beat)

We will go back along the track and meet you at Winninowie Fuel Station off the Prince's Highway. There's a phone signal there. Ring me whenever you get a signal, keep checking your screen.

Waru nodded. The two vehicles separated, both throwing trails of orange, brown dust that drifted slowly westward.

FADE OUT

INT/EXT. CORDILLO DOWNS STATION. SIMPSON DESERT. NIGHT.

Michelle listlessly pushed items of clothing into her bag and sat on the bed. Outside it was fully dark and starlit, the faint glow of a lantern out on the veranda lighting the edges of the windowpanes yellow. Somewhere in the house a generations old clock ticked on a mantel.

A guttered candle-stub was lit on her bedside table, wax pooling on the stained wood. She pushed her finger into the warm wax, leaving the print cleanly defined like ancient proof that she had been there.

She stood like she had made a decision. Outside it was cool and no wind and a thin grey reef of lighter sky floated on the eastern rim of the World. She walked out into the desert a little way and stood breathing it in. A calf bawled somewhere, and she heard movement in a shed. She shivered and went back into the house.

The kitchen was lit with a lantern, the smell of coffee and warm bread. She sat at the table, not knowing what to do next. Billy Bob came in, paused when he saw her, then hung his hat on a peg next to tangles of coats and leather tack. He went over to the stove and took out a baked loaf, set it on the table with two plates and butter, went back for the coffee. Before he sat down, he touched her shoulder lightly with his fingertips. For some inexplicable reason it made her cry.

MISH ROGAN
I'm sorry. I don't remember ever crying so much since I was a child. I have no idea what has happened to me in the last few days.

Billy Bob poured coffees, straddled his chair and sat like an old cowboy, all boots, jeans and elbows. She realized with a jolt that she could be falling in love with this exasperating man who had burst seismically into her ordered world. They both looked down at the food, both feeling vaguely afraid to meet each other's eyes.

Billy Bob took a breath, shifted the focus.

BILLY BOB MASON
(Glancing around)
This house was built in 1876. My grandfather lived and died in it. He ran sheep and cattle; he was first to bring Texas Longhorn into Australia.

Billy Bob grinned at her, his teeth flashing impossibly white.

                    BILLY BOB MASON (CONT'D)
Once you ate that beef you was hooked
you know. Sweet and lean like wild
creatures. Back then Cordillo was
25000 acres, hard to estimate really
because there's hardly any fences.

                    MISH ROGAN
Is there any other family Billy Bob?

                    BILLY BOB MASON
My Granddaddy had eight boys and a
girl. Only the girl, my mother, lived
past 25. The boys was snake-bit,
gored, kicked, sunburnt and shot.
None of them boys died in a bed.

She felt warmth blossom inside her. Surprised by
the feeling, she touched the scarred knuckles
on his hand.

                    MISH ROGAN
What will you do Billy Bob?

He poured more coffee in both cups, pushed one
towards her, holding her gaze.

                    BILLY BOB MASON
When all this is done, if they don't
kill me, I will bring you back here
and marry you Michelle Rogan.

Never thought that I would ever say
that.
          (A beat, eyes on her)
Every time you cry, I want to be
there where I can see you, and you
can see me.

Both chairs toppled backwards as they came into each other's arms in a breathless embrace that was beyond articulate thought, her mouth open against his grizzled cheek, seeking his mouth, his breath full in her face, crushing her against the hard muscle of his chest.

Michelle closed her eyes, overwhelmed in the moment, falling into an abyss of timeless primal submission that not a single moment of her 37 years of life to date had prepared her for.

They kissed a long time, his hand knotted into her hair, their bodies welded together. Eventually she pulled away from him, breathless, her pupils dilated, a full colour flush on her cheeks, a lifetime and a million miles away from the cool detached and highly controlled city creature that had arrived at Cordillo Downs a few days back.

He cradled her head back to his chest, fingers entangled in her hair, letting their passion subside.

            BILLY BOB MASON (CONT'D)
            (Ragged breath)
    Are you OK?

              MISH ROGAN
    Yes, I think so.
        (A beat, husky)
  Wow...

They kissed again, more lightly, her hand on the back of his head, pulling him in towards her. He broke the kiss, taking her hand decisively, pulled her towards the door. They fell onto the old brass bed in his bedroom and fucked voraciously like primitive creatures until they were both exhausted and spent.

Afterwards she lay in the tangle of sheets, her head against his chest and looked at the austerity of his room. No bookshelves, some old prints on the wall and just a bedside table with a drawer and a light.

                    MISH ROGAN (CONT'D)
          What's in this drawer Billy Bob?

He slid the drawer open and took out a Colt 45 handgun, checked it, laid in on the tabletop. She smiled at him, questioning, lost in the moment.

                    BILLY BOB MASON
              (Murmuring)
          Snakes.
              (A beat)
          It's loaded with dust-shot. They get
          in here sometimes.

She rolled over, balling her fists and punching him lightly in the chest, her laughter natural, childlike, tinkling like a bell.

                    MISH ROGAN
              (In wonder)
          Now, how is possible that I have
          lived in this country all my life
          Billy Bob, and never known that you
          might need to shoot a snake in your
          bedroom?

                                        FADE OUT

EXT. WINNINOWIE GAS STATION. PRINCE'S HIGHWAY. EVENING.

Pump Jockey was gassing a souped-up Chrysler Valiant 360 V8 when she saw Birani Pemba's pickup circle down the ramp towards the pumps. She finished the job, then drifted across to her 4*4 and leaned on the door, her arm through the open window, fingers trailing down inside touching the dull steel of the Remington 12 gauge.

Birani parked away from the pumps, then exited with two other Aboriginal men, and strolled over to the coffee vendor. He saw her and lifted a finger to his hat brim, nodding gravely. She nodded back. She watched them surreptitiously, but he made no move in her direction.

Two other vehicles pulled in and she considered but had little option but to serve them. One of the Aboriginal men climbed onto the flatbed and went to sleep, the other sat drinking in the passenger seat. Birani leaned, nursing his coffee, now and then checking his screen. The pump area cleared, Pump Jockey considered, then stepped over to Birani's pick-up.

> PUMP JOCKEY
> Birani.

> BIRANI PEMBA
> PJ. How's it going?

She leaned, alert, decided, then took the risk.

> PUMP JOCKEY
> (Quietly)
> It was me Birani. I rescued the Cantrells.

Birani jumped as if he'd been stung.

He looked critically at her for a few moments, then motioned her away from where his companions could hear. They stood at the counter and ordered two coffees, then sat at nearby bench.

                    BIRANI PEMBA
        Tell me.

                    PUMP JOCKEY
        I met a black Range Rover on the
        Hawker Road with three very handy,
        and very tooled up boys. Ray bans,
        black suits, no violin cases on show,
        but you know what I mean.
            (A beat, succinctly)
        They were looking for the Cantrells.

Birani held her gaze, shocked, taking in new information.

                    PUMP JOCKEY (CONT'D)
            (Dry observation)
        You fellers got no holes in you,
        so I'm guessing you didn't run into
        these boys.
            (A beat)
        I worked it out and got there before
        them. Took the Cantrells and the
        other guy out the back way. Dropped
        them at Port Augusta hospital.

Birani watched her intently. Pump Jockey looked past him, watched the down ramp from the Highway behind his head. He saw that and turned, following her look.

                    BIRANI PEMBA
        You think they might turn up here?

PJ shrugged noncommittally.

                    PUMP JOCKEY
        It's a fuel stop. Everyone stops here.
            (A beat)
        Am I in some danger Birani?

                    BIRANI PEMBA
        Not from me PJ, never.

                    PUMP JOCKEY
        Those two men were sick Birani. I
        mean very sick, like they was food
        poisoned.

PJ looked intently at Birani. He looked away,
blinking, uncomfortable. She suddenly stood,
like she just knew something.

                    PUMP JOCKEY (CONT'D)
            (Horror)
        Oh, fuck no Birani, no. You didn't,
        not the Bunyip...
            (A beat)
        No-oo...so that's why they were sick?

She turned on her boot heel, spinning around,
outward whistling breath, then came back to
face him, her normal composure gone, horror
etched into her face.

                    PUMP JOCKEY (CONT'D)
        So, it was true then... Hell fire.
            (A beat)
        How long does it take to incubate?
        Will the hospital find the eggs?

                    BIRANI PEMBA
    Too soon yet I reckon. Maybe if they
    operated, not sure.

Birani looked at her in torment, then his face
softening.

                    BIRANI PEMBA (CONT'D)
    You did what you thought was right
    PJ. There is no danger from me, or
    my people.
            (A beat)
    I don't know who these other guys are.
    That is news to me, maybe Government
    agents?

PJ shook her head vehemently.

                    PUMP JOCKEY
    No, not Government mate, definitely
    not, these boys were more like mafiosi,
    maybe Russian, not sure.

PJ sat down opposite Birani again, her normal
laconic and laid back composure momentarily
shaken, but now returning.

Over by the pumps, an RV pulled up, the driver
getting out, looking over towards them. She
waved at him, then stood, lingering for a beat,
her eyes on him.

                    PUMP JOCKEY (CONT'D)
    I gotta go Birani.
            (Pausing, haunted look)
    Will it kill them, you know, in
    the end?

                    BIRANI PEMBA
I don't know PJ.
        (Head in hands)
I don't know, maybe. That's why we
have to be there.

PJ gassed the RV, watching Birani from a distance.
He sat there for several minutes, then went over
to his pickup truck, got in the driver's seat.
The other two men got in and she watched the
truck roll up the ramp to the highway, then
indicate south towards Adelaide.

PJ finished up, then got in her own truck. She
circled past the black cave of the garage open
door, slowing. Straw-Hat came and leaned. She
raised a finger to him; he touched his hat
brim. PJ accelerated away, circled up the ramp,
turning north towards the Simpson.

                                        FADE OUT

INT. PORT AUGUSTA HOSPITAL. POST MORTEM. DAY.

The outer room was bleak. Plastic plants and
chairs and discreetly curtained windows.
Several people sat silently, waiting. A police
photographer; Two Uniforms; an ALTERN 'Suit;
and two of Jandi's 'family' members, Birani
Pemba and Waru Iluka. The tension in the room
was palpable.

The Coroner, pressing a clapboarded file to
his chest, and a green clothed Medic entered.
Everyone stood.

                    CORONER
Good afternoon everyone.

He turned to Birani Pemba and Waru Iluka.

> CORONER (CONT'D)
> (Gravely)
> I am very sorry for your loss
> gentlemen. Thank you for attending
> here today, this must be very hard
> for you.

The Coroner paused, his glance sweeping all present, then turning specifically to address Birani.

> CORONER (CONT'D)
> I realize and acknowledge that you
> strongly disagree with the decision to
> perform this procedure on religious
> and spiritual grounds.
>
> However, I can assure you that the
> decision to proceed today has been
> elevated to the highest level in the
> country.

Birani and Waru acknowledged his words with sombre nods.

The Coroner nodded to the Medic and he led the way into the starkly lit Post Mortem room. Except for the Medic, everyone filed into the row of witness seats along the side of the room. An assistant to the Medic stood quietly to one side. The room smelled strongly of an awful mix of disinfectant and putrefaction.

Jandi's body lay totally motionless on a stainless-steel table with white plastic sheeting stretched across. The floor was tiled in dazzling white with several drainage grills.

Empty tubs, jars and vials sat ready on a rolling cart along with arrays of stainless-steel tools and strangely shaped equipment. Without preamble, the Medic stripped the plastic sheet from the body in a single dramatic sweep, handing it to the assistant. The body was naked and washed but no incisions had been made yet.

Jandi didn't look like he had died last week. His eyes were black, his jaw open and his protruding tongue purple, his skin was mottled in shades from grey to deep black. His gut was distended upwards, and his scrotum ballooned to the size of a beach balls. The Medic pulled on gloves and faced the group, nodding to the Coroner.

MEDIC
This postmortem has been ordered by the Coroner because of the unusual circumstances of this person's death.

If any of you feel unwell during this process, please leave the room immediately. There are washrooms adjacent to the outer room. Please let the assistant know if you need help.
    (A beat)
Before we begin, I will quickly explain the normal procedure. I will make a 'Y' shaped incision from each armpit across to the sternum, then vertically down to the lower abdomen.
    (A beat)
Specifically, today, because of the medical interventions prior to death, I am focused on abdominal pathological conditions such as abscesses, bowel perforations or infarction.

The Medic turned towards the body and the Assistant took up position on the opposite side of the table. Birani and Waru were in a state of high tension as the first 'Y shaped cut was made.

Both were unprepared for the physicality of the process, the sound of bones being clipped, and the sheer strength and force that was necessary to open up the body for examination. As the cut extended into the lower abdomen, accumulated gasses escaped with a loud whoosh and the distension of the abdomen collapsed downwards grotesquely.

An unbearable stench billowed into the room offending everyone but the three professionals, who had seen it all before.

As the flaps of tissue of the abdomen were folded back, both the Medic and the Assistant exchanged low conversation. At the side, the Coroner leaned forward, trying to hear. The Medic reached down into the abdominal cavity, his hands out of sight. Birani and Waru were mute with tension.

The Medic worked for several beats inside the cavity, then paused registering surprise. He glanced across at the Coroner, then the Assistant also reached down to work inside the cavity. The Medic bent slightly, cutting carefully deeper inside the abdomen, then staggered backwards in shock.

Birani stepped forward involuntarily, and one of the Policemen immediately held his arm to restrain him.

The Medic stepped forward again, the Assistant holding back tissue to further expose the contents of the abdomen. Everyone strained to see, and not see. Even the Coroner broke protocol by stepping away from the designated witness area.

Within seconds everyone in the room crowded around the body and its exposed content. The collective shock was palpable, even Birani and Waru were deeply affected, even though they were at least mentally and spiritually prepared for what they would see.

Laying in Jandi's abdomen in the glare of the stark white lighting were two pale blue eggs the size of small melons. One was slightly larger than the other, both streaked with blood.

The Assistant placed his hand on the larger one, his eyes wide with shock, looking from the Medic to the Coroner.

                    ASSISTANT
          How can this be even possible?
               (A beat)
          How the fuck... I don't believe what
          I am seeing here. This man has been
          been dead for 5 days.
               (Louder)
          He's got some sort of eggs in him,
          and they are warm!

                              FADE OUT

INT. 408 NELSON ROAD. PARA HILLS.
ADELAIDE. DAY

John wandered the house and garden restlessly
trying to deal with the discomfort and shooting
pains in his lower abdomen. He didn't mention
this to Sarah, fearing another spell in hospital
if she called the Medic. Several times a day he
stood by the window looking at passing traffic
and watched the eucalyptus copse where the
Aboriginal camp had been but saw nothing that
captured his interest.

Sarah went about her daily activity saying
little. She cast worried looks at him from
time to time, but their daily routine began to
re-establish itself. John had little appetite
and seemed to be losing weight, apart from
his stomach, which was distended, the skin
stretched and taught.

John stood in his habitual place and looked along
Kesters Rd. He noticed a well-built bareheaded
man in shirtsleeves walking in the direction of
the junction. The man got to the junction and
looked each way, seeming to be perplexed as to
which road to take. John watched for a beat,
then went out through the carport.

                    JOHN
     G'day, you lost?

                    DMITRI OLVO
     Oh hello. Which road do I take for
     the big shopping centre?

The man came across the road and stood by the
trunk of the Holden.

                    JOHN
Well, Tea Tree Plaza shops are left,
but it's probably five miles. In this
heat, that's a long way mate. I
wouldn't recommend walking it.

                 DMITRI OLVO
Wow is it really. I think I misjudged
the distance. I thought I'd walk
before it got too hot. I haven't been
here long, it's all a bit new to me.

                    JOHN
You should be wearing a hat as well
mate. Look, can I get you some water?

The man reacted gratefully.

                 DMITRI OLVO
Really? Thanks very much, that's very
kind of you.

John went into the house. When he returned the
man was leaning casually against the back of
John's Holden. He gave him a cold bottle from
the fridge. The man drank, then handed the
bottle back.

                    JOHN
No, you keep it mate. No worries.
     (A beat)
I was you; I'd head back and get your
car and drive to Tea Tree Plaza. Too
bloody far to walk, you'll end up
with sunstroke.

The man saluted him with the bottle, crossing
the road and heading back along Kesters.

                    DMITRI OLVO
               (Over his shoulder)
          Thanks again. Good advice. I'll be
          seeing you.

John went back in the house. Sarah had been
watching from the window.

                      SARAH
               (Guarded)
          Was he lost?

                      JOHN
          Said he wanted to go to Tea Tree
          Plaza shops, walking...

Sarah leaned to watch the man disappear down
the hill. She was puzzled.

                      SARAH
          Weird.
               (A beat)
          John, I'm going to the shops anyway,
          but I wouldn't be giving no strangers
          a lift.
               (A beat)
          Nobody walks around in the sun, that's
          really odd.

John drank cold water from a bottle and watched
her idly as she got shopping bags, her cell
phone and keys.

                 SARAH (CONT'D)
          I won't be long John. Do you need
          anything?

John shook his head, then went to window and
watched as she reversed expertly out of the

carport onto Nelson Rd. She raised a hand to him and sped away. He sat, running his hands over his abdomen, glad not to be pretending for a while. It was getting worse, not better.

His cell phone rang, he glanced at the screen, unknown number.

CELLPHONE CONVERSATION.

> JOHN
> John Cantrell.

> MEDIC
> Hello, Mr Cantrell. This is the Doctor from Port Augusta hospital. How are you feeling today, Sir.

> JOHN
> Oh, I'm OK. Getting there, you know.

> MEDIC
> Mr Cantrell, we would like you to come back for some further tests. Are you at home right now?

> JOHN
> What tests?

> MEDIC
> Mr Cantrell, are you at home? We will be sending an ambulance to pick you up in the next two hours. Can you throw some things in a bag please. You will be with us for a couple of days.

                    JOHN
    I don't want to go back to hospital.
    I'm fine. Thank you for ringing, but
    please leave me alone.

                    MEDIC
    Mr Cantrell, I...

John hung the call, throwing his cell phone
across the table top in annoyance.

The next thing he was on the floor in a terrifying
spasm that left him breathless, crabbing around
in a circle, his knees drawn up to his chest.
He got back onto his chair after a few minutes,
drank some water and tried to regain some
control.

He heard Sarah pull into the carport.

                    SARAH
    It's mad out there at Tea Tree. The
    bloody aircon is down. Lots of the
    shops closing for the day until it's
    fixed.
            (Looking at him)
    You OK John?

                    JOHN
            (Bleakly)
    I'm good, don't go on.

She watched him for a beat, uncertain, then
went into the bedroom. His eyes followed her,
calculating. He got up, picked up his chair and
followed her silently. She was in the bedroom,
the door ajar. He pulled the bedroom door closed
and jammed the chair under the door handle with

force, kicking the legs hard into the carpet. She came to the door on the other side.

                    SARAH
          John, what the fuck are you doing? I
          can't open this door.

He didn't reply, a dark calculating smile passing over his ravaged face.

                    SARAH (CONT'D)
                    (Shouting)
          John, open this door. I mean it! This
          isn't fun.

She was now banging on the door frantically, her initial anger turning to worry.

                    SARAH (CONT'D)
          Please John. What are you doing baby,
          comon, let me out of here. I'm serious.
                    (Loud banging)
          Open this fucking door you bastard...

John limped to the front room, throwing a few clothes and bottles of water into a bag, looking around for wallet, cell phone and car keys. He stood looking around him, suddenly weary and sad beyond anything he had ever felt before. He brushed tears away, took a deep breath and headed for the door, ignoring the racket coming from the bedroom.

                                        FADE OUT

INT. RANGE ROVER. KESTERS RD SHOPS. PARA HILLS. DAY

Dmitri tapped on the blazing hot door panel and the Range

Rover's lights pulsed as Sergei released the locks. Dmitri

climbed in, leaning back as the blissful aircon surrounded

him in cool.

> DMITRI OLVO
> Done it. The tracker is under the back bumper. It will work from an iPhone.

Sergei grunted and pulled out his iPhone, touching the

screen.

> SERGEI
> Hang on...
> (A beat)
> Yep, got it! Excellent. Well done

mate. Wherever he goes now we can

track him.

FADE OUT

INT. HALF MOON ST. LONDON. NIGHT.

LONG DISTANCE PHONE CALL.

Ekaterina, alone in the house, took the call,
Sergei's face

showing on her screen.

She walked over the window and stood looking
along Half Moon St, the rain sweeping in waves
in the pools of orange light beneath each
lamppost.

                    EKATERINA LEBOV
        Sergei, my love. I have missed you.

                    SERGEI
        And I you Ekaterina. I have been out

        of phone signal for long periods. We

        are back in Adelaide now.

                    EKATERINA LEBOV
        Are you safe?

                    SERGEI
        We are safe, no problem. How is

        Andrei?

                    EKATERINA LEBOV
        He is very brave, but he is going
        down in small ways each day. Have you
        any news for me?

                    SERGEI
Yes, we are close. It has been difficult
to get to the Cantrells for all sorts
of reasons, but now we are almost
ready to deal with them directly. We
have a tracker on their car also, in
case an opportunity presents itself
away from their house.

                EKATERINA LEBOV
Do they still have the BUNYIP flesh
do you think Sergei?

                    SERGEI
We think so. The wife, Sarah has
been very circumspect whenever she
has been interviewed on TV. The news
reports are slowing down now. The
Bunyip is hardly mentioned. The big
media circus at their house has now
disappeared.

Ekaterina kissed the screen in her excitement,
then wiping away lipstick in annoyance.

                SERGEI (cont'd)
            (Grinning)
Ekaterina, if we get the Bunyip flesh,
is it possible that you and Andrei
could fly out to Adelaide.

That would be preferable to us
trying to smuggle the flesh out on an
international flight.
            (A beat)
Could Andrei make the flight?

Ekaterina caught a sob in her throat, then
controlling herself.

EKATERINA LEBOV
Yes, he will make the flight.
(A beat)
What has he got to lose? Be safe my
love, ring me when you have news.

Ekaterina broke the connection, poured a vodka,
listened to the rain on the window.

FADE OUT

**INT. CORDILLO DOWNS STATION. SIMPSON DESERT.
NIGHT**

Billy Bob dragged the glow of the cigarette
down to nothing and arced it away in a shower
of sparks over the veranda rail.

He went into the dark house and sat at his
desk in the old swivel chair that was his
Granddaddy's. He flicked on the desk light with
the green shade leaving the corners of the room
in darkness. On the desk was a glinting brass
calendar that changed dates when you tipped it
over. It still said February 17th, 1947.

There was an ashtray and a glass paperweight
and a tattered blotter that had MCCARTHY'S FEED
SUPPLY written on it. Lying face-up was his
mother's graduation photo in a silver frame, he
reached and set it so he could see it.

The room smelled of old cigarette smoke. He
turned off the light and sat there in the dark
missing Michelle Rogan more than he could have
anticipated. Through the window he could see
the starlit desert falling away to the north,
black crosses of telegraph wire stark against

shooting stars. He leaned, crossing his boots on the desktop.

The clock struck 11.00 in the hallway.

He felt a movement deep in the earth. He crouched down, his hand flat to the floor. He got up, picked up the Colt, and went out on to the veranda. The headlights, still a long way off, rose and fell with the corrugations in the road, sometimes disappearing, then coming on again stronger.

He pulled back the loading gate on the COLT, checking the glint of brass cartridge as the vehicle finally pulled into the yard, the headlights dying down to an ember, then gone.

The dark bulk of the 4*4 becoming apparent against the low horizon.

The driver sat there in the darkness for several beats, the engine ticking as it cooled. Realization dawned. Billy Bob put the Colt into the waistband of his jeans, a slow grin flashing.

                    BILLY BOB MASON
        Now, don't you go blubbing on me now.

Pump Jockey stepped out of the driver's side door carrying her Remington Pump in her left hand. She stepped into the shaft of light falling out of the doorway, stood for a beat, then moved smoothly into Billy Bob's arms.

                    PUMP JOCKEY
        Hello Daddy.

                    BILLY BOB MASON
       Hello Louise Victoria Mason.

LATER

PJ, freshly showered, feminine and soft, came
into the kitchen and sat at the kitchen table.
She pulled a steaming coffee towards her,
cradling it.

                    PUMP JOCKEY
       So, who was she?

                    BILLY BOB MASON
       Who was who?

                    PUMP JOCKEY
            (Wide grin)
       Dad, I can smell her. Is she gonna be

       my new Mammy?

                    BILLY BOB MASON
       Maybe.

She cast a critical eye at him, an older male
representation of herself, his genes driving her
entire value system and persona, her love for
him without limit or description. He had set
the bar so high for her that no other male had
even tilted towards it, or approached it.

                    PUMP JOCKEY
       Dad, I need to talk to you. I think

       Birani is in some sort of big trouble.
       He's growing Bunyip eggs in two men.
       One of them is a white guy.
            (A beat)

I heard yesterday that other one, the
black feller carrying eggs, has died
in Port Augusta hospital.

Billy Bob was thunderstruck. He came to his
feet wide eyes looking down at her. Then, still
processing the momentous information, picked up
her point.

> BILLY BOB MASON
> Bloody hell Louise, they will do an
> autopsy?

> PUMP JOCKEY
> (Nodding)
> Yep.

> BILLY BOB MASON
> Fuck!

Billy Bob was shocked into silence, for a few
seconds, then immediately less shocked as
the logic took over. He began to speak, she
interrupted.

> PUMP JOCKEY (CONT'D)
> Dad, there's more...
> (A beat)
> Three Mafiosi boys in a black Range
> Rover are after the Bunyip. I don't
> think they don't know about the eggs
> yet, but maybe they will soon.

> FADE OUT:

EXT. 408 NELSON ROAD. PARA HILLS. ADELAIDE. DAY

Sergei gunned the Range Rover along Kesters Rd, crossed the junction and pulled up alongside the Cantrell's carport.

> IGOR STEPAN
> Fuck, his car is gone. Do you think she is here?

> SERGEI
> OK, we are here now. Let's check.

The three men exited the car and went through the carport to the house door. Sergei knocked, then leaned into the door, listening.

> SERGEI (CONT'D)
> What the fuck is going on in there? Can you hear that racket?

They all listened, looking blankly at each other. Without another word, Sergei shoulder charged the door. On the third charge the door splintered open. They ran through the house, seeing the chair locking the bedroom room in place, Dmitri kicked it away and suddenly they were face to face with a tearful Sarah Cantrell.

She recoiled in shock.

> SARAH
> Oh my God, who are you?

Sergei, immediately backed away, both hands held palm outwards.

                    SERGEI
Please don't be frightened Sarah, we
have just rescued you. We heard the
racket. Where is your husband? What's
happening here?

Sarah backed away and sat on the bed, very
frightened. Sergei gestured to the others and
they both backed away and went into the kitchen.
He knelt in front of Sarah a meter away, palms
spread earnestly.

                SERGEI (CONT'D)
Sarah, Mrs Cantrell, My name is
Sergei, please believe me when I say
I have no intention of harming you.

Sarah stared, realization dawning.

                    SARAH
You are the men in the Range Rover.
You have been watching us.

                    SERGEI
Yes, that is true. But not to harm
you or your husband in any way. In
fact, if things go as we hope, we
want to make you and your husband
very rich.

Sarah exerted huge control to calm herself.

                    SARAH
Where is John, my husband? He locked
me in.

                    SERGEI
Sarah, I'm sorry, but I don't know
where he is, or why he would even do
that.
          (A beat)
The car is gone. Why would he lock
you in the bedroom? Is it for a joke
maybe?

Sarah looked at him, regaining her composure
slightly. She ignored his question.

                    SARAH
What did you mean, make us rich?

Sergei smiled winningly at her, getting to his
feet, his hand out to her solicitously.

                    SERGEI
Let's go sit with a cold drink in the
kitchen Sarah. Come...

Sarah, still very wary, followed him into
kitchen Both other men rose from their seats
around the table, bowing slightly as she took a
seat. Sergei gestured; Dmitri got cold drinks
from the fridge. Sarah stared at him.

                    SARAH
You are the man who was lost earlier.
I knew there was something odd about
that story. You were checking us out.

Dmitri acknowledged her words with a slight
bow and an apologetic smile. Sergei leaned in
earnestly.

                         SERGEI
    Sarah, I will be direct with you. We
    represent our boss back in UK. He is
    terminally ill with not much time
    left.
         (A beat)
    We believe that you have in your
    possession the means to cure him
    and maybe save his life. We, and his
    wife, love him. We are devoted to
    saving him if we can.

Sarah stared at him, realization dawning.

                         SARAH
    The Bunyip.

                         SERGEI
    Yes Sarah, the Bunyip. Do you still
    have the flesh?

Sarah paused, her eyes calculating and scheming.

                         SARAH
    I may have.
         (A beat)
    What might be on the table if I did.

Sergei smiled, handsome and immediately boyish,
relief flooding his entire physiology. All the
men smiled.

                         SERGEI
    Oh, Sarah, you have no idea how happy
    that makes us all. I need to make
    some phone calls. Can you assure us
    that you have the Bunyip flesh?
         (A beat)

We have no intention of stealing it
from you, we will pay.

The men exchanged glances. Dmitri got up and
looked in the fridge, then checked the freezer,
turned and shook his head. Sarah was immediately
tense. Sergei reached and touched her hand.

                    SERGEI (CONT'D)
          It's OK Sarah. Bear with me. I will
          make a call.

Sergei held her gaze and dialled.

TELEPHONE CONVERSATION

                    SERGEI (CONT'D)
          Ekaterina, its Sergei. Can you speak?

                    EKATERINA LEBOV
          Sergei, it's 0200 in the morning. Are
          you OK?

Sergei smiled reassuringly at Sarah.

                    SERGEI
          Ekaterina, are you alone?

                    EKATERINA LEBOV
          Wait please...
               (A beat, movement)
          OK yes, I can speak.

                    SERGEI
          I want you to speak to Sarah Cantrell
          here please. She is open to discussing
          a possible financial arrangement
          with you.

This may lead to you and Andrei flying
here at short notice in the next 24
hours.

There was movement on the other end of the call.
When Ekaterina's voice came back it was clear
and authoritative.

                    EKATERINA LEBOV
          Put her on please Sergei.

Sergei handed the cell phone to Sarah.

                    SARAH
          This is Sarah Cantrell. Who am I
          speaking to?

                    EKATERINA LEBOV
          Hello Mrs Cantrell.

          My name is Ekaterina Lebov Mrs
          Cantrell. Sergei and the other two
          men work for my husband. Please can
          you tell me, do you have the Bunyip
          flesh in your possession?

          This is very important.

                    SARAH
          Yes, I do. It is deep frozen.

Ekaterina breathed a huge ragged emotionally
charged sigh of relief. There was silence for
several beats, then,

                    EKATERINA LEBOV
          Mrs Cantrell, we will be prepared to
          pay you 1 million US dollars for the

Bunyip meat. My husband and I will
fly to Adelaide immediately.

He is terminally ill with a very
short time left. The Bunyip is now
our only hope.
(A beat)
It may fail, but that will not be
your fault in any way. You will be
paid, whatever the outcome. Sergei,
Dmitri and Igor will stay with you
and your husband until we get to you.
They will protect you, and I assure
you, that no harm will come to you.
(A beat)
You are about to become a very rich
lady.

Now please put me back to Sergei.

Sarah, tearful and shaken, handed the cellphone
back to a beaming Sergei.

                EKATERINA LEBOV (CONT'D)
Sergei, I will arrange flights
immediately. Secure the house and do
not raise alarms in the immediate
neighbourhood. Stay in touch.
(A beat)
Oh yes and check on the Bunyip meat.
Ring me if any issues.
(A beat)
Thank you, dear Sergei, you will
always have my love.

The phone hung. Sergei put his hands to his face
for a beat, allowing relief to flood through him.
Igor and Dmitri both beamed happily.

Sarah stood, went to the rear of the house, came back with a frozen foil wrapped package. She thudded it down solidly to the table with a look of triumph.

                    SARAH
        The Bunyip.

                                    FADE OUT

INT. 162 WESTON CREEK RD. CANBERRA. AUSTRALIA. EVENING.

162 Weston Creek Rd was four miles from downtown Canberra, set back from the road in deep foliage, manicured, trimmed, smoked glass and the seductive promise of delectable BBQs, Sth Australian wines, and an infinity pool.

Arthur McCloud MP and Minister had lived there for the four years he had held a Cabinet Ministerial post. Pulled in under the trees were Michelle's Prius, Jeff's Mercedes CLS and Arthur's chauffeur-driven Bentley.

They all leaned back in easy chairs under the pergola, by the softly lit infinity pool. The debris of dinner was pushed away into the centre of the table.

Arthur's wife Joyce, former lingerie model, raised a wine bottle with a question in her eyes.

                    JOYCE MCCLOUD
        Drop of red Jeff?

                    JEFF UTERI
What is it, Joyce?

                   JOYCE MCCLOUD
           (Shrugging)
It's a red, I don't know the make.

                  ARTHUR MCCLOUD MP
Oh   for   fuck's   sake   Jeff,   live
dangerously, just this once. It's a
Barossa red, what more do you want
to know.

Jeff conceded, Joyce poured, Arthur smiled.

Michelle gazed off into the foliage, distant,
barriers up. Joyce eyed her, with the bottle
still raised, then gave up with a weary look
towards Arthur.

            ARTHUR MCCLOUD MP (CONT'D)
Mish, you have a face like a slapped
arse, is there anything you want to
share with us?

Michelle swept an icy gaze across them all, then
looked away as if the sight offended her. After a
long moment she turned to them, speaking mainly
to the two men.

                    MISH ROGAN
           (Cold, precise)
How   can you just decide Arthur,
just like that, over a BBQ for God's
sake, to destroy a generations old
Australian family dynasty, a man, and
most likely his daughter's life.

                         257

If he fights for his heritage and his property, your goons will probably kill him.
          (A beat)
I don't get that guys. This is not what I signed up for. This is legalized state murder of our own citizens.

People who have committed no crime, other than owning something you want to take from them.

Arthur cast a flinty eye at Jeff, a warning in his posture. Jeff flinched minutely, looking down. Arthur knocked back half a glass of white, and nodded.

                    ARTHUR MCCLOUD MP
I do take your point Mish, and I absolutely concede that on the face of it, it is a very hard decision.

Michelle, you are very talented, principled, and forceful woman.
          (A beat)
Perhaps I'm being desperately shallow, but in my opinion, this situation is unprecedented. What's out there cannot be owned by a person, Michelle.

However awful this sounds, those rare earth metals on the Cordillo Downs Ranch must be, they absolutely have to be, utilized and secured for the public good.

I know this is hard for you to take but the process by which it transfers ownership to become available for the public's use, is not actually of interest to me.

That part is yours, and Jeff's job, I don't want to know.

Arthur reached and poured himself another glass of white. He looked at her, a lopsided grin on his face.

ARTHUR MCCLOUD MP (CONT'D)
I'm vaguely surprised, given your track record, that it is even a problem to you.

He laughed suddenly, the sound shaky and harsh, but genuine enough to catch everyone's attention. He cleared his throat.

ARTHUR MCCLOUD MP (CONT'D)
Look Mish, I don't want to get into the ethics of State Sponsored assassination, homicide, or murder. Better brains than mine have been arguing these issues for generations.

The fact is, whether we like it or not, all States do it.

When an individual, for whatever reason, earns this unique and distinctive status, for the greater good, we, The State, will remove that person, then argue the vindication afterwards, but only if we are exposed.

Arthur looked around at everyone, then dropped his eyes petulantly, studying the content of his glass. Michelle stared at him, eyes glittering, but he would not meet her gaze.

The atmosphere had chilled. Joyce's hostess skills rose to the surface.

                    JOYCE MCCLOUD
          So, here we all are then. Can we
          lighten up a bit please.

Joyce leaned, flicking something from her knee, her eyes on Michelle, humorous and knowing, pushing her luck.

                    JOYCE MCCLOUD (CONT'D)
               (To Jeff)
          So, what's he like then Jeff, this
          cowboy? Sitting out there on his
          desert empire, boots on the table,
          skinning jackrabbits on his front
          porch, the master of all he surveys.

She wriggled suggestively, her cleavage rippling.

                    JOYCE MCCLOUD (CONT'D)
          Do you think he's a good fuck?

Jeff sipped, grimacing slightly, pushing away his glass.

                    JEFF UTERI
          Not for me to say Joyce.

Michelle stood abruptly, checking her watch, cell phone. She produced a wintry receptionist smile to Arthur and Joyce.

MISH ROGAN
Thank you so much for the food and
wine Arthur and Joyce. So sorry, I
have to go early before we get to the
singing and dancing part.
(To Jeff)
I'll see you back at the office.

She stalked away without a backward glance,
they all watched her go silently.

JOYCE MCCLOUD
More wine anyone?

Arthur, still looking at the moving branch
where Michelle had passed under it.

ARTHUR MCCLOUD MP
You need to get that lady in line
Jeff. I'm serious. Either you do it or
I will.
(A beat)
That fucking cowboy is not going to
stand in the way of this country's
progress. He may be shagging your
right-hand man, and I use the term
advisedly, but that will not stop
us clearing the decks wherever and
whenever we deem it necessary.
(A beat)
The money offer has failed, so now we
move to the next stage of compulsory
purchase, at 25% of our original offer.
(A beat)
He will obviously refuse that, so our
options close down.

Hard look at Jeff, index finger upwards.

                    ARTHUR MCCLOUD MP (CONT'D)
          Don't they Jeff?

                                          FADE OUT

**INT. TOYOTA PRIUS. A LAY BY IN CANBERRA.
EVENING**

Michelle pulled in off the road, trying to deal
with angry tears. She took some deep breaths
and calmed herself with a supreme effort. She
dialled.

CELLPHONE CONVERSATION

                    MISH ROGAN
          Billy Bob, its Mish.

                    BILLY BOB MASON
          You on your way back here anytime
          soon?

                    MISH ROGAN
          No, I'm not. I can be more protective
          of you from here right now Cowboy.

She heard him strike a match, imagined him
blowing out the match with blue smoke curling
in concentric circles in the superheated air.

                    BILLY BOB MASON
          I take it this isn't a cybersex call
          then babe?

                    MISH ROGAN
          Fuck you, Billy Bob.
              (A beat)

Someone will come. I don't know who,
how, where, or when. They are moving
to option three.

The phone went silent for several beats, she
thought he had hung, then,

                    BILLY BOB MASON
          Are you safe Mish?

                    MISH ROGAN
          Yes, I'm OK Billy Bob, they wouldn't
          dare do anything to me here.

                    BILLY BOB MASON
          You should come here, now, then, I'd
          be sure.

He heard her catch her breath.

                    MISH ROGAN
          Again, fuck you Billy Bob Mason,
          how the hell do you always make me
          bloody cry?
                    (A beat)
          I love you.

                    BILLY BOB MASON
          I love you too.

                                        FADE OUT

EXT. PORT AUGUSTA HOSPITAL CARPARK DAY.

The pickup was parked in a corner of shade.
Both men leaning against the wing. Birani Pemba
ground out his cigarette under a boot-heel,
thrusting his chin in the direction of an

obscure doorway. Waru Iluka followed his eyes. An old Aboriginal man with dreadlocks came out, went across to a row of huge bins, then disappeared back through the doorway.

                    BIRANI PEMBA
          That's him I reckon.

Waru nodded.

                    WARU ILUKA
          Freddie Buna. Haven't seen old Fred
          for a long time.

Birani glanced around the car park, then set off towards the doorway. Waru followed. As they got near the door, it opened again, and the old man came out carrying a plastic bag. He saw the two men and stopped in his tracks, then a huge smile spread across his lined face.

                    BIRANI PEMBA
          Hello Freddie. Long time eh.

Freddie stepped up to Birani, looking deep into his eyes.

                    FREDDIE BUNA
          You's turning into your Daddy Birani.
               (Turning to Waru)
          G'day Waru. Oh man, this is a good day.

The three men embraced, tears streaking down Freddie's ancient face. Freddie pulled away, looking around warily, then gestured for the men to follow him.

                    FREDDIE BUNA (CONT'D)
     My place is in here boys. Come and
     visit with old Freddie.

They followed him down a stuffy concrete corridor
smelling of disinfectant and urine. He went in a
door and hit a switch. The room was packed with
brushes, boxes, and utility equipment. A small
table and a kettle stood against a wall. Freddie
pulled some boxes into position, indicating.

                    FREDDIE BUNA (CONT'D)
     Sit boys. Cold drink? I have my own
     fridge here.

He pulled three beers from a battered fridge
and popped them. They sat looking at each other
for a beat. Birani leaned, clicking his can
against the other two. They all grinned at each
other.

                    BIRANI PEMBA
     Freddie, you the Hospital Janitor
     here, right? We need you to help us.

                                        FADE OUT

EXT. COUNTRY ROAD NEAR CANBERRA. DAY.

Jeff Uteri drove out of the city towards grey
cloud and the promise of rain. For thirty miles
he crested ridges, hammered down the other side,
took long slow graceful bends, then gradually
the black ribbon of bitumen straightened into
an arrow line over the horizon, and he clicked
85 mph on the cruise control.

A thunderous crack in the heavens above his head jolted his wandering attention back to full alert as the rain came down in torrents. The plains on either side became waving seas of brown grass, and watercourses along the edges of the bitumen raged into muddy froth, and Jeff, his brain synapses firing frantically, brought the skidding Toyota down to a manageable 35 mph, then after several beats, gave up and sloshed the car to a stop on the streaming shoulder. Five minutes of deafening noise, then the tap switched off leaving him breathless. Another few beats and a beautiful vivid rainbow painted itself across the clearing sky. Jeff rolled down the window, cool air in his face, the smell of earth, the colours of the countryside distinct and over bright. He pulled back on the road in a haze of sunshine and steam.

A late model Falcon came into his mirror fast, two indistinct shapes behind sun glinting on the windscreen. He watched it pace his speed even though the road ahead was clear to the horizon.

On the passenger seat, his screen came to life, the sound crackling through the car's speakers. 'Unknown Caller', he hit 'Accept'.

TELEPHONE CONVERSATION

                    LUIS DEWAYNE
    Mr Uteri, my name is Luis Dewayne, my
    partner is Enzo Matteo. We are right
    behind you.
            (A beat)
    3 miles ahead left is a Service Area.
    Please pull in and we will meet you
    in the snack bar area.

                    JEFF UTERI
    Will do.

Jeff hung. The Falcon accelerated past him,
tunnelling into flat white sunlight through the
rising steam off the bitumen.

                                        FADE OUT

**EXT. PRINCES HIGHWAY NORTHERN SUBURBS OF
ADELAIDE. DAY.**

John Cantrell pulled onto the vast parking area
of the FLINDERS ROADHOUSE and cruised slowly
through the high-rise forest of massive road-
trains. He got as close as he could to the
washrooms, then sat and waited, watching who
went in and out.

After ten minutes, he decided to risk it. He
went through the doorway, hitting the stench
immediately. All the toilets in the row were
close to overflowing. He chose the least full
one where the water was a clear inch below the
top of the toilet.

He sat, cramped with shooting pains, and tried
to perform. No use. After a while he got up and
looked down into the bowl. It was bright red.
He tried to flush; the bloody water gurgled but
didn't go down. He gave up, leaving it. The tap
worked so he was able to wash his hands. He bent,
washing his rear quarters as best he could.

A small man with a Hawaiian shirt came in,
walked along the row of toilets shaking his
head. He looked at the toilet filled with bloody
water, then looked at John questioningly.

                              JOHN
          Not me mate. This whole place is a
          fucking war zone.

The man went out through the door. John followed,
slightly doubled over in his discomfort.

Inside the restaurant area, most of the tables
had one man sitting, lost in their own world.
John found a table by a roped off area and sat. An
elderly waitress circulated with a coffeepot. She
called everyone 'DOLL' and seemed permanently
annoyed. She cast a flinty eye at John.

                           WAITRESS
          We got Burgers and Dogs Doll,
          everything else is gone.

                              JOHN
          Burger please, no fries.

                           WAITRESS
          Burgers come with fries. Don't eat
          them, I don't care.

                              JOHN
          I don't want fries.

The waitress blew a long outward breath, looking
around helplessly. She composed herself, then
fixing him with a malevolent stare.

                           WAITRESS
          Burgers come with fries. That's it. So
          do you want a fucking burger? Or not?
               (A beat, looking around)
          I really do not give a shit either way.

John got laboriously to his feet, favouring his right side.

JOHN
I'll leave it. Thanks.

By the time he got back to his car he was almost delirious with pain. He sat in a dark canyon between two massive trucks and closed his eyes.

When he awoke, the trucks had gone, and his car was exposed on all sides in a mix of dirty yellow lighting and pale moonlight. He rolled down the side window, taking deep breaths. His phone screen told him seven calls were unanswered.

He got out of the car to try the toilet again.

FADE OUT

INT. HEATHROW DEPARTURES. LONDON. DAY

There was five-hour delay for the Adelaide flight. New departure times screens were flickering in black type over yellow. There was a pervading air of tension and annoyance everywhere.

Ekaterina placed her hand protectively over Andrei's arm as they sat on high stools at the circular Oyster Bar.

Andrei was perfectly groomed with darkened lenses hiding the grey pallor around his eyes. He smiled deprecatingly at the huge sign in the centre of the massive building.

ANDREI LEBOV

Departure Lounge is vaguely appropriate for us, well me anyway, don't you think Baby?
(A beat)
Defibrillators everywhere as well, they must have known I was coming.

EKATERINA LEBOV
(Impatiently)
Not very funny Andrei. If you are going to be like this for a 23 hour flight, you can go on your own.

Andrei smiled at her, bitterness showing being the darkened lens.

Ekaterina searched his face, then looked away. A TV was playing just above her head, He stared at it. A TV newsreader was speaking silently, glancing between a sheet of paper and the autocue. After a while he turned to the doll-like weather girl with a nervy fake smile.

The barman saw Andrei watching and made a gesture to turn up the volume. Andrei shook his head. The barman smiled politely.

The weather doll clasped her hands in front of her midi-skirt and read out the temperatures. The painted map behind her was draped with spiked magnetic lines. She looked strained as she moved southwards through the weather regions. For some reason Andrei felt sorry for her.

The tannoid stuttered metallically.

ANNOUNCER
This message is for all passengers
on Flight BA75aLHR to Adelaide, South
Australia. The flight has been delayed
due to bad weather conditions.

The ground crew are de-icing the wings
of the aircraft. The new departure
time is now 10.50am. Please accept
our apologies for the inconvenience.

Andrei watched Ekaterina's lips compress
slightly, a small sign of annoyance. He touched
her arm.

ANDREI LEBOV
It will be nice for you to see Sergei
again; do you think darling?

She looked for irony in his Ray Bans, saw none,
relaxed.

EKATERINA LEBOV
I want to see you well again my love.
This is our last hope you know. We
are all focused on that.

ANDREI LEBOV
I do know that my darling.
(A beat, bitterly)
My continued existence on this earth
is dependent on a mythical creature
that most people do not believe even
exists. You will forgive me if it all
feels vaguely tenuous.

Tears sprang into her eyes, he was outwardly
contrite, inwardly indifferent.

                ANDREI LEBOV (CONT'D)
          (Smiling)
     But it is truly exciting also Ekaterina,
     you have brought the spirit of Harry
     Potter into my disappearing world of
     stark realities.
          (A beat)
     That is truly amazing. I love you
     very much my darling.

                              FADE OUT

EXT. PORT AUGUSTA HOSPITAL CARPARK. AUSTRALIA.
0300AM.

Birani Pemba woke up hurting all over when
Freddie Buna tapped on the side window of the
pick-up truck. Beside him Waru also snapped
awake, a naked blade appearing momentarily.

Freddie grinned, his broken teeth flashing yellow
in the street lighting. 200 meters away across
the carpark the hospital was ablaze with light,
business as usual.

                    FREDDIE BUNA
          Follow me boys. Keep heads down, don't
          look up at CCTV cams.

Freddie took off across the empty carpark,
motioning them to follow him in the pickup. They
parked under a tree in semi-darkness away from
CCTV and switched their cell phones to silent.
Freddie led them past huge waste bins, between
skips, through a dark doorway into aircon cold
and along several dimly lit corridors that
disappeared away to points of perspective.
Eventually he stopped, his finger to his lips.

He carefully unlocked a door and peered in, then gestured them to follow. A dimly lit room, then the powerful smell of disinfectant and putrefaction that Birani remembered.

Freddie expertly unlocked another door, and they were in the neat, tidy, spare, Post Mortem room, were Jandi's body had been examined.

Freddie stood back by the door, pointing towards several refrigerated storage units along a side wall. Both men carefully pulled out the sliding shelves out of the stainless-steel wall. On the third attempt, Waru hissed, he was holding back a white plastic shroud covering Jandi's body.

Birani went over, pulling the shroud away. Jandi had been roughly stitched up in a massive 'Y' shaped scar like a horror movie, the skin pulled and distorted like rubber.

Birani and Waru exchanged glances. Waru produced his knife and with no hesitation ran the blade along the fresh stitches. An awful stench billowed out as the flesh relaxed back loosely, the body settling and gaping grotesquely on its base.

Holding his breath, Birani plunged his hands, up to his elbows into the yawning abdomen area, feeling around in the icy cold mess, his face turned away to take gulps of clean air. Both Freddie and Waru turned away, taking ragged breaths.

                    BIRANI PEMBA
        Oh God, they've just dumped everything
        back in here.
                (Rising panic)
        There's no eggs here. They've gone!

273

WARU ILUKA
What the fuck do you mean gone,
nothing? Gotta be there...

Birani stood back, his arms dripping gore onto
the white tiles, breathing hard. Waru stepped
up, plunged his own hands in, Feeling around,
his face gradually despairing.

WARU ILUKA (CONT'D)
What the hell do we do now?

Birani was momentarily defeated. He dripped
blood over to a nearby sink and sluiced his
hands and arms. Waru followed suit, both men
miserable. Over by the door Freddie slumped
against the frame, looking at both younger men
for the next move.

Suddenly Birani had an inspiration.

BIRANI PEMBA
They were warm weren't they? The eggs
were warm?

Waru read his thoughts instantly.

WARU ILUKA
Incubators? They will be incubated.
(Looking at Freddie)
Where Freddie?

Freddie was following the thinking, nodding,
gesturing to hurry. He motioned them to shut
the refrigerated storage units, quickly mopping
blood from the tiles.

FREDDIE BUNA
Come with me, I know where the
incubators are.

He led off again, more corridors. At one stage they
had to pass across a brightly lit thoroughfare
where beds were being moved back and forth on
silent rubber wheels. They crossed the open
area, hearts thumping. Freddie led onward. They
came to a small reception area where Freddie
engaged an indifferent aboriginal nurse behind
glass. They knew each other, and while Freddie
joked with her, Birani and Waru slipped past
and though a door.

The incubator room was dimly lit and empty,
except for one brightly lit cubicle. They went
to it, then stopped in awe. Two melon sized
pale blue eggs were lying on white blankets,
kept warm like new-born babies. The heating
bulbs shining down on them, Objects of ethereal
beauty. Several gauges showed flashing data in
illuminated figures. Birani touched the glass,
it was warm.

Freddie stood by the door, anxious, making
hurry up gestures. Waru looked around, found
an insulated carrying container for babies. He
placed more blankets in it while Birani opened
the glass doors of the incubator. He carefully
lifted both warm eggs into Waru's carrier,
covered them, zipped it, and then they stood
behind Freddie as he checked out the corridor
ahead.

Instead of passing the occupied glass Reception
Area, Freddie led them down another corridor,
then a left turn and they were suddenly outside,
out of the cold building and into the warm

Australian night. They checked for CCTV, then keeping close to walls, circumnavigated the carpark to their vehicle. Birani held Freddie's bony shoulder.

                    BIRANI PEMBA
        Freddie, you have made this possible.
        You need to keep a low profile for a
        day or two...

Freddie shook his head emphatically.

                    FREDDIE BUNA
        No mate, I'm done here.
             (Wide grin)
        I'm coming with you fellers. You have
        the bloody eggs.

        I'm gonna see that Bunyip before I
        die mate. Oh yes.

Birani searched the old man's watery eyes. There were uncompromising. He glanced at Waru, who nodded. Birani grinned at Freddie and the three men climbed into the pickup truck and drove quietly off the carpark and up the semi-circular ramp to the highway.

Halfway up the ramp they put the vehicle lights on. On the highway, they turned north towards the Simpson.

                                    FADE OUT

EXT. DUNWARRA ROAD HOUSE. 70 NORTH EAST OF CANBERRA. DAY

A chain-link fence, holding back scrub, appeared on Jeff's left side, looping and dipping, then falling away and dissolving into vast car parking with rows of massive high-sided vehicles. Jeff Uteri pulled in, coasting to a stop next the empty Falcon.

INTERIOR: SNACK BAR

The two dark suited men sat, incongruously, next to each other with coffees. Another coffee placed at the empty seat opposite.

Jeff sat down, feeling inadequate. Luis Dewayne, oozing self-confidence and masculine power had more muscles than he could count. Impossibly wide, with jet black hair, full lips, sunglasses probably worth more than Jeff could earn in a month. Enzo Matteo was a slightly smaller clone, reeking in cologne, tattooed neck, both men wearing expensive suits and western boots.

>   JEFF UTERI
>   Hi, thanks for...

Luis raised a hand, silencing him.

>   LUIS DEWAYNE
>   (Authoritative)
>   Wait.

They all sat in silence while an ACT (Australian Capital District) Police Cruiser rolled across the car park. It slowed next to their cars, then rolled on to the Lorry Section. Enzo got up, went to the window, and watched for several beats, came back, sat down again, shrugging.

                    LUIS DEWAYNE (CONT'D)
          OK Mr Uteri, we already know who and
          what, all we need from you is payment
          method and disposals.

                    JEFF UTERI
          You know who?

                    LUIS DEWAYNE
          We were there, at Cordillo Downs
          earlier, with all the press.

Jeff was still non-plussed, they both stared at him as he floundered.

                    JEFF UTERI
          Disposals? Sorry, what do you mean
          disposals, what the hell does that
          mean?

                    LUIS DEWAYNE
                    (Wearily)
          He said you were up to speed, obviously
          not. Fuck it.

The two men exchanged glances, drained their cups and made to stand up.

                    JEFF UTERI
          Hang on, can we go back to basics a
          bit here. Who has briefed you so far?
          I thought I was doing that.

They sat down again, both staring at Jeff.

                    LUIS DEWAYNE
          (Patiently)
     The Minister.

     He said you would deal with the
     practical's. So Mr. Uteri, let's do
     payments first shall we?

                     JEFF UTERI
     OK, I can arrange cash. But I...

                     LUIS DEWAYNE
     Its $40k. $20k each. 50% up front by
     tomorrow.
          (A beat)
     Disposals?

Jeff looked at them blankly.

                LUIS DEWAYNE (CONT'D)
          (As if speaking to a child)
     The bodies. Its extra if you don't
     want them found. Otherwise, we can
     just snipe from a distance, cheaper
     option.

                     JEFF UTERI
          (Aghast)
     Bodies, like plural? You are going to
     kill him, and his daughter?

Luis Dewayne closed his eyes in despair, then
spoke to Enzo.

                     LUIS DEWAYNE
          (To Enzo)
     Jeez, don't you just hate dealing
     with fucking amateurs.

(To Jeff)
OK, I'll assume you want bodies
disposed of, that will be an extra
$10k on the total.

He wrote on a napkin, pushed it across the table
to Jeff.

LUIS DEWAYNE (CONT'D)
That'll be $25k direct transfer to
that account before banks close
tomorrow.

Enzo rose and went to the counter. Luis regarded
Jeff as if he were an insect, then stood abruptly
and stalked away from the table. Enzo followed
him out through the doors into the stark
whiteness of the concrete car park. Jeff, shocked
and angry, watched them go.

The Falcon V8 pulled majestically off the car
park, the rear end settling as it accelerated
west towards Canberra.

Jeff pulled his cell phone.

CELLPHONE CONVERSATION

JEFF UTERI
Mish, can you talk?

MISH ROGAN
(Cool)
Go on, I'm alone.

JEFF UTERI
Arthur has already told them to kill
Billy Bob and his daughter. It's a
'fait accompli'. No negotiation, no

more offers, nothing. I have to pay them half their fee tomorrow.

Jeff heard her sharp intake of breath, then silence for several beats.

                    MISH ROGAN
          (Shaky)
     Fuck!

She hung. Jeff, outraged, stared at his screen as it cleared.

                              FADE OUT

EXT. CORDILLERA DOWNS STATION. VERANDA. NIGHT.

Billy Bob hung his cell phone, glancing at PJ.

                    BILLY BOB MASON
     Two of them, on their way in. Anytime
     soon.

                    PUMP JOCKEY
     I'm staying here Dad, don't try to...

Billy Bob held up a finger, silencing her.

He rolled a cigarette, taking his time. The moment extended impossibly. PJ watched, held her breath until the match exploded in slow motion, sparks and pungent blue smoke flaring outward, then the blazing glow of the cigarette like a new planet being born. Finally, the outward rush of smoke laden air extinguishing the burning match.

Time caught up with a snap. He turned his blue eyes to her, the single most precious creature in his universe.

        BILLY BOB MASON
        (Conceding)
    OK baby, I won't.
        (A beat, slow grin)
    Your Mother once said to me that
    I should treat you at least as an
    equal, or even better maybe.

They sat in silence looking out over the desert where it merged into the limitless firmament. After several beats, PJ reached and took Billy Bob's hand.

                            FADE OUT

EXT. ADELAIDE INTERNATIONAL AIRPORT. DAY

Sergei Narratova watched his boss walk towards the Range Rover in stark sunlight and 38c temperature.

Beside him walked Ekaterina, impossibly cool, remote, and unapproachable behind oversized shades. Since Sergei had last seen Andrei, he realized that he had deteriorated a lot, he was groomed and ray-banned, but he looked weak and frail despite the obvious effort he was making. Sergei could only guess at the immense personal toll it was taking for him to make that walk.

Sergei got out of the Rover, opened the rear door. Andrei faltered at the last step, but Sergei caught him deftly, muscles bunching as he took the sudden weight. In the car, Andrei leaned back with his eyes closed, taking deep breaths, fighting down his heart rate. He didn't speak.

Ekaterina, glasses off, gazed gratefully into Sergei's eyes, silently thanking him, then glasses back in place, looked away. Dmitri and Igor stood respectfully, closed the doors, then carried suitcases to another hired black Range Rover.

The two identical Ranger Rovers drove in convoy 25 minutes to the Glenelg hotel, where Sarah Cantrell waited, staying within speed limits.

FADE OUT

EXT. BLINMAN. FLINDERS RANGES. 400 MILES NORTH OF ADELAIDE. DAY.

Blinman is a township in mountain high country scrub desert. It has a hotel, a post office and a general store. The main street is from a western movie, wide dusty, baking in relentless heat, deserted.

Several 4*4 are parked haphazardly under shade and the air-conditioned Blinman Hotel bar has three drinkers, two of which are in a blind stupor. The 3rd drinker is desperately unwell, but on the face of it, in a similar condition to the other two. The Landlord ignores all three of them, totally conditioned to an incapacitated clientele over a lifetime.

John Cantrell sips from a cold beer, hugging his gut, turned away from the room. The hotel toilet was clean and disinfected, but his recent visit there was mostly unsuccessful. He was now beyond ill, convulsing and tormented in a nether world of pain and misery, a demoniacal zombie-like walking corpse. Some strange and dynamic inner power source of energy kept him moving, his pulse beating so quickly that he felt the palpitations in every artery and vein and could even see it moving in the corners of his watery eyes as he looked around. He would sit, his muscles and joints seemingly rendered incapable of further movement, then somehow, an inexplicable and hideous strength would pour into his legs, driving him upward and onward.

All logical thought processes were now gone, but in its place, John was driven by some unworldly animate force which gave him clear direction and navigation towards an unknown goal.

Traveling relentlessly north, his route from Adelaide had been faultless, each road change taken without hesitation or any conscious effort from him.

John drove himself upright from his chair, stood still for a beat to get some balance, then staggered to his car, the sprung door banging closed behind him. The Landlord watched him go, shaking his head, fully accepting normal life in Blinman.

Nothing new to see here.

FADE OUT

EXT. A20 EASTBOUND. RENMARK. SOUTH AUSTRALIA. DAY

Michelle Rogan followed the Murray River east towards Adelaide appreciating the lush green country route rather than the stark B75 outback route Jeff had taken on their last trip. She took the B74 Goyder Highway towards Burra, the landscape becoming brown and dry as she left the river, striking slightly northeast.

She was frantic with worry for Billy Bob and his daughter. She had warned him that unknown thugs would be coming for him but had not been able to give any idea of details.

He had received the information coolly with short laconic questions and replies, seemingly accepting that this was an unavoidable consequence of owning property in this harsh and abrasive landscape. 'Sometimes you have to fight for it' embodied his attitude.

The end of her phone conversation with him stayed in her mind. She had told him that she was driving to Cordillo Downs immediately to be with him. He had been worried about her doing the 30-hour drive. She said that she heard him, but was coming anyway. A roundabout flight would take longer and still involve a long drive.

He had been silent for two minutes. She thought he had gone, then she heard a movement through the handset. He had then said something that chilled her and excited her in equal measure.

                    BILLY BOB MASON
I told you that when all this is
done with, I'll come for you Michelle
Rogan. I meant it.
        (A beat)
Nothing will change that, nothing.

She replayed those words over and over as
she drove. He had shown no trace of fear or
uncertainty and she wondered what experiences
he must have lived through to give him that sort
of self-assurance.

LATER

Michelle nosed her vehicle into the carpark of
the Royal Exchange Motel at Burra. She stood
by the car and stretched, then opened the rear
door for her travel bag.

Across the carpark a black Volvo XC90 pulled
into a parking place. Luis Dewayne glanced at
her from a distance, frowning.

                                        FADE OUT

INT. GLENELG HOTEL. ROOM 231. ADELAIDE. DAY.

Room 231, Andrei and Ekaterina's room, looked
out across a flat blue sea, its surface barely
marred by wind. In the near distance a lone
figure sat motionless astride a surfboard, like
a rider on a horse, calmly balanced, scanning
the horizon, searching the vast blue undulations
for tell-tale signs of an approaching swell.

Andrei Lebov watched the surfer. He sat in a
shaft of sunlight chewing, a glass of water

by his side, gazing across the balcony. He felt strange powerful movements inside his body. The radically altering nature of his physiology gradually leaching through his sub-consciousness, like waking into a new day after a big night, with an ashtray brain and an empty wallet.

He was experiencing a sensory onslaught, starting anew.

On the tray next to his water, was a plate with an OXO cube sized piece of raw meat. He had eaten one 30 minutes earlier. He reached for the second, gagging slightly, then swallowing it down resolutely with a slug of water.

He kept focusing on the motionless surfer as his muscles bunched and relaxed, blood surged in his veins and dizzying sensations heaved and strained inside his body. He clutched his chest, then pushed his hand away in an outward gesture, a claw warding off evil.

Ekaterina reached for his hand, wincing as he gripped her, then he let go, holding onto the chair with both hands, doubling over. She looked helplessly at Sergei as Andrei bucked and twisted in his seat.

Then suddenly he was still, his chin down to his chest. Sergei touched his carotid, waited, then nodded to her.

She wrapped a blanket around him and they all sat looking across the flat blue sea, waiting for something, neither knew what it was going to be.

CONTINUOUS

ROOM 232

In the next room, Sarah Cantrell sat with her
hands clutched together in her lap trying to
control her emotions.

There had been no sounds from next door since
Ekaterina had taken the two OXO shaped pieces
of thawed Bunyip meat on a plate to Andrei.
Opposite her sat Dmitri and Igor in easy chairs,
legs splayed. Igor slept; Dmitri looked at his
phone screen.

Sarah wondered at the events of the past weeks.
Her life radically and irrevocably changed,
never to be the same again. £1M pounds sterling
had been transferred into an account for her
in St Maarten in the Caribbean. The deposit
had been confirmed an hour ago and she had the
codes.

John was missing, no return calls from him.

She waited, vague sounds from the next room,
she looked expectantly at the door.

                                        FADE OUT

**INT. ROYAL EXCHANGE MOTEL. BURRA. SOUTH
AUSTRALIA. EVENING.**

Michelle gazed at herself in the bathroom mirror.
The habit of applying makeup as ingrained as
breathing. Somewhere she could hear water
running, then bumps and a door closing.

She grudged the stopover at Burra, but knew she had to stop and sleep. Another long drive tomorrow and she would be there.

The room had a door onto the 1st floor veranda that ran all the way around the building. She went outside, the warm air hitting pleasantly. She stood at the rail looking down a softly lit main street with vehicles pulled in diagonally along each kerb. A row of bedraggled trees ran down the centre of the road. A 'SIZZLING CHOOK' takeaway was doing business with a few people sitting at outdoor benches, the smell of grilled chicken wafting on the wind with sounds of conversation and laughter.

Instinctively she looked towards the sparsely populated carpark, checking her vehicle. A tall man was walking across the bitumen, he passed by her car, pausing briefly to glance inside. She ducked slightly back from the rail, watching him, a chill running through her. He walked on and she relaxed. He passed underneath her into the main entrance without looking upwards. She went inside, sat on the bed, dialled.

TELEPHONE CONVERSATION

MISH ROGAN
Billy Bob, its Mish

BILLY BOB MASON
Where are you?

MISH ROGAN
Exchange Motel, Burra.

He thought about that.

289

                    BILLY BOB MASON
So, you'll be here around suppertime
tomorrow then, yeah?
      (A beat)
Any other news?

                    MISH ROGAN
Nothing. I've had several missed
calls from Jeff, I didn't reply. Arthur
McCloud has also rung me twice.

                    BILLY BOB MASON
The politician?

                    MISH ROGAN
Yes. He's Jeff's boss. He heads up
ALTERN.

                    BILLY BOB MASON
Are you going down into the bar?

She smiled indulgently, hugging herself.

                    MISH ROGAN
Why Billy Bob? Is that a hint of
jealousy maybe?

                    BILLY BOB MASON
From ACT Canberra there are only two
routes here babe. Think about that.

She suddenly remembered the tall man taking an
interest in her car.

                    MISH ROGAN
      Fuck...

He reacted quickly.

                    BILLY BOB MASON
What? Have you seen something?

                      MISH ROGAN
Maybe nothing Billy Bob. A guy walked
across the carpark. He seemed to look
hard at my car... maybe I imagined
it. Don't know.

                    BILLY BOB MASON
Did he see you?

                      MISH ROGAN
No, I was up on the veranda 1st floor. I
ducked back. He didn't look upwards.

                    BILLY BOB MASON
Stay inside the window, but take a
look across the carpark Mish, see if
anything sticks out. Any big flashy
stuff?

Mish stood by the edge of the window. The
carpark was lit with pools of orange light.

                      MISH ROGAN
Not seeing anything Billy Bob. Only
unusual one is a big black Volvo
estate. Other stuff is usual small-
town stuff.

                    BILLY BOB MASON
Can you see the reg number? Has it
got VHD?

Sarah rummaged in her pack looking for an old
pair 8*40 binoculars. She found them, went to
the window, focused.

MISH ROGAN
Billy Bob, how the fuck could you
know that?

BILLY BOB MASON
Canberra hire vehicle all have that
number.
(A beat)
It might be nothing. Listen, pack
your stuff quietly. Take off, take the
B64 until you hit the Prince's Highway
A1 at Port Pirie. Then head north to
Winninowie Fuel Stop. They know me
there. Ask for Straw Hat Man.
(A beat)
Do it now baby. Hang up. Ring when
you have a signal.

Billy Bob hung. She sat on the bed, deflated,
frightened, highly alert. She packed her bag,
quietly went out to the carpark through a rear
door. The area was deserted, lit with pools of
light. She reversed with lights out and cruised
onto the main road, taking the B64 to Port
Pirie.

FADE OUT

INT. EXCHANGE MOTEL BAR. BURRA. SOUTH
AUSTRALIA. NIGHT.

Luis Dewayne and Enzo Matteo hunched over beer
midis, piles of cash change in front of them.
From time to time the barman filled their glasses
with a Beer Pistol as he passed, then he passed
back the other way taking money from their cash
piles. No-one spoke to him, neither did he ask

them what they wanted. Several other men along
the bar took part in the well-worn ritual.

Both men were quiet. Luis's phone rang.

TELEPHONE CONVERSATION

                    LUIS DEWAYNE
    Luis.

                    JEFF UTERI
    It's Jeff Uteri. Did your money go
    through OK?

                    LUIS DEWAYNE
    Well, we are both here. On our way
    to Cordillo Downs. We will be there
    tomorrow sometime.
        (A beat)
    Any problems?

                    JEFF UTERI
    Maybe.
        (A beat)
    Billy Bob Mason will be expecting you.

                    LUIS DEWAYNE
    What? How? Who?

Jeff was silent for several beats, gathering his
equilibrium.

                    JEFF UTERI
    Michelle Rogan. She works with me but
    is not happy with things.
        (A beat)
    She is fucking Billy Bob. She is not
    answering her phone. We think maybe
    she is heading there to be with him.

Luis exchanged glances with Enzo, nodding. Then a thought occurred to him.

>   LUIS DEWAYNE
>   What does she drive?

>   JEFF UTERI
>   A white Toyota Camry. ACT plates.

>   LUIS DEWAYNE
>   (To Jeff)
>   Hang on...
>   (To Enzo)
>   Go see if that Toyota with the hot
>   lady is on the carpark.

Enzo took off, returning, shaking his head.

>   LUIS DEWAYNE (CONT'D)
>   She was here, I think. Pulled onto the
>   carpark. I thought she was familiar.
>   (A beat)
>   Fuck it. She was here 30 minutes
>   back.

Luis broke the connection. Finished his beer and scooped his change into his pocket.

>   LUIS DEWAYNE (CONT'D)
>   Comon Enzo, we are on the road mate.
>   We'll catch her. Not much traffic on
>   these country roads.

>   FADE OUT

INT. CORDILLO DOWNS STATION. KITCHEN. MORNING

Billy Bob stood up from the debris of breakfast and stretched. There was fine dust in the air that shafted the sunlight into solid beams, flaring bright wherever they hit a surface. PJ pushed back her chair and pulled on high heeled boots, dropping her jeans down over them.

PUMP JOCKEY
How will they come Billy Bob?

Billy Bob went to the window, staring west across the blinding scrub hardpan where the track arrowed away to a point.

BILLY BOB MASON
They might already be here baby, but I doubt it. I slept on the floor last night; I would have felt it I reckon.
(A beat)
They can't drive in. We'd see them walking in, so I reckon if I was them, I'd shoot from as far away as I could guarantee a hit.

PUMP JOCKEY
They've got to get 200 meters or thereabouts then. Unless they are military grade snipers with all the kit.

Billy Bob buckled on a brass laden gun-belt, opened the loading gate of the Colt 45 and softly spun the cylinder, then holstered it. He shouldered a pack of essentials and pulled down his hat brim, turning to her, his eyes in shadow.

                    BILLY BOB MASON
Don't give them a target Louise. Keep
the Sat phone charged. I'm going up
on the high ground behind the ranch,
I'll see them from there. Call me on
Sat Phone to say hello.

They held each other's gaze for two beats,
then he picked up his Marlin lever action and
stepped through the shafts of sunlight onto the
veranda.

She heard his boots tramp across the boards,
then the house fell silent. She rocked back
until her head touched the wall, the Remington
across her knees.

                                        FADE OUT

**EXT. WINNINOWIE GAS STATION. PRINCE'S HIGHWAY.
MORNING**

Michelle Rogan sat opposite Straw Hat Man, both
with a coffee. Around them was a mind-boggling
array of engine parts, tools, weird machinery,
tires, and partially dismantled vehicles, some
on hydraulic stands, others rocked over onto
their side, exposing underbellies.

Everywhere was the reek of oil and diesel. On
a nearby wall was a rack of several firearms.
As Straw Hat Man rocked down flat, she saw the
glint of a handgun in his belt.

                    MISH ROGAN
Thank you for last night Bruce, I'm
grateful. It must have been a surprise,
this strange woman turning up.

Straw Hat Man watched the pumps and the down ramp behind Mish through the gaping opening. The outside concrete shimmered in white heat. He shook his head and squinted at her.

> STRAW HAT MAN
> Nothing surprises me these days Ma-am, glad to help out. Anything for a friend of Billy Bob.
> (A beat)
> Cordillo Downs is close to 500 miles from here, some of that ungraded road. Its a long hard drive, even if it goes well.
> (A beat, grimace)
> Most likely only be you and them boys on that road. Chances are you will pick up their dust, or them yours.
> (A beat, hard look)
> You are understanding what I'm a-saying here, ain't you?

Michelle didn't reply and he looked sharply at her, saw the glitter in her eyes.

> STRAW HAT MAN (CONT'D)
> You and Billy Bob something?

She nodded, shifting in her seat.

> STRAW HAT MAN (CONT'D)
> Them boys after him for something big?

She nodded again, eyes brimming, not trusting herself to speak. Then she saw him stiffen slightly, his posture changing subtly. He was looking past her.

                    STRAW HAT MAN (CONT'D)
            They are here.

She turned in her chair, watched the black
Volvo XC90 roll down the ramp, pulling up at
the pumps. Straw Hat Man stood and stretched,
adjusting the handgun in his waistband, glancing
down at her.

                    STRAW HAT MAN (CONT'D)
            Stay out of sight Michelle. They won't
            come in here.

He strolled out into the sun, stepping over to
the pumps as Luis Dewayne exited the car and
stretched, stomping his boots.

                    STRAW HAT MAN (CONT'D)
            Fill her up Mister?

Luis glanced imperiously at him, nodded. Looked
around the vast concrete area dotted with
vehicles of all shapes and sizes.

                    LUIS DEWAYNE
            Looking for a friend of mine, she's
            driving a late model Toyota Camry. I
            guess she will be on the road north
            somewhere around here
                    (Turning to look at Straw
                    Hat Man)
            Seen anyone like that?

Straw Hat Man finished up, clanked the pump
nozzle back into it's holder on the side of the
pump.

                    STRAW HAT MAN
            Nope.

                    (Thrusting his chin)
          Pay over at the cabin.

Luis thoughtfully watched the old man head
back into the huge black opening of the garage
workshop. Then got back into the driving seat

                    LUIS DEWAYNE
          Friendly fuckers around here Enzo.

He spun the Volvo around, cruised slow around
the various parked vehicles, saw nothing of
interest, then accelerated away up the semi-
circular ramp, heading north.

Straw Hat Man resumed his chair opposite
Michelle, grinning. Despite her churning fear,
she couldn't resist a vague smile back at him.

                    STRAW HAT MAN
          Finish your coffee Ma-am, come look
          around the back.

He headed off around the side of the building,
threading through a vast array of dusty machinery
and partially dismantled vehicles and parts.
Out on the concrete pad facing away down a
runway, was a Piper Cherokee PA28 four-seater
light aircraft. He looked proudly at the plane,
then grinned with blackened teeth at Mish.

                    STRAW HAT MAN (CONT'D)
          She will do Cordillo Downs in under
          4 hours from here.

Michelle felt gratitude flood through her, all
her city values being decimated with each new
revelation of Australian outback life.

                    MISH ROGAN
          Why are you doing this Bruce? You
          don't know me.

Straw Hat Man tipped his hat back, mopping his
brow with a wrist, then tugged it back down.

                    STRAW HAT MAN
          Fuck, its hot out here. Let's go back
          inside.

They resumed their seats inside the workshop.
Straw Hat Man poured more coffees. He squinted
at her fondly.

                    STRAW HAT MAN (CONT'D)
          You are right Ma-am, I don't know you.
          But I knows Billy Bob, and his baby
          girl PJ. I knows them well enough.

He watched Mish over the rim of his coffee. She
looked at him with a question in her eyes.

                    STRAW HAT MAN (CONT'D)
          Billy Bob married my daughter. PJ is
          my grand daughter. Normally she works
          the pumps here. Right now she's there
          with Billy Bob at Cordillo Downs.

Michelle was shocked. Colour draining from her
face.

                    MISH ROGAN
          Billy Bob is married?

                    STRAW HAT MAN
          Was.
               (A beat)

Long-time back. My baby girl, his
wife, was snake-bit in the Simpson
15 years back. Billy Bob carried her
home 20 miles on his back, dead.
            (A beat)
She's buried at Cordillo. He's been
on his own ever since. He'll never
leave there.

Michelle was devastated, tears springing into
her eyes yet again. Straw Hat Man got up, came
back with a box of tissues.

                STRAW HAT MAN (CONT'D)
Ma-am, you could cry for Australia.
            (A beat, shrewd look)
It's like you just discovered it.

With a huge effort Michelle brought her raging
emotions back into control. Straw Hat Man waited
patiently, his eyes through the door, watching
the ramp.

                MISH ROGAN
I love him, Bruce. I need to get
to him.

                STRAW HAT MAN
I know it girl. We'll get to that. No
rush. Them boys ain't going far.

                MISH ROGAN
Bruce, if they drive all night, they
could make it by tomorrow morning.

Straw Hat Man rocked backed, a wide grin slowly
spreading. It was not a pretty sight.

                    STRAW HAT MAN
     They'll maybe make another hundred
     mile, maybe less. Engine will blow.

Straw Hat Man reached into his jeans pocket,
pulled out his fist and slowly let a white
granular substance trickle onto the table top.
Mish leaned to look at it. She touched it.

                    MISH ROGAN
          Is it sugar?

Straw Hat Man grinned happily, nodding.

                                        FADE OUT

INT. GLENELG HOTEL. ROOM 231. ADELAIDE. DAY.

Andrei sat very still, upright on the bed.
Ekaterina, Sarah and Sergei all watched him in
trepidation. He didn't look at them, keeping
his eyes downward as he experienced a range of
sensations.

Minutes ago, he had had violent racking spasm of
coughing accompanied by a horrible liquid sound
in his chest. He tried now to get some control,
but panic was just a heartbeat away. Sweat
poured off his forehead, stinging his eyes. His
fingers, clutching the bedclothes, were swollen
obscene sausages, blue and mottled.

Sarah was in her own private hell. She was richer
than she could ever had believed possible, but
she a powerful feeling that these people would
kill her and somehow recover the money if
Andrei died.

Ekaterina held up a vial of nitro-glycerine to Andrei, he shook his head, then tensed, holding his chest. A boring squeezing pain began to mushroom outward from beneath Andrei's breastbone and up into his neck. He leaned back, nodding, accepting his oncoming death with a strange paradoxical calm, his breathing slowing until he was taking a breath every few seconds.

                    ANDREI LEBOV
          OK, yes. Bring it on.

Sergei looked at Ekaterina, she was white with shock as she watched her husband die. He reached for her hand across the bed, but she snatched her hand away, biting her bottom lip. Sarah began to stand, but a look from Sergei warned her to remain seated.

Andrei gradually stilled, his breathing stopped, and he began a strange sinking motion where he seemed to reduce in size. His left foot twitched several times, then he became totally still.

The silence was complete for several minutes, then an involuntary sob from Ekaterina. She immediately suppressed it, looking tenderly at Andrei. She reached with a tissue and gently wiped his immobile porcelain face, the others looking away, not wanting to intrude on the privacy of that intimate moment.

Finally, after 15 minutes, Ekaterina stood, regal and distant in her grief. She moved away from the bed, stood for a moment looking down at Andrei, then went into the other room. Sergei and Sarah followed, closing the door. No-one looked at each other, each in their private world. Sarah felt like she should be apologizing but realized how inappropriate that would be.

There was a sound from the other room, a bump, then another, louder. They all looked at each other, nonplussed. Sergei went to the door, opening it as if a terrifying monster would come bursting out. He stood in the doorway staring, then went in. Sarah and Ekaterina stared after him, then both followed him through the door.

Andrei had moved. One hand was thrown out over the edge of the bed, hanging like a claw, fingers moving spasmodically. His head was turned away from them as if he was examining something on the other side of the room. He spoke without turning to look at them.

> ANDREI LEBOV (CONT'D)
> It's not true you know.

All three of the other occupants in the room were in total shock. Andrei slowly turned his head, his blue eyes impossibly bright.

> ANDREI LEBOV (CONT'D)
> It's all shite, about that tunnel and heading into the white light. Didn't happen. It all just fucking hurt.

Ekaterina fell to her knees by the bedside, clutching Andrei's hand, flooded with tears. Sergei staggered against the door frame in disbelief. Sarah moved through her initial shock quicker than the others because part of her had not fully accepted that the Bunyip would fail. She felt a surge of relief that her future wealth was assured.

Andrei painfully sat up, feeling his chest in wonder. He motioned to Sergei, and Sergei went to help him stand by the bed, his other hand still held tightly in Ekaterina's clutch. He took several deep breaths, the liquid sounds in his chest had gone.

A long slow smile began to form. Sergei smiled with him. Over at the door, Sarah was laughing. Still on her knees, Ekaterina sat back on her haunches, her eye make-up wrecked, shaking her head in disbelief, still in shock.

                    ANDREI LEBOV (CONT'D)
          Who was that feller with the quote,
          something like "The rumours of my
          death are a load of bollocks". It was
          Mack somebody wasn't it?

                    EKATERINA LEBOV
               (Faint smile)
          Close Andrei. He was called Mark
          Twain.

                                        FADE OUT

EXT. B83. OUTBACK HIGHWAY. LEIGH CREEK. NORTHBOUND. DAY.

Birani Pemba swung the pickup left off the Outback Highway and into the slip-road containing several dilapidated shops and a Pub. He pulled up in the shade of a eucalyptus and stretched. Freddie gazed around him.

                    FREDDIE BUNA
          What's here?

                    BIRANI PEMBA
    Oh, there's the Leigh Creek tourist
    centre over there if you want to
    sample the local delights Fred.

Freddie spat out of the car window, taking the
comment seriously.

                    FREDDIE BUNA
    I'll leave it.
          (Straining to look)
    Its not even open anyway.

Birani and Waru exchanged glances with wry
grins.

                    BIRANI PEMBA
    I'll go get some drinks.

Birani walked off, returning with a armful of
cold cans and nibbles. Breasting up to a window.

                BIRANI PEMBA (CONT'D)
    Can you get these please, they are
    bloody cold.

No-one reached to help, Birani struggled, then
lost a can onto the dust road surface. It burst,
spraying COKE in all directions that fizzed and
spluttered.

                BIRANI PEMBA (CONT'D)
    Fuck's sake guys, help me out here.

Birani caught sight of Waru's face and stopped
in his tracks.

                BIRANI PEMBA (CONT'D)
    What's happening Waru, what is it?

Birani leaned into the driver's door, dropping all the purchases onto the seat, then looking into the back seat where Waru sat with the Egg Carrier open.

                    WARU ILUKA
        One of the eggs is dead Birani. Its
        cold. Its the smaller one.

Birani slumped in shock and despair.

                    BIRANI PEMBA
        Fuck. You sure?

Waru nodded, his face distraught, tears on his weathered cheeks.

                    WARU ILUKA
        Ice cold mate. The other one is OK.

Freddie watched both men, his eyes flitting back and forth, picking up the mood.

                    FREDDIE BUNA
        It's still OK with one live egg boys?
        Isn't it? We can still do this? Yeah?

Birani moved the purchases and dropped into the driver's seat.

                    BIRANI PEMBA
        We can still do it Fred. Let's be
        positive here. Two more days and we
        will be there.

They all took an ice cold can and ate potato chips, staring aimlessly out of the dusty windscreen.

                                    FADE OUT

TV NEWS REPORT. CHANNEL 9.DAY.

POLICE ARE INVESTIGATING A BIZARRE THEFT FROM PORT AUGUSTA HOSPITAL. IT SEEMS THIS THEFT IS RELATED TO THE RECENT BUNYIP STORY THAT GAINED WORLD-WIDE INTEREST LAST MONTH.

SOMETIME IN THE SMALL HOURS OF THURSDAY JUNE 17, STAFF AT PORT AUGUSTA HOSPITAL CALLED POLICE REPORTING A BREAK IN TO THE POSTMORTEM UNIT. FOR OBVIOUS REASONS, SECURITY IS NOT HIGH AROUND THIS UNIT, SO NO CCTV FOOTAGE IS AVAILABLE. IT APPEARS THAT A BODY, WHICH HAD ALREADY UNDERTAKEN A POSTMORTEM AND WAS STITCHED UP, HAD BEEN OPENED UP AGAIN, AND SOME BODY PARTS HAD BEEN TAKEN.

HOSPITAL STAFF ARE KEEN TO DISPEL IMMEDIATE CONSPIRACY THEORIES THAT THE BODY CONTAINED TWO BUNYIP EGGS. SOME PEOPLE APPARENTLY BELIEVE THAT THE EGGS COULD SOMEHOW BE FERTILIZED TO EVENTUALLY PRODUCE AN INFANT BUNYIP.

IT SEEMS THAT THE BUNYIP STORY REFUSES TO DIE. MORE ON THIS INVESTIGATION LATER.

INT. GLENELG HOTEL. ROOM 231. ADELAIDE. DAY.

Andrei switched off the TV, leaning back thoughtfully, still watching the darkened screen. Sergei, Dmitri and Igor sat around the table with coffees, exchanging glances, waiting.

                    ANDREI LEBOV
          Interesting.
             (A beat)
          Eggs. So, what do we know about Bunyip
          eggs?

Sergei, grinned uncertainly at the others, then spoke to Andrei.

> SERGEI
> The aboriginals that we spoke to totally believe that the Bunyip exists, and that it apparently lays blue coloured eggs. They also believe that these eggs can be carried by other species, including humans, until they are ready to fertilized by a female Bunyip.

Andrei looked at each man closely. They met his eyes, waiting for him to burst into laughter, so they could release their tension and join in.

> ANDREI LEBOV
> A couple of weeks ago, I wouldn't have believed all sorts of shite like this. The fact that I am sitting here is beyond parody, but here we all are.
> (A beat)
> So, now I believe that some fucker has probably stolen some Bunyip eggs.

He gazed around at them, his face serious.

> ANDREI LEBOV (CONT'D)
> I do, I really do.

Andrei stopped, his hand going involuntarily to his stomach.

> ANDREI LEBOV (CONT'D)
> Shit, I might even have one in me.

Andrei got up and paced, all the others eyes followed him. In another room they could hear the sounds of running water as Ekaterina showered. He sat down again, lighting up a cigar in clouds of blue smoke.

> ANDREI LEBOV (CONT'D)
> Can you imagine the value of a Bunyip egg? If it exists of course. I mean, can you?
> (A beat)
> I know you can't, but just try. The most powerful people in the World would give anything to own one. The most powerful sick people in the World would give up their entire fortune to simply touch one.
> (A beat)
> Men, I an not prepared to gamble that Bunyip eggs do not exist, and that they are figments of wild people's, and native Australian's, fevered imagination.
>
> I cannot take that risk, and I do NOT accept the concept of conspiracy theory. God, I hate that term.
> (A beat)
> Somebody is out there with a fucking Bunyip egg, or eggs. You guys must find them, track them down.

Dmitri looked like he was going to speak. Sergei gave him a look and he leaned back. Andrei spotted the exchange.

> ANDREI LEBOV (CONT'D)
> OK guys, let's leave it for today, I need to get some rest.

Andrei leaned back, gesturing to dismiss the other three. They got up and trooped out.

>   ANDREI LEBOV (CONT'D)
>   Dmitri, can you stay for a moment
>   please.

Dmitri paused, looked briefly at Sergei, who shrugged, then closed the door behind him. Dmitri returned to his seat, sitting bolt upright, hands flat to his thighs.

>   ANDREI LEBOV (CONT'D)
>   (Softly)
>   So, tell me what you were about to
>   say Dmitri.

Dmitri gathered his thoughts, glancing up several times. Andrei waited.

>   DMITRI OLVO
>   Boss, when we captured Sarah Cantrell,
>   her husband had left her and driven
>   off. Apparently, he was very ill with
>   severe stomach pains. He hasn't been
>   heard of since.

Andrei watched Dmitri's face, but he was not really seeing it. Eventually he snapped back from his deep train of thought.

>   ANDREI LEBOV
>   So... what do think was making him
>   ill Dmitri?
>   (A beat, slowly)
>   You think he may be carrying an egg?

                    DMITRI OLVO
Well I don't know Boss, we got the
other Bunyip meat from the Cantrells',
its possible. Maybe?

Andrei paced, thinking it through, then decisive.

                    ANDREI LEBOV
Bring Mrs Cantrell in here, lets have
a little talk with that lady.

Dmitri got up, went into the outer room. All
eyes turned to him. Dmitri, revelling in his
Boss's attention, grinned importantly at them.
He spoke to Sarah.

                    DMITRI OLVO
Sarah, could you come into the other
room with me please.

Sarah looked at the others. Sergei shrugged
again. She got up and followed Dmitri.

                    ANDREI LEBOV
Mrs Cantrell, please sit down.
        (A beat)
I am trying to get to the bottom
of something here. You and your
husband where abducted by a group
of Aboriginals and taken to a remote
place, were you not.

                    SARAH
        (Tentatively)
Well, yes. I don't know where it was.
It was a derelict farm in the desert.
We were there a few days.

ANDREI LEBOV
What happened to you there Mrs
Cantrell?

Sarah immediately became emotional, and Andrei
solicitously leaned forward, pouring a crystal
glass with water.

SARAH
They did something to John, my husband.
I wasn't present. They said no woman
should see it. When I came back, he
and Jandi, an Aboriginal man, were
both traumatized and very ill.

I was only separated from them an
hour or so.

ANDREI LEBOV
Go on please Sarah, is it OK if I
call you Sarah?

SARAH
It's fine.
        (A beat)
They went off and left us then. Told us
us to sit quiet and they would come
back for us. Left us with water etc.
        (A beat)
A young girl, a white Australian,
saved us, took us to Port Augusta
hospital.

Andrei glanced at Dmitri, nodding.

SARAH (CONT'D)
Jandi, the Aboriginal man, died
there. John came back home for a few

days, then was increasingly strange, then he left me. Took the car.

ANDREI LEBOV
The Aboriginal man, Jandi, you say, he died at Port Augusta?

Sarah nodded, dabbing her nose with a tissue.

ANDREI LEBOV (CONT'D)
Thank you, Sarah, you have been amazing. You have been very helpful.

Sarah sat there uncertain. Then got up and Dmitri ushered her through the door. Came back and sat down. Andrei looked triumphantly at Dmitri.

ANDREI LEBOV (CONT'D)
The TV NEWS report said some body parts had been stolen from a body at Port Augusta, then they talked about the possibility of Bunyip eggs being carried by other creatures, including humans.
(With finality)
Well fuck me, I reckon those two men were both carrying Bunyip Eggs Dmitri.
(A beat)
Chances are the buggers that broke into the hospital were the lads that abducted the Cantrells. They impregnated those two men... One died; they were getting the eggs out of him. We don't know where the other feller, John Cantrell is.

Andrei felt his stomach again, fingers digging in.

ANDREI LEBOV (CONT'D)
Maybe that's the price of being cured.
You end up carrying a Bunyip...

Andrei gestured to Dmitri to leave him. Dmitri
wanted to speak, but Andrei waved him away
irritably. Dmitri hovered.

ANDREI LEBOV (CONT'D)
(Sharply)
What the hell Dmitri, fuck off when I
tell you. Enough already.

DMITRI OLVO
(Quickly)
Boss, I put a tracker on her husband's
car, John Cantrell. I can find him.

Andrei stubbed his cigar in a shower of sparks,
looked at the dying embers for a few seconds,
then raised his eyes to Dmitri's, with a long
outward breath.

ANDREI LEBOV
The other egg Dmitri, bloody hell.
(A beat)
You are able to find the other
fucking egg?

FADE OUT

**EXT. BIRDSVILLE TRACK NORTHBOUND. SIMPSON
DESERT. DAY.**

The XC90 rolled north at 70 mph on graded dust,
the orange cloud behind them stretching out like
a meteor trail. The bitumen Outback Highway had
ended abruptly at Marree and since taking that

315

right turn onto gravel, the noise level inside the normally silent motor, was like sitting in a thunderous waterfall.

                    ENZO MATTEO
     Fuck this, Luis. We haven't seen
     another car on the road for hours. I
     lived in OZ all my life and I never
     seen this. Didn't even know all this
     desert stuff even existed.

Luis didn't reply. It didn't really warrant a response other than to grunt. A roadside sign appeared on their left, as usual it was riddled with bullet holes and rust. He slowed slightly to read.

                    LUIS DEWAYNE
     There's a town up ahead called
     Mungeranie. We can stop there and
     eat, get fuel.

They passed several ruined stone buildings, fragments of wall like broken claws reaching into the white-hot sky, then the sign on the right to the town. Luis slowed, took the turn. Enzo gazed around.

                    ENZO MATTEO
     There's nothing here mate. Where's
     the town?

Sporadic buildings appeared, some ruined, everything rust colored. Then a long low shed with a fence and scrub bushes appeared. 'Mungeranie Hotel' written along the side in meter high white paint.

ENZO MATTEO (CONT'D)
Looks like this is it mate.

Luis pulled up near the entrance. A fuel pump stood on its own nearby. He rolled on to the pump, then sat and let the dust settle. Enzo got out and paced around with a disgusted look on his face. Presently a fat man in over sized shorts came out and nodded.

FAT MAN
Fillerupmate?

LUIS DEWAYNE
What?

The man paused, pointed to the pump.

FAT MAN
(Patiently)
This is a fucking gas pump. It don't do steak and chips. If you park next to it, then my next logical question is, do you want to have the tank filled.

He pointed to the door of the building.

FAT MAN (CONT'D)
If you go and stand next to the bar in there, I promise I won't ask if you want fuel. I won't even ask you if and how you want your fucking steak. It comes as it comes mate, I don't give a shit either way.

Luis digested what the man said, then laboriously climbed out of the driver's door. Closed it, crossed himself, then walked over to the Fat

Man and hit him hard between the eyes. The man fell on his back spreadeagled and lay there looking up at Luis.

                    LUIS DEWAYNE
          I am in a real bad mood. Fucking bad.
          A sensitive person would pick that up
          and treat me accordingly. But you...

Enzo grinning broadly, helped the Fat Man to his feet, brushing him down. The man spat blood, shook his head and put his hand back on the pump.

                    FAT MAN
          Fillerupmate?

                    LUIS DEWAYNE
          Yes, thank you.

TWO HOURS LATER

They walked back to car with bellies full of steak and fries. It wouldn't immediately start. Luis tried several times. It fired, then died. They looked at each other, perplexed.

                    LUIS DEWAYNE (CONT'D)
          Now what.

They got out, opened the hood, and looked disconsolately inside at the dust covered engine. The Fat Man drifted up and looked as well. Luis decided that some male bonding might be in order.

                    LUIS DEWAYNE (CONT'D)
          Any ideas old mate?

The Fat Man looked for several beats, then reached in and put his hand on the engine block. He held it there a moment, then put it back in his pocket, walked off, came back with a hammer. He reached down deep into the Volvo's innards and tapped a few times. He nodded to Luis. Luis climbed in and tried, the engine spluttered, then roared into life.

                    LUIS DEWAYNE (CONT'D)   *
          So, what was it?

                    FAT MAN
          Don't know, maybe some shit in the
          fuel line. Happens all the time on
          this road.

                    LUIS DEWAYNE
          Can I buy that hammer off you?

The Fat Man considered the request with a sad expression. He hefted the hammer a few times, looking closely at it.

                    FAT MAN
          Hammers are real hard to come by
          around these parts. This one belonged
          to my Granddaddy, it's been in the
          family my whole life.

Enzo winked at Luis, then pulled $50 off a roll. The man looked at it, shrugged, took it and passed the hammer over, and walked off.

                                        CONTINUOUS

319

EXT. EYRE DEVELOPMENT ROAD. 3 MILES SOUTH OF BIRDSVILLE

Luis hammered the Volvo north as the first vague signs of human occupation began to show along the sides of the track.

A hand-painted road sign on their left said 'Birdsville Race Club' then another road sign on the right with a large 14. Handwritten in white paint beneath was 'Cordillo Downs 158 miles.' Luis spun the wheel to the right and the Volvo expired with the death rattle sound of metal breaking deep in its innards.

They shuddered to a stop and sat there, dust settling. After a while, Luis hit the steering wheel with a fist.

FADE OUT

INT. GLENELG HOTEL. ROOM 231. ADELAIDE. DAY.

Ekaterina paced the floor. Andrei, now apparently cured, was no longer her 'pet project' and she is looking for other things to take up her interest. For the past 24 hours he has shown zero interest in her. Preferring the men's company. She waited for him to go into bedroom, then pounced.

> EKATERINA LEBOV
> (Loving, warm)
> Andrei, how are you feeling my darling? You seem so energetic and focused, its hard to believe you are cured and back to your old self.

Andrei rummaged in a drawer, his back to her, irritated. He ignored her entreaty.

> EKATERINA LEBOV (CONT'D)
> (Patiently)
> I know this has happened, but it's still hard to believe that you are not only cured, but stronger than I have seen you for years.

Andrei loses it.

He pulls out the entire drawer and throws it across the room in frustration. Clothes and effects cascade everywhere, the drawer splinters against the wall. Ekaterina is shocked and dismayed. He rounds on her.

> ANDREI LEBOV
> (Shouting)
> Why can't I find anything? I'm looking for my fucking Ray Bans. Every time I put something down, you pick it up and hide it somewhere entirely illogical where no one but you can find it.

He turns to her, his face twisted into a frightening mask of aggression that she never seen before.

> ANDREI LEBOV (CONT'D)
> Leave me the fuck alone Ekaterina. Stop badgering me. Right now I do not need your company, or your counsel. I'll let you know when I do.

Ekaterina was mute with shock and horror. She crumbled in front of him, falling into the

settee, her knees drawn up, her eyes wide with
alarm. He was relentless.

                ANDREI LEBOV (CONT'D)
    Oh for God's sake, don't start all
    that hurt female shite with me. Piss
    off out of my sight then I don't have
    to see it.

Ekaterina ran from the room, passing Sergei in
the doorway. He looked at Andrei with concern.

                SERGEI
    Everything OK Boss?

                ANDREI LEBOV
      (Bitterly)
    Oh, the loyal and truehearted Sergei,
    the veritable bridge over troubled
    waters, who incidentally, happens to
    be fucking my wife.

                SERGEI
    Comon Boss, be cool. You are just
    getting your strength back.

Andrei became enraged, his eyes wild with a
savage violent energy. He reached behind his
back and pulled an automatic pistol, clicking
off the safety, its muzzle pointed directly at
Sergei's face.

                ANDREI LEBOV
      (Icy calm)
    You may be living your last moments
    on this earth Sergei, choose your
    next words with care.

Sergei stood very still. He had faced enough potential shooters in his criminal career to know when the deadly point of no return had been passed. Andrei held the handgun on him for several long moments, a muscle twitching in his temple, then dropped his hand to his side.

He looked away, suddenly tired, his arm raised towards Sergei in a throw away gesture of dismissal.

FADE OUT

EXT. BIRDSVILLE TRACK TWO MILES SOUTH OF BIRDSVILLE. SIMPSON DESERT. DAY.

Luis and Enzo, bareheaded, walked along the deserted dust track towards Birdsville in early afternoon heat.

The sound of gravel hitting the underside of a vehicle turned them. Coming along from behind them a late model Ford sedan rolled to a stop, the driver leaning across the passenger seat, window sliding down

FORD DRIVER
Are you boys OK? Is that your Volvo back there? I can take you into town no problem.

Luis grinned his tanned, white toothpaste smile.

LUIS DEWAYNE
Gee, thanks mate. Yep, the Volvo is sick, and we have a way to go yet.

                    FORD DRIVER
OK, no worries, jump in boys, too
bloody hot to be on foot.
        (Grinning)
You are pointed towards Cordillo
Downs. You heading out to see old
Billy Bob?

Luis's smile faded. He glanced at Enzo, then
went around the car to the driver's door. The
Ford driver slid down his window, grinning up
him, his face a picture of innocent naivete.
Luis returned his smile, leaned down and shot
the man in the face, blood and brain matter
spraying across the front seat. The man sat
where he was, face caved in, shattered head
lolling back.

Enzo surveyed the scene with distaste.

                    ENZO MATTEO
For fuck's sake Luis, look at the mess
on the seat.

They quickly pulled the man's body out of the
car and into the scrub bushes by the highway,
kicking sand and undergrowth over him. Luis
scooped and scattered handfuls of dry sand onto
the seats, soaking up the gouts of blood and
brain matter. There was some clothing on the
back seat, Enzo spread items across the seats
onto the dry sand, and they quickly piled into
the car, spinning it around in the road.

A brief stop by the Volvo, transferring sports
bags and guns, and then they were on their way
south on the last leg towards Cordillo Downs.

                    LUIS DEWAYNE
              (Thoughtfully)
     This guy knew Billy Bob. So, Billy
     Bob will know his car.

After a mile, Enzo leaned forward to switch
on the Ford radio, looking for a country music
station. He found Willy Nelson singing 'On the
Road Again' and grinned at Luis.

                    ENZO MATTEO
     I just love Willy Nelson.
              (Puzzled)
     He must be getting on a bit by now,
     do you reckon? In his eighties maybe?

                                        FADE OUT

**EXT. HIGH GROUND BEHIND CORDILLO DOWNS
RANCH. DAY.**

Billy Bob lay on a warm flat rock and adjusted
his gun-belt under his belly. Next to him lay
his lever action Marlin 1895 chambered in 45-70.
The rifle had buck-horn open sights and no scope;
the old Marlin model newly issued by Ruger.
The 45 calibre round could also be chambered
by the Colt in the worn leather holster on his
hip. In this way he only carried one calibre of
ammunition interchangeable for both guns.

The hardpan desert stretched away into pale
shimmering haze. He glassed the ranch buildings
200 meters below him. No sign of any movement.
The cattle sheds were empty and the cowboy crew
of six Aboriginals who had worked the ranch
for years were all on leave at Birdsville. He
imagined PJ, her open choke Remington loaded

with '00 Buckshot', across her knees, watching the same view through her ground level window.

The track stretched 85 miles through broken country to meet the euphemistically named Eyre Development Road where it improved somewhat, then another 90 miles on to Birdsville. For 300 meters out from the ranch building, there was little cover. Any movement in that 'Kill-zone' would be an easy target.

Billy Bob kept an eye behind him and to the sides but was sure they would come as far as they could using a vehicle along the single track. Even walking short distances in featureless desert was highly dangerous without directional equipment.

Billy Bob's Sat-Phone trilled.

SAT-PHONE CONVERSATION

> BILLY BOB MASON
> Billy Bob.

> STRAW HAT MAN
>   (Static)
> How's it going mate? Bruce here. Obviously they didn't get there yet?

> BILLY BOB MASON
> Hey Bruce.
>   (A beat)
> No sign yet. Where are you?

> STRAW HAT MAN
>   (Static)

8000 feet over Marree mate. With you in 50 minutes or so. Is the road clear?

                    BILLY BOB MASON
Yep. Mish?

                    STRAW HAT MAN
          (Static)
She's here. All good.

Straw Hat Man hung and the phone screen died. Billy Bob did a 360, checking for raised dust. As he came back facing front, he saw it, several miles away. He dialled.

                    BILLY BOB MASON
PJ, you OK?

                    PUMP JOCKEY
Yep, OK here.

                    BILLY BOB MASON
Incoming along the track.

                    PUMP JOCKEY
OK.

PJ hung. Billy Bob glassed the dust cloud. It was too far off to make out detail. He did another careful 360 check knowing it was dangerous to focus on an obvious target.

The dust cloud grew. After a while he could tell that the vehicle wasn't a Volvo. He watched it though the glasses, his tension decreasing.

SAT PHONE CONVERSATION

> PUMP JOCKEY (CONT'D)
> Yep.

> BILLY BOB MASON
> It's a blue Ford sedan.

> PUMP JOCKEY
> Jack Lucas?

> BILLY BOB MASON
> Hang on...
>> (A beat)
> Yep, its Jack. Its OK baby. Let him
> come in. Keep watching though. I'll
> stay up here. Give him a drink.

> PUMP JOCKEY
> Will do.

> CONTINUOUS

INT. BLUE FORD. CORDILLO DOWNS TRACK. DAY.

Luis kept a steady pace along the corrugated surface as the Ranch building grew closer. Beside him, Enzo was silent and watchful, cradling a lightweight AR15 Colt 5.56 calibre semi-automatic rifle with a 20-round magazine and Red-Dot sight. Another identically setup rifle was wedged between the seats for Luis's use. Luis brought the Ford to a stop in a slight depression, engine ticking over. Squinting forward, focused.

ENZO MATTEO
What do you reckon, shooter up on
that hill behind the buildings?

Luis watched the rim against the sky for several
beats.

LUIS DEWAYNE
Yep, I would. Then someone in the
house.

ENZO MATTEO
Options?

LUIS DEWAYNE
Well, go in fast and he will shoot
at the windscreen for sure. Best is
to get out of the car and into the
scrub.
(A beat)
Hmm, but he knows this car, and the
screen is tinted. If we can get behind
the building, the shooter will have
no shot from that hill.
(Deciding)
We'll drive on in. If we take any
incoming fire, dive out both sides.

Enzo nodded, flicking the rifle to 3 shot repeat.

CONTINUOUS

**EXT. HIGH GROUND BEHIND CORDILLO DOWNS
RANCH. DAY.**

Billy Bob relaxed as Jack Lucas's Ford rolled
towards the ranch. He dialled.

SAT PHONE CONVERSATION

> BILLY BOB MASON
> Jack is coming in. Don't watch him
> PJ, watch along the track. If they
> are seeing this, they will use him
> as a distraction.

> PUMP JOCKEY
> Will do.

The Ford rolled to within 30 meters of the house
and parked. Billy Bob could only see the tail
end because it had drawn under the roof line
of the house.

He brought up glasses and watched the far horizon.

Suddenly with a force that jolted him, a cluster
of several shots rang out at the house below.
Then the boom of PJ's Remington, then another
single shot, then silence. White smoke drifted
from below the roof line.

With a feeling of the deepest dread, Billy Bob
knew he had fucked up.

He galvanized to his feet, horror stricken,
running, and sliding down the steep scree in
a cloud of red dust. Then at the bottom of the
hill, he dropped into cover behind a boulder,
his heart thumping. He peered around the rock,
low down. Jack Lucas's Ford was parked with
both doors open. There was no sign of anyone.
He waited, his heart in his boots. He had
been overconfident, and maybe it had killed his
daughter.

He dialled, sweat dripping onto the handset.

SAT PHONE CONVERSATION - STATIC

> BILLY BOB MASON
> Bruce, where are you?

> STRAW HAT MAN
> (Static)
> 5 Minutes, road still clear?

> BILLY BOB MASON
> Mate, they have got PJ, most likely
> she's down Bruce, I don't know.
>
> Do not land, repeat do not land on
> the track. Put down wherever you can,
> even if it's rough. They are in the
> house with her.
> (A beat, broken voice)
> I fucked up mate. They came in with
> Jack Lucas's Ford. I have no idea what
> might have happened to Jack.

Billy Bob could hear static and snatches of
aircraft engine for a minute. Straw Hat Man came
back cool and controlled.

> STRAW HAT MAN
> (Static)
> Shoot out at least two of the tires
> of any vehicles you can see Billy
> Bob. Then we are all locked in. Let
> me get this baby onto the ground.

Straw Hat Man hung.

Billy Bob resisted the urge to call PJ's handset.
With luck she may have hidden it, it could prove
to be an asset. He rolled out into the open,
past the rock, and shot out the Ford's tires,

then did the same with his 4*4. He rolled back, then hunkered up and sat with his back to the warm rock.

>   BILLY BOB MASON
>   (Calling out)
>   Hello the house. I want to come in
>   and check on my daughter.
>
>   You can watch me.

The house was silent for several beats. Then a male voice he had never heard before.

>   LUIS DEWAYNE
>   Your daughter has taken a round Billy
>   Bob. It's not good mate. What's your
>   plan?

Billy Bob winced, a deep surging anger in his chest. He controlled it.

>   BILLY BOB MASON
>   OK, I'm going to stand up.
>
>   I'll leave my guns here where you can
>   see them. Then I'll walk in the door.
>   (A beat)
>   Is she conscious?

>   LUIS DEWAYNE
>   Nope.

>   BILLY BOB MASON
>   Did you fellers kill Jack Lucas?

>   LUIS DEWAYNE
>   Who?

                    BILLY BOB MASON
        The Ford you drove in with.

                     LUIS DEWAYNE
        Yep.

Billy Bob spat in disgust and sorrow.

                    BILLY BOB MASON
        Someone will come a-looking from
        Birdsville, for sure.
                          •
He heard Luis laugh, and from another part of
the house, another guffaw.

                     LUIS DEWAYNE
        They better, cos you done shot out
        all the fucking tires Billy Bob.

Billy Bob stood in plain sight awaiting an
impact. He levered the rifle open and leaned it
against the rock, then placed the Colt 45 on the
flat top, half-cock, gate open. He expected to
be shot anytime, but his choices were used up.

After a while he walked to the house, stepped
up onto the veranda, tramped along and pushed
through the swinging mosquito barrier.

PJ was chalk white, sitting upright against the
far wall where she had been impacted by the
AR15 round. Her Remington butt was splintered
and broken where a round had hit. Her Sat Phone
was on the floor, splintered into bits.

Luis Dewayne stood alert in the kitchen area,
Billy spun in a slow circle, his hands raised.
Luis stepped over and ran expert hands around
Billy Bob's body. There was no sign of the other

shooter. Billy Bob nodded, walked over to PJ, his heart broken. He knelt down onto one knee and bent to look closely at her.

She was unconscious, breathing steady. The round had hit her in the front and side kidney area. He moved her minutely to look at her back for the exit wound. He heard Luis move behind him, then another set of footsteps came in the room. Billy Bob didn't look round.

> BILLY BOB MASON
> Can I look at her back please mate? I want to sec the exit wound.

Another voice spoke.

> ENZO MATTEO
> What the fuck does it matter. No-one is walking away from here today, Billy Bob.

Billy Bob turned to look at the other man with contempt.

> BILLY BOB MASON
> You got a daughter, or a sister, or anyone at all?

Luis Dewayne shrugged.

> LUIS DEWAYNE
> Let him look Enzo. She's fucked anyway, they both are.

Billy Bob reached and gently pulled her away from the wall. The round had exited into the wall. In the back of her waistband was Billy Bob's bedside colt loaded with dust shot for snakes. He didn't hesitate or think about it, all his were options were used up.

He drew the Colt from her belt, spun and shot Luis Dewayne full in the face, a red cloud of stripped flesh flying off him. He screamed and sat down hard on the base of his spine, his gun going off, then spinning away. Billy Bob rolled, pulling back the hammer with the heel of his hand. Enzo made the cardinal error of looking at his partner as he fell.

Billy Bob fanned the Colt and Enzo took five blasts of dust shot, each one stepping him backwards, the final one bumping his head violently against the wall. He dropped like a log, falling into himself.

Billy Bob galvanized to his feet, pouncing on Luis, pulling back his right arm and driving the Colt down hard with deadly force, breaking his collar bone with a loud snap. Luis shrieked through his ravaged mouth, dribbling blood. Billy rolled off him and onto Enzo, who was unconscious, and methodical broke his collar bone also.

Billy Bob stood, breathing heavily, flooded with adrenaline.

He collected guns and frisked the two men. Both men were incapacitated. Luis's left eye glittered from his bloody face, his other eye a ragged mess. As Billy Bob stepped forward, his leg snagged, it was numb. He looked; Luis's bullet had hit the Sat Phone on his belt. The Sat Phone had deflected the bullet, he wasn't hit but he was bruised.

Enzo stirred, then moaned in agony, holding his arm to his chest. He looked across at Billy Bob and nodded bitter approval through gritted teeth.

ENZO MATTEO
Fair play to you mate.

Billy Bob went to PJ, knelt, and pulled her eyelid back. She was comatose but breathing steady. She wasn't in immediate danger, but they were a long way from medical help.

Footsteps sounded outside on the veranda. Straw Hat Man called.

STRAW HAT MAN
Billy Bob, you are still alive?

BILLY BOB MASON
Come on in Bruce.

Straw Hat Man came in the room with handgun drawn, immediately moving his back to the wall, his eyes taking in everything. He looked at Billy Bob, nodded briefly, then slid the firearm into his waistband.

STRAW HAT MAN
You hit?

Billy Bob shook his head.

STRAW HAT MAN (CONT'D)
(Whistling)
Good result mate. Looks like you rescued at least some part of this clusterfuck.

He crossed to PJ and bent to look closely at her wound and the exit, then gently leaned her back, and touched her face with his fingertips.

                    STRAW HAT MAN (CONT'D)
                 (Softly)
         My little baby...
                 (To Billy Bob)
         Looks like the round has gone on
         through, small exit. These AR15s are
         small calibre and fast. If they don't
         hit a bone, they don't tumble or
         deform.

We need to get her to Port Augusta.

He and Billy Bob moved PJ gently into a head up prone position and strapped her wounds with belts keep pressure on them. They both sat back, looking down at her.

                    BILLY BOB MASON
         Where is Michelle?

                    STRAW HAT MAN
         She's fine mate. Sitting under a tree
         out there. Go find her, I'll keep an
         eye on stuff here.

Billy Bob stood, getting his balance. He nodded, stepped through the mosquito barrier. Straw Hat Man looked down at Luis and Enzo his blackened teeth grinning with contentment.

                    STRAW HAT MAN (CONT'D)
         Well now, it looks like you two pretty
         boys are my babies now.

                                        FADE OUT

EXT. SCRUB BEHIND CORDILLO RANCH-HOUSE. DAY

Billy Bob walked through soft sand towards a small stand of eucalyptus. He was suddenly weary as the adrenaline came down from its peak.

> BILLY BOB MASON
> (Calling out)
> Michelle Rogan, show yourself. Its Billy Bob.

Mish stood up tentatively from cover 40 meters ahead of him, her hands up to her face, tearful and shaken. Billy Bob stood and looked at her like a man who had come to end of something and started something else. The silence drew out for several beats, then Mish launched herself at Billy Bob sending them both sprawling in the sand.

She covered his face with breathless kisses, murmuring incoherent sounds, squirming against his hard body. He relaxed into her embrace, letting go of everything for an ecstatic few moment.

> MISH ROGAN
> Oh Billy Bob, I thought I'd never see you again. Oh, my lovely man, you are safe.

She drew back to look at him, her face concerned.

> MISH ROGAN (CONT'D)
> What is it?

He returned her look unflinching, his eyes glittering.

                    BILLY BOB MASON
I fucked up bad Mish. It's my fault,
PJ, my daughter Louise, has been shot.
        (A beat)
It's a through shot, but we are a
long way from anywhere here, it could
kill her before we can get her to any
medic attention.

Michelle sat up, her face registering the
enormity of what he had said.

                    MISH ROGAN
Oh Billy Bob, I'm so sorry.
        (Sudden horror)
Oh my God, the plane, its wrecked.
We broke the undercarriage when we
landed.

He had to land on rough ground because
the track where he usually landed was
too dangerous,

Billy Bob looked away towards the ragged outline
of blue hills lost on the heat haze. She leaned
against him, feeling the hard muscle in him,
rigid with the physical pain of his distress.

                                    CONTINUOUS

INT. CORDILLO DOWNS RANCH-HOUSE. DAY.

Ignoring the noise of their physical pain,
Straw Hat Man pulled Luis and Enzo into a
sitting position, then hunkered down against
the opposite wall and looked at them. Neither
were seriously injured by the dust shots with
its 3-meter effective range, but nonetheless

shocked. Both were holding an arm across their
chests to support their broken collar bones.

Luis, his face ravaged by the first dust shot,
squinted at Straw Hat Man.

                    LUIS DEWAYNE
        What the fuck did he do to us old man?

Straw Hat Man grinned delightedly.

                    STRAW HAT MAN
        Well son, he shot you with dust shot.
        We use it for snakes mostly. It's
        fine ground lead, spreads out like a
        shotgun. After 3 meters or so it's
        useless.
            (A beat)
        Then he broke both your collar bones.
        Best way to slow a dangerous man down
        I reckon.

Luis nodded bitterly, hugging his arm to his
chest.

                    LUIS DEWAYNE
        So, what the fuck are you gonna do
        now old man?
            (A beat)
        You have a serious problem don't
        you. Your mate Billy Bob has just
        shot two agents of the Australian
        Government, who were carrying out
        official Government business.

Straw Hat Man frowned, thought about that.

                    STRAW HAT MAN
That Ford you were driving, belongs
to a friend, Jack Lucas. How'd you
fellers come by that?

                    LUIS DEWAYNE
          (Grinning)
Our Volvo burnt out, so's we had to
requisition another mode of transport.

                    STRAW HAT MAN
And Jack?

                    LUIS DEWAYNE
He objected, so we had to insist.

                    STRAW HAT MAN
I know Jack, if you'd a asked him to
bring you here, he would have done
that like a shot. Been glad to.
          (A beat)
So, you killed him huh?

                    LUIS DEWAYNE
Yes.
          (A beat, firmly)
In order to complete our mission, we
did what we had to do.

Beside him Enzo stirred, in pain but resentful
and vicious.

                    ENZO MATTEO
          (To Luis)
Why are you talking to this stupid
Hill Billy bumpkin Luis. He's a
fucking no account nobody like that
other female piece of shit lying over
there. Given the chance she would

                    341

have shot us point blank with that
Remington, God knows what she's got
loaded in it, probably rusty nails
or worse.
(A beat, to Straw Hat Man)
It was me that shot her old man, pity
all that was interrupted. We would
have had a sweet time with her.
(Grinning savagely)
I do love a bit of anal.

LUIS DEWAYNE
(To Enzo, irritably)
Shut the fuck up Enzo.
(To Straw Hat Man)
I imagine you fellers have Sat phones.
Best is that you ring some numbers I
can give you. They will confirm that
we are agents of the Government. Then
arrangements can be made to get us
to medical attention.
(A beat)
That will mitigate your collective
punishment for all this. Better for
you in the end mate.

You think about that.
(A beat)
Governments don't lose you know mate,
small fry like you lose, that's life.

ENZO MATTEO
Yes, and don't you be pondering on
these things too long old man.
(Thrusting his chin towards PJ)
She ain't gonna be lasting too much
longer I reckon.

Straw Hat Man got laboriously to his feet, nodding, acknowledging Enzo's remarks.

                    STRAW HAT MAN
          Well boys, I hear what you say, and
          I guess you may be right. So, let's
          be get on to the next bit without any
          more discussion shall we fellers.

A tiny flicker of alarm showed in Luis's eyes.

                    LUIS DEWAYNE
          The next bit? What next bit?

Straw Hat Man grinned grotesquely at him with blackened teeth, his eyes hard and uncompromising.

                    STRAW HAT MAN
          Well, your little friend raised the
          issue of loving a bit of anal, so I'd
          better not be disappointing him.

Both men squirmed in their seated positions and became very alert.

                    STRAW HAT MAN (CONT'D)
          These here folks are my kin. This ranch
          and its land goes back generations in
          our family.
                    (Nodding to PJ)
          That little lady over there is my
          grand daughter, the lady that you
          travelled all the way out here, and
          you then shot.

          Oh yes, and then you fellers was
          gonna have a little sport with.

Vague alarm was now communicating to Enzo as
well. Both men watching Straw Hat Man intently,
growing fear behind their eyes.

                    LUIS DEWAYNE
                  (Urgently)
          Hey, you kill us old man, and your
          life is over. They will come after
          you for sure.

                    STRAW HAT MAN
          Aw now, I ain't gonna kill you fellers,
          that would be way too easy. I want to
          make remembering this day a regular
          occurrence for both you boys.
                  (Musing)
          You know, I lived for a few years in
          Papua New Guinea. It's a country just
          directly north of The York Peninsula,
          but a whole world away really.

          The people there are primitive and
          sort of sophisticated all at the same
          time. The PNG folk believe there are
          several ways to die, only one of them
          is what they call 'Diepinis'. Or 'die
          finish'.
                  (A beat)
          They say that's the easy one, much
          worse way to die is of rejection, or
          of humiliation.

He looked at both faces registering puzzlement.

                    STRAW HAT MAN (CONT'D)
          You ain't got a fucking clue what I'm
          talking about do you. I'll try to
          demonstrate.
                  (Grinning at Enzo)

We'll do you first shall we, the man
who enjoys a little bit of anal.

Straw Hat Man put his guns out of immediate
reach then advanced on Enzo. Enzo recoiled in
sudden panic; his eyes wild.

Luis shrank against the wall. Straw Hat Man
pulled Enzo shrieking away from the wall,
holding him, undoing his belt, then turning him
over and ripping down his pants to his knees.

Enzo screamed into the dust on the floor. Luis
was choked with horror.

>   LUIS DEWAYNE
>   (Shock horror)
>   Oh my God, are you gonna fuck him?

Straw hat Man grinned at Luis, nodding.

>   STRAW HAT MAN
>   Yep, I am, but not in the way you
>   think.

With incredible strength, Straw Hat Man hauled
up Enzo and slung him over the arm of the settee,
his naked rear quarters thrusting grotesquely
upwards. Enzo's screams of pain from his broken
collar bone were lost in the dusty cushions.

Straw Hat Man reached behind him and drew out
a long evil looking Bowie knife from his belt.
Without pausing, he parted Enzo's buttocks and
thrust the knife its entire length into his
anus, then looked around at Luis to get his
reaction. Enzo was beyond pain and horror. He
lay silent, taking gulps of air, totally still,

not daring to move, his head turned away into a cushion.

Straw Hat Man worked the knife, then withdrew it, holding it up bloody and steaming to Luis, holding it well away from his face.

> STRAW HAT MAN (CONT'D)
> (To Enzo)
> Now that my son, was for my grand-daughter Louise, who you was gonna have some fun with.

He threw the knife into the floor, where it stuck there quickening, blood, and shit pooling onto the wood floor. He looked at Luis, nodded.

> STRAW HAT MAN (CONT'D)
> You are next now son. Best if you just relax into this, less pain.

Straw Hat Man hauled Enzo's pants back up, then tumbled him off the arm of the settee onto the floor unceremoniously. He lay moaning, clutching his knees to his chest.

> STRAW HAT MAN (CONT'D)
> So, you see, he's all done, one to go. This is way better than killing you boys.
>
> You see, I just want to discourage you, and any of your other little agent mates from heading back up here to Cordillo Downs anytime soon.
> (A beat, grin)
> Mind you, next time I see you fellers I'll recognize you from the fact that you'll both be wearing man nappies.

I know how's you city folk likes to be fashionable, well, maybe they'll do some wider fits to accommodate your new situation.

Anyways up, you'll remember your little sociable visit to Cordillo Downs most days, and you know what, down the line you'll experience many deaths before your big one, so I wish you fellers good luck with all that.

Straw Hat Man settled into his narrative.

                    STRAW HAT MAN (CONT'D)
You see boys, your little job of being an agent is now all over and done with. I guarantee your boss ain't gonna want to be seen with you fellers dressed all up in your new baby gear, shitting yourself freely all over his nice plush office, and all of them nice pretty little secretaries wrinkling up their noses in your direction.
         (A beat, patiently)
So, from here on in, nappies is your only option because you know what it's like, taking a crap can happen when you least expect it.
         (A beat, grinning)
I mean damn it all to hell, it could be right there in the middle of a conversation with a beautiful woman.

Enzo was on the floor whimpering, his face turned away.

Straw Hat man advanced on Luis. Luis roared in horror, straining back against the wall, feet scrabbling.

FADE OUT

INT. GLENELG HOTEL. ROOM 231. ADELAIDE. DAY.

Andrei paced relentlessly; his rising energy levels were increasingly difficult for him to manage. Ekaterina had withdrawn into her bedroom. Sergei was quiet and introspective.

Most of Andrei's dialogue was now directed at Dmitri, who revelled in his new importance, smirking at Sergei whenever he got the chance.

Dmitri sat working at his laptop.

> DMITRI OLVO
> (Exclamation)
> I found him Boss!
> (A beat)
> Bloody hell, he's miles away. He's way north of here, looks like desert country. What the fuck is he doing up there?

Andrei came to stand behind Dmitri, looking down at the screen. Dmitri zoomed in on the screen.

> DMITRI OLVO (CONT'D)
> Not many roads in this area. He's at a place called Tiboorura.

Andrei leaned in, his hand resting on Dmitri's shoulder.

ANDREI LEBOV
Zoom right down Dmitri, is it a town?

Dmitri zoomed down to street level.

DMITRI OLVO
An old gold town by the looks of it
Boss, not now though. There was only
140 people at last census.

There seems to be a store and a
hotel. Why would anyone want to live
there?
(A beat, zooming to street level)
The store has fuel pumps outside it.

Dmitri continued working, Andrei continued
pacing.

DMITRI OLVO (CONT'D)
More Boss.
(A beat)
Looks like there's an airstrip 6k
from Tiboorura. We can fly Adelaide
to Broken Hill, then a local flight on
to Tiboorura.
(A beat)
No car-hire anywhere in the whole
region though. Oh yes, there's a
helicopter service between Broken
Hill and there as well.

Andrei grinned savagely, teeth flashing.

ANDREI LEBOV
Book it Dmitri.
(Looking around)
We are on our way to Tiboorura boys.
(To Dmitri)

Extend our hotel stay and pay for another two weeks, and no disturbance please. Tell them we are sightseeing, so we want to retain the rooms, but will be away.

CONTINUOUS

INT. GLENELG HOTEL. ROOM 231. ADELAIDE. DAY.

Ekaterina could hear sounds of movement in the big room but stayed silent in her's and Andrei's room. She was very upset and angry at Andrei's unprecedented behaviour. In the several years they had been together, he had always treated her with impeccable manners, great respect and deference.

His outburst several hours back had left her very confused, and not a little frightened. She was also shocked at his treatment of Sergei, who had been loyal to him for many years.

There was tap on her door.

> EKATERINA LEBOV
> Yes.

The door opened tentatively; Andrei stood in the doorway.

> ANDREI LEBOV
> (Politely)
> I have sent the men out to prepare for a trip into the desert. Before then I would like to have a brief meeting with you and Sergei, if that's OK with you Ekaterina.

Andrei came further into the room, standing over by the window. Sergei followed him, hands thrust into pockets, his eyes downcast, he sat in a chair and didn't meet Ekaterina's eyes.

> ANDREI LEBOV (CONT'D)
> (Brightly)
> It is amazing you know, each day I feel stronger and have more energy. This is all thanks to both of you that this miracle has happened.
> (A beat)
> Both of you believed in this, and it is your passion and your focus that has cured me from what a short while ago, seemed inevitable.

Both Ekaterina and Sergei felt a great weight being lifted from them, they were both reading Andrei's eloquent apology with great relief.

In a roundabout way, he was saying sorry for his bad behaviour. After all, they reasoned, he had been through the most extraordinary experience, gazing into the abyss, then not only surviving, but being restored to better health than he had enjoyed for years. It was a lot to cope with.

> SERGEI
> Boss, it's OK, I was out of order interrupting...

Andrei held up his hand silencing him.

> ANDREI LEBOV
> Please let me finish Sergei, it's important for me to say these things.
> (A beat)

In my reduced state over a long
period, both of you did everything
that you could to bring me comfort,
and I will always be grateful for
that. You have...

                    EKATERINA LEBOV
               (Rising, emotional)
          Oh Andrei...

Andrei again raised his hand.

                    ANDREI LEBOV
               (Sharply)
          Please, both of you, let me finish
          what I have to say.
               (A beat, quietly)
          As I was saying, even being grateful
          for the things you have both done can
          never mitigate your betrayal of me.

          In my vastly reduced state, your
          betrayal seemed inconsequential,
          somehow trivial, when I had a mere
          few days left on this earth.
               (A beat)
          Now that has changed.

He regarded them both, seeing the first stages
of shock begin to register.

                    ANDREI LEBOV (CONT'D)
          In this changed situation new rules
          of behaviour apply; a new moral code
          must be observed.

          Your betrayal and your treachery
          cannot now be tolerated or belittled
          or pushed into the past.

Both of you have made me a cuckold in
front of the World, a laughingstock, a
weak and fallible man who demonstrably
could be pushed beyond the limits
that any husband could bear.
(A beat, bitterly)
You made me into a poor sick joke,
that in my death, it would be what
I was remembered for, nothing else.

Ekaterina and Sergei were white, both mute
with shock and apprehension. There was a small
movement from Sergei, and a handgun magically
appeared in Andrei's hand.

Sergei settled back and stayed immobile, hardly
breathing, his eyes blazing, alert, on Andrei.

                    ANDREI LEBOV (CONT'D)
Please, don't make this hard for me.
I am completing an inevitable and
incontrovertible duty to preserve my
legacy, and in doing so, eradicate
the defilement and misery that your
sordid little affair has brought to me
and my family.

Sergei, all hope gone from his soul, knew where
this was going.

He launched himself powerfully out of his seat
at Andrei. Andrei shot him in the forehead
in mid-air, with no hesitation. The silenced
handgun making a loud click. Sergei dropped
to the carpet like a rag doll, brain matter
dripping down the wallpaper behind him. He
lay twitching, his dying synapses still firing
potent messages to his muscles.

Ekaterina, now fully focused on Andrei, was rigid with horror.

> EKATERINA LEBOV
> (Broken voice)
> Andrei, please my love, do not do this, please.

Andrei dispassionately sighted along the gun barrel and shot her three times in the chest, the impact bouncing her back hard against the bed frame. She settled over slowly to her side, the light in her dying eyes on him, dimming.

He watched her die, a brief surge of sadness in him, the handgun by his side, white smoke curling from it. Then, stirring himself, he went out of the room, locking the door and putting a 'Do not disturb sign' on the handle.

He stood in the large room alone, sweeping it for things he might need, turning slowly around, then, gun holstered against his spine, he backed out into the outer corridor, closing the entrance door with yet another sign hanging on the handle.

He walked away quickly down the corridor, shooting his cuffs.

                                    FADE OUT

INT. CORDILLERA DOWNS RANCH HOUSE. DAY.

Billy Bob and Michelle made their way several hundred meters back to the Ranch. Billy Bob entered from the veranda, sweeping back the hanging mosquito curtain. Straw Hat Man was kneeling beside PJ, whose eyes were open. Billy Bob, ignoring the other two men lying against the wall, knelt beside her searching her eyes.

                    BILLY BOB MASON
          Louise, my baby I...

                    PUMP JOCKEY
                    (Weak grin)
          Stop calling me Louise Billy Bob. It
          probably means I'm gonna bloody die
          on you.

Billy Bob rocked back on his haunches, momentarily lost for words. He grinned weakly down at her, his eyes glittering.

                    PUMP JOCKEY (CONT'D)
          Is that your new lady friend back
          there?
                    (A spasm hits)
          Whoa, that fucking hurts.

Her knees came up, she slowly lowered them as the spasm lessened.

                    BILLY BOB MASON
          We need to get you to some help PJ.
                    (To Straw Hat Man)
          Can we have a discussion outside
          Bruce?

Straw Hat Man nodded. They trooped onto the veranda. Mish joined them, feeling better outside. Billy Bob lit up, blowing blue smoke.

                    BILLY BOB MASON (CONT'D)
          OK, let's review our options?

    (A beat)
Both vehicles here have tires shot out, but I'm pretty sure there are spares in one of the sheds, we can make one working vehicle for sure, maybe even two.
    (A beat)
Birdsville is 8hrs drive on ungraded road; Port Augusta, that's way too far, forget it.

Billy Bob looked at Straw Hat Man.

     BILLY BOB MASON (CONT'D)
Mish said you had a rough landing, Bruce? Can the Piper be fixed?

Straw Hat Man shook his head, looking down.

      STRAW HAT MAN
No chance, both wheels ripped off, landed on her belly.

Bill, PJ will have septicaemia in that wound in a day from now. Another day after that and she is gone mate.

Billy Bob slumped, his eyes searching Straw Hat Man's face. Michelle put her hand on Billy Bob's shoulder. He glanced at her, touched her fingers. Straw Hat Man looked away into the distance, then stood, stepped off the veranda and paced in the sand.

Billy Bob was motionless for several beats, then he spoke so softly, that Straw Hat Man couldn't hear him.

                    STRAW HAT MAN (CONT'D)
What?

                    BILLY BOB MASON
There is another option Bruce

Straw Hat Man stopped pacing, slowly turning to
face Billy Bob.

                    STRAW HAT MAN
                  (Tentatively)
If there is, I don't know it Bill.

Billy Bob stood as if he had made a decision.

                    BILLY BOB MASON
Bruce, she will not survive 8 hrs
drive on an ungraded road, she just
won't.
                  (A beat, succinctly)
We take her to the Bunyip.

Straw Hat Man sat down abruptly in the sand,
colour draining from his face. Michelle thought
she had miss-heard, she looked helplessly from
Billy Bob to Straw Hat Man.

                    MISH ROGAN
                  (A small voice)
I'm not sure I heard that correctly.
Did you really say, you're going to
take her to the Bunyip, Billy Bob?
                  (A beat, shaking her head)
Please tell me you didn't say that.

Billy Bob ignored her question, still fixing
Straw Hat Man with his stare. Straw Hat Man
finally spoke quietly.

                         357

                    STRAW HAT MAN
              (Wonder in his voice)
        You know where the Bunyip's lair is
        Billy Bob?

Billy Bob nodded.

                   BILLY BOB MASON
        Maybe 17 miles from here. Across
        country. No roads.
              (A beat)
        I'll carry her. I carried her Mother
        Bruce.

                    STRAW HAT MAN
              (Gently)
        I know you did son, I know that. But
        she was dead wasn't she.

                   BILLY BOB MASON
              (Decisive)
        Bruce, there's no choice. I'm doing
        it. She's light as a feather anyway.

Michelle couldn't take any more of this.

                    MISH ROGAN
        Hey whoa up there cowboys, comon,
        hang on here guys.
              (A beat)
        You two are not making any realistic
        sense here. The fucking Bunyip does
        not exist guys.

        It has never existed. It is a mythical
        beast made up over centuries by
        primitive people, it is a story to
        frighten children, it is the worst
        form of daytime television.

(Incredulous)
Going to the Bunyip Lair to cure
a girl who has been shot with an
automatic weapon is the craziest
unbelievable thing I have ever heard
outside of Lord of the Rings and the
Disney channel.
(Bitterly)
Hey, I admit Bruce here would make
a fair to middling GANDALF, but
Billy Bob, Frodo the HOBBIT, you are
definitely not.

She gestured to the open doorway.

MISH ROGAN (CONT'D)
Billy Bob, honestly, I am not really
making fun of this situation, and
neither should you.

You daughter is in there, she has
been shot. Surely there is something
else that can be done. You have a Sat
Phone?

BILLY BOB MASON
Wrecked, it took a bullet.

She looked at Straw Hat Man, he shook his head.

STRAW HAT MAN
The radio smashed when we crash-landed.

Mish stood, helpless.

Billy Bob turned away, began preparing. He got
some saddle harness, linking strips of leather
together for PJ to sit in. Straw Hat Man loaded
two shoulder packs with water, rifles, handguns

and ammunition, binoculars, flashlight, mirror, sun protection, blankets and first aid.

                    STRAW HAT MAN (CONT'D)
                    (To Mish)
          You take that pack; I'll take the other one Mish.

Michelle stepped in front of Billy Bob, interrupting his work, her hands to each side of his face, her eyes earnestly on him.

                    MISH ROGAN
          Billy Bob, please don't do this my love. I'm crazy about you, but this is madness.

                    BILLY BOB MASON
          Mish, I need you to help us out here, work with me. PJ is going to die, she might anyway.

          It's my stupid fault.

                    MISH ROGAN
          Hey look, I'm sorry, you think I'm being scornful and making fun of you, I really want to meet you daughter, spend quality time with her, and be friends with her sometime down the line.

          Not mourn her passing Bill.

          Just supposing you can't find this non-existent Monster. Or if it happens to be out working on the latest Disney fantasy film set?

> (Backing away, voice breaking)
> And, if you did happen to find it,
> how the hell will you persuade it to
> help PJ?

> It's a Monster for fucks sake, Monsters
> aren't reasonable.

Billy Bob gave up, turned away, motioned to Straw Hat Man to help him hoist PJ into the makeshift harness. She had passed out again which made the process easier. He was out the door in an instant, hiking away from the Ranch House.

Straw Hat Man stepped over to Luis and Enzo. They looked up at him with pain-filled eyes.

> STRAW HAT MAN
> (To Luis, no pity)
> We are gone boys. When we get back,
> you had better be the same, or
> believe me, I will finish the job I
> started. There are spare wheels in
> the shed, get them on a car and get
> gone from here, don't ever meet me
> again, because I will not hesitate.
> (A beat)
> If she dies, you and your bosses are
> dead men walking, believe that.

He held both men's gaze until their eyes dropped away.

> LUIS DEWAYNE
> How are we supposed to...

                    STRAW HAT MAN
               (Losing interest)
I don't care how you do it. Be
inventive.

Mish and Straw Hat Man hefted their packs and
went after Billy Bob, he was already 200 meters
away.

                                    CUT TO:

EXT. TIBOORURA TOWNSHIP. SOUTHERN SIMPSON. DAY

The Rex Express flight from Adelaide's Old
Noarlunga airport circled Tiboorura then headed
6 kilometres west to the tiny aerodrome with
two crossed airstrips, one black sticky bitumen.
The other orange dust.

Andrei, Dmitri and Igor climbed down the steps
into 38 degrees centigrade of still air, hefting
shoulder bags.

They stood, non-plussed looking around them.
Behind them the 14-seater plane swung away, as
if shunning its recent passengers, and taxied
back to the head of the strip for take-off. They
watched it nose up into the superheated air,
the pilot giving them a thumbs up.

Silence and dust descended.

                    DMITRI OLVO
               (Looking around, helpless)
There are no airport buildings here,
nothing.

When he turned, Andrei and Igor were already walking towards Tiboorura in their shirtsleeves.

TWO HOURS LATER

The three men stood in the middle of a wide dusty crossroads. Clumps of eucalyptus and a few sporadic buildings, no people.

Andrei led on ahead without hesitating. Finally, they came to a street that seemed to promise at least the hope of seeing another human. A huge white sign 'Corner Country Store' loomed, a long low structure behind it with a huge dust laden aircon unit. A Mobil sign highlighted two rusted oil-stained fuel pumps standing like sentinels either side of the entrance.

They trooped into shockingly cold aircon, rows of laden supermarket shelves, a fierce looking elderly woman sat behind a bar looked up momentarily, then resumed knitting, her hands working automatically. Andrei stepped over to her, dropping his shoulder bag gratefully, sliding onto a stool, elbows on the bar.

                    ANDREI LEBOV
                  (Winning smile)
          Good day to you Madam. May we have
          some cold drinks please. It sure is
          warm out there.

The old lady nodded, finished her row, then shuffled along and pistoled three midi glasses of cold beer, then paused, beer pistol hovering. The three men stepped over and necked the drinks appreciatively, she immediately filled

them again, then went back to her knitting. They
drank again, slower.

>   ANDREI LEBOV (CONT'D)
>   Ma-am, thank you. May I please ask
>   you for some information?
>
>   We are looking for a friend who may
>   have passed through here in the past
>   few days.

The old lady squinted critically at them, leaning
to take in their dark suits, their dusty and
sweat stained shirts. She settled back, nodding.

>   OLD LADY
>   City folks huh?

>   ANDREI LEBOV
>   Yes Ma-am, we surely are. We work for
>   the Government, and we are looking
>   for someone. The man we are after may
>   be very ill and possibly dangerous.
>   He is driving an old Holden Kingswood
>   estate car.

The old lady continued knitting.

>   OLD LADY
>   (Snorting)
>   Humph well, most folks around here
>   are fucking dangerous if'n you crosses
>   them the wrong way. They'll shoot you
>   down like a dog in a heartbeat.
>   (A beat, grimace)
>   The one's driving old Holdens are
>   worse'n all the others.

Andrei took a breath and and nodded an inward "Ok', then he smiled winningly. He winked at Dmitri.

ANDREI LEBOV
We will have three more beers please Ma-am, if that's OK.

She laboriously stowed her voluminous knitting again and pistoled three more midis, wiped spilled foam and went back to her knitting.

OLD LADY
I reckon maybe the feller you is after was here two days back.

Looked like he is looking for someplace to die if you ask me. He fuelled up, bought water, an' headed north towards Eromanga, didn't talk.

20 meters behind them the entrance door opened and slammed shut on its noisy springs. Everyone turned to look.

A middle-aged cowboy, lean and tall, stepped in on dusty high heeled boots. He nodded to the old lady, then wandered, collecting armfuls of provisions around the shelves.

Eventually he stepped to the bar with his purchases and necked the beer that was waiting. He wiped his mouth on a sleeve and looked curiously at the three suited men, then he spoke to the old lady as if they weren't there.

COWBOY
Cops or Gangsters?

                    OLD LADY
          (Grinning)
Government they say. Ha, same thing
probably.

                    COWBOY
          (To Andrei)
What y'all doing way up here boys?
Tracking somebody down?

Andrei stepped up the Cowboy with his hand out.

                 ANDREI LEBOV
Hi, I'm Andrei. We are indeed tracking
someone. He's very ill we believe and
could infect others. He may also be
dangerous because of his illness. We
work for the Government's Environment
Agency.

The Old Lady discarded her knitting and came
to lean on the bar, interested.

                    OLD LADY
Infect you say?   .

                 ANDREI LEBOV
Yes Ma-am. He is carrying a dangerous
infection that he could pass on to
other innocent folks.

                    OLD LADY
          (To Cowboy)
I think maybe this man was here two
days back Cowboy, there's not many
strangers pass on by here.

Holden Kingswood Estate car, all
beat up. He looked like one of these
fellers out of zombie movie.
(To Andrei)
This here is Cowboy McNeil. He's from
a Ranch Homestead 80 miles north of
here, Noccundra.

Cowboy nodded to Andrei, looking coolly at
Dmitri and Igor. He looked pointedly at the Old
Lady, and she nodded briefly.

He took a breath.

                    COWBOY
          (Slowly)
Well boys, I reckon I might know
something, don't know how much use it
is to you fellers. We have a cattle
waterhole along Warry Gate Road, its
a dust track way north of here.

There's an old, battered Holden pulled
off into the scrub there. It was there
when I flew down here anyways two
hours back. I'm guessing its maybe 60
miles north of here.
          (A beat)
Looks like he had pulled off the road
and driven out into the donga for
some weird reason, then maybe he got
bogged in some soft sand, I don't
know. I dropped down low and circled,
but there was no sign of anyone alive
there that I could see.

Andrei reacted.

                    ANDREI LEBOV
You flew?

                      COWBOY
Chopper.

We use it for commuting, mustering
sheep, stuff like that. It's a Bell 47.
Normal mode of transport round here.

Andrei grinned briefly catching Dmitri's eye.
Dmitri smiled.

                    ANDREI LEBOV
            (Leaning in, earnest face)
Sir, this is a big ask, because you
don't know us, but would you take us
to that Holden in your Bell Chopper?

We will of course pay you handsomely
for your time, and for the vehicle
use, fuel etc.
            (A beat, reaching for his wallet)
Would $1000 dollars cover it?

Cowboy and Old Lady exchanged glances.

                      COWBOY
            (To Andrei)
You say this here Holden feller could
pass on some serious infection? And
he's already ill.

The old lady nodded, leaning on her elbows.

                     OLD LADY
He's ill all right. I seen him boys.
Didn't look to me like he had more'n
a few hours left in him.

Cowboy drained his glass, paid, nodded to the Old Lady, tugged down his hat brim and headed for the door. He turned to glance back in the doorway.

                    COWBOY
          You fellers coming?

                                        FADE OUT

EXT. SIMPSON DESERT OUTBACK. STH AUSTRALIA. DAY

Billy Bob led an unrelenting pace, stopping only to give PJ sips of water and check her condition. She was welded to his back by strips of leather tack and sweat, so to some extent her wounds were supported. She never complained once as she moved in and out of consciousness.

Straw Hat Man and Michelle kept as close as they could to Billy Bob's pace, catching him up when he stopped briefly to administer to PJ's needs. At some point he stopped in the shade of a huge red boulder, hunkering down at its base, cradling PJ, giving her water. Straw Hat Man and Mish gratefully dropped down beside him.

Michelle drank, slugging the water down. Straw Hat Man restrained her with a strong grip to her arm.

                    STRAW HAT MAN
               (Gently)
          Don't Mish, a little, often.

Michelle leaned back against the warm rock, catching her breath.

                    MISH ROGAN
    We've been walking five hours now
    Billy, how long do you reckon?

                  BILLY BOB MASON
    Another couple hours maybe.

Mish glanced at Straw Hat Man, his eyes slid
away. She put her hand on Billy Bob's arm.

                    MISH ROGAN
    Billy Bob, we have to talk about this
    now don't we. What the fuck are we
    going to do when we get to wherever
    we are going?
         (Looking around)
    There's nothing here Billy Bob.
    Nothing...

Billy Bob groaned, pushed his hat back, wiping
away rivulets of sweat, eyes closed.

                  STRAW HAT MAN
         (Earnestly)
    She's got a point Billy Bob. We need
    some sort of plan at least. Probably
    we gonna have to hunker down and wait
    till we get a clear kill shot at this
    fucker.
         (A beat)
    Could take a while you know.

Michelle snorted, getting angry, climbing to
her feet, glaring down at the two men.

                    MISH ROGAN
    Shoot it...Oh my God!
         (A beat, becoming emotional)

Billy Bob, we are humouring you at
the cost of this girl's life. What the
fuck are you doing man?

She sat slumped, forehead down on her knees,
defeated, crying openly.

> MISH ROGAN (CONT'D)
> You know, I can't stop you guys doing
> this. I'm a stupid idiot woman, worse
> than that, I come from the big city.
> I keep on following you deeper into
> this wasteland because any minute I
> think you will stop and come to your
> senses, but you don't.
>
> And now we are almost somewhere,
> you say, but I don't see anything,
> somewhere - where Bill? - there's
> nothing here.
> (A beat, resigned)
> Look, I know you said that you shot
> something back then, but for God's
> sake, a Bunyip... really?
>
> Comon guys, I'm lost for words here.

Billy Bob softened towards this strong opinionated
and passionate woman. He put his hand on her
shoulder.

> BILLY BOB MASON
> Michelle, whatever you think, please
> go with me on this. I know the Bunyip
> is a stupid myth to you, I do know
> that. Believe me, but it isn't a myth
> out here.

For us, it's as real as you and me sitting here. Not just real to native Aboriginal People, but to all of us who live their life out here in this place.

Billy Bob leaned into them, his eyes earnest and focused.

> BILLY BOB MASON (CONT'D)
> I must get something of the Bunyip onto PJ's wounds. Maybe some remnants of saliva, maybe some fragments of flesh. Maybe, like Bruce here says, I'll have to shoot it to do that. I honestly don't know right now.
> (Eyes glittering)
> I'm gambling here Mish.

By her other side Straw Hat Man reached to squeeze her hand. He looked at her and nodded.

> MISH ROGAN
> (To Straw Hat Man)
> You believe this as well don't you Bruce?

Straw Hat Man met eyes, held the gaze, and nodded.

> STRAW HAT MAN
> (Business-like)
> Comon now, let's haul Billy Bob upright with his precious package. We need to get there before dark.

FADE OUT

INT. BELL 47 CHOPPER. 300 FEET HIGH. SIMPSON DESERT. DAY.

Cowboy gunned the Bell 47 Chopper hard, nose angled slightly down, north from Tiboorura. He followed Warry Gate Road, the orange dust strip snaking through hardpan scrub desert unrolling 300 feet below them. Andrei was by his side, Dmitri and Igor behind in jump seats. Cowboy spat out of the open side.

COWBOY

This is the way to travel the desert boys. Everything else is bloody hard work.
(A beat)
Your man drove this track north out of Tiboorura, then for some reason, I don't know what that might be, went purposely off road into no place donga.

It seems like he kept going fairly straight for maybe another 12 miles or so on the scrub, a long way. Then maybe got bogged in soft sand or something, or maybe the car gave up on him, hard to know.
(A beat)
Anyways, the Holden is setting down there, I circled it a couple of times, my money says he's probably dead by now, particularly if you say he was already bad.

If I was going to look for him, or maybe his body, I'd look along a straight line he took from the road.

I reckon that son of a bitch was
going somewhere, and he knew where
it was.

Cow boy glanced briefly at Andrei, his eyes
serious behind the shades.

> COWBOY (CONT'D)
> Things happen out here you y'know
> city boy. People who live here don't
> look for reasons.

Andrei watched the ribbon of dust track unfold
under him. No other vehicle was in sight. Hot
air buffeted him on his left side.

> COWBOY (CONT'D)
> (To Dmitri in mirror)
> I saw you looking. You familiar with
> the Bell 47 Chopper?

> DMITRI OLVO
> Flew one in Kosovo few years back.

> COWBOY
> The war huh?

> DMITRI OLVO
> Yep.

Cowboy nodded, respect in his eyes behind his
shades.

> COWBOY
> Guys, if you watch below, you'll see
> our water hole over there just to left
> of the track. It's sort of square, 120
> meters across, see it now, catching
> the sun?

Andrei pointed down to his left side. Cowboy
nodded.

                    COWBOY (CONT'D)
        That's it.
                (A beat)
        That there is where he left the track
        and went out bush. If you look closely,
        you can see his tracks leading off.

Below were definite signs of a vehicle tracking
away from the dust road into the featureless
desert. Cowboy dropped down to 120 feet and
swung the Chopper along the twin tire trails
left by the Holden.

Five minutes later the Holden came into view,
like a sunken vessel sitting motionless on the
sea floor. Cowboy circled lower, raising swirls
of orange dust.

                    ANDREI LEBOV
        Can we land Cowboy, take a look?

Cowboy nodded and settled the Chopper into
a deepening cloud of choking dust. They held
their hands across their faces and ears to
protect them.

                    COWBOY
                (Shouting)
        Keep your heads down when you exit
        boys. Bend and run away from the
        bird a good 40 meters before you look
        upwards.

Cowboy closed the engine and the four men exited
the chopper. They collected at the Holden as

the dust slowly settled and the slowing rotor
blades drooped lower and lower.

Cowboy looked expectantly at Andrei.

> COWBOY (CONT'D)
> Now what Mr Andrei?

Dmitri and Igor moved casually away from Cowboy,
leaving him standing separate. He glanced at
them curiously, then looked back at Andrei
expectantly, a slow grin forming.

Without another word Andrei drew his handgun
from behind his waistband and shot Cowboy point-
blank in the forehead.

Blood and brain matter erupted from the back
of his head, spraying out in a fan shape across
the sand. His muscle structure gave way, and
he dropped vertically down where he stood,
instantly dead. He twitched several times, his
boots digging into the sand, then was still.

> ANDREI LEBOV
> Get the Chopper keys off him Igor,
> search him for anything else we might
> need. Get his Sat-Phone as well.

Andrei looked at the Holden, thoughtful.

> ANDREI LEBOV (CONT'D)
> This guy is heading somewhere very
> specific. He took a dead straight line
> from when he come off that track back
> there.
> (To Dmitri)

Fly us along that same compass point
Dmitri, low and slow, lets see where
this fucker was going.

He squinted in the direction of travel.

                ANDREI LEBOV (CONT'D)
There's something out there for us,
we can't see it yet, but I can feel
it in my bone's boys.

                                FADE OUT

**EXT. BUNYIP LAIR. SIMPSON DESERT. LATE
AFTERNOON.**

Billy Bob led through broken scrub country,
ragged shards of rock poking through blankets
of sugar soft sand, their muscles raged as they
dragged their feet free of each forward step,
the next step plunging ankle deep, their thigh
muscles in relentless pain.

Ahead of them the land shimmered into heat
distorted distance on three sides. Directly in
front the ground thrusted majestically upwards
from the desert floor. Massive, rounded boulders
reared 30 meters up from their base. Billy Bob
paused to let the others catch up with him. He
nodded to his left at a boulder 3 meters across
etched with a pictogram perhaps a thousand
years old.

Michelle looked at it and shuddered.

                MISH ROGAN
    A Bunyip?

He nodded.

> BILLY BOB MASON
> Maybe. We are getting close now.

PJ stirred; her face buried in Billy Bob's neck.
He turned his face towards her slightly.

> BILLY BOB MASON (CONT'D)
> Water Louise?

> PUMP JOCKEY
> (Weakly)
> I told you Billy Bob, stop the fuck
> calling me that. I reckon you and Maw
> had a grudge against me that day.

PJ settled again. Billy Bob moved forward,
bending into another cluster of rounded boulders,
hunkered down in deep shade.

> BILLY BOB MASON
> Bruce, pass me them glasses?

Bruce knelt down beside him, rummaged and
passed him the binoculars. The ground in front
of them rose steeply with massive, rounded
boulders stark against the hard blue-orange
sky, blown sand silted against their base. There
was a sharp smell of iron in the air they could
almost taste.

> MISH ROGAN
> What's that smell?

Beside her, Straw Hat Man hefted a rifle, checking
the loads, the metallic lever action sound clear
and sharp.

STRAW HAT MAN
Bunyip.

Michelle shuddered, staring at him in disbelief.

Billy Bob methodically glassed the rocky mountain landscape in front of them. Here and there ragged clumps of Cat-claw bush clung to the boulders, their unworldly black roots exposed and tangled. Etchings were everywhere on the boulders; some were faded where they took direct sun. In shaded areas they were fresh, vibrant, and animated, resonant with ancient history and a race, old as time, that survived and lived out their tribal existence in this raw and savage land.

The iron smell was stronger now. Billy Bob reached to his holster, checking the Colt, rotating the cylinder with soft snicks, hints of bright brass showing.

BILLY BOB MASON
Mish, stay behind Bruce please.

Billy Bob pushed painfully to his feet with PJ on his back, beginning the incline towards the huge rock formation. The effort turning his shirt black again with fresh sweat. There was a sound ahead, he stopped dead, his hand out to stop followers.

High in front, a Wedge-Tailed Eagle settled onto a huge boulder. Folding its wings, it watched them impassively for several beats, then turned, looking down, became focused and dead still. Billy Bob glassed it, it was watching something below. It half flew and hopped onto another rock, settled again. Billy Bob glanced back at Straw Hat Man.

            BILLY BOB MASON (CONT'D)
    Its seen something down there mate.

            STRAW HAT MAN
    You want this rifle; you have a better
    eye than me.

Billy Bob shook his head. At the back, Michelle sank her clawed hand into Straw Hat Man's sinewy shoulder, living her personal nightmare. The massive rock formation was turning dark red, deeply shadowed in the late sunlight. After a few beats, Billy Bob gestured, and they moved tentatively forward again.

The Eagle took off in a skedaddle of beating wings. The mood of the sky changed as rain curtain clouds with hearts dark as soot formed, their edges blazing red. They hung over the pale blue plain to their left as the light began to fail.

            BILLY BOB MASON
    We need to get settled down somewhere
    guys, we left it late getting here.

He moved to his right, kneeling by a small cliff of red stone. He undid leather straps and laid PJ carefully with her head slightly raised against the rock. Straw Hat Man knelt and scooped sand to make a seat for Mish. He laid their packs in front of them making a fortress, rifle laid on top pointing outwards, then sat himself, his back against the stone which still held the heat of the day.

                    STRAW HAT MAN
          (To Mish)
It'll get cold later Mish. Get your
stuff out of the pack now. Ain't
nothing gonna happen now till first
light maybe.

TWO HOURS LATER

Straw Hat Man dozed, his chin down to his chest,
breathing lightly. PJ was quiet, her temperature
raised but not high.

Around them the desert took on an ethereal
light. The shadows black but softer detail
showing where starlight reflected white on sand.
To the east, the sky was black with the sharp
bright studs of early stars. To the west, a
long streak of purple lay against low blue-
black distant mountains. A low three quarter-
moon hung in the southern firmament, empyrean,
sublime and remote.

                    BILLY BOB MASON
          (To Mish)
Mish, don't be alarmed, I'm going to
take a look around.

He took out his Colt, held it towards her butt
first.

                    BILLY BOB MASON (CONT'D)
Take this Mish. You haul back the
hammer like this, point it and pull
the trigger to make it shoot, that's
it. If you have to shoot to make a
noise, best point it in the air.

She took the gun, holding it like a live bomb. Billy Bob gently took her hand and pointed the gun away and downwards.

> BILLY BOB MASON (CONT'D)
> Anything at all, fire it off, and I'll be back here straight off.

He bent slightly to see her face, it was washed blue white in the moonlight. She leaned into him, kissing him gently, her lips warm and soft with passion for this man who continually amazed and excited her beyond words. Her journey from smoked glass city office to this mountain in remote desert was greater for her than any APOLLO mission, or any wild fantasy she could ever conceive.

Billy Bob smiled reassuringly at her, he reached and touched PJ's cheek lightly, checked and hefted the rifle, and stepped away into the darkness.

He stood, studying the star positions for several minutes, memorizing his position, gazing around where the rocks rimmed jet black outlines against the sky. He moved slowly towards the highest boulder, remembered from his last exploration, from time to time he stopped, motionless in deep shadow, watching for any movement. The iron smell in the air was constant now and he knew he was close to the cave.

He suddenly stopped, alert.

The world changed. He felt minuscule movement deep in the earth and the hair on his arms prickled. He stopped his next move, settling back to watch and wait. Nothing moved in his field of view for ten minutes, but the feeling persisted. He waited again, then he saw it. The shape of a man merged silently out of a deep shadow 20 meters in front of him. The brief moonlit glint of a rifle barrel showed briefly, held across his chest Aboriginal style.

The man dropped down, sitting cross legged, entirely motionless. He was in open sand, lit softly with starlight down one side. Billy Bob could see he was bare chested and well built, something vaguely familiar in his self-assurance.

                    BIRANI PEMBA
        Come and sit Billy Bob, its safe.

The acute moment of shock immediately subsided. Billy Bob stood away from the shadow, spinning slowly around, alert to any other flanking movement, there was none. He stepped over to Birani, and sank down on his haunches several feet away.

                BIRANI PEMBA (CONT'D)
        You are carrying somebody on your
        back mate?

                BILLY BOB MASON
        Pump Jockey. She's been shot.

Birani looked quickly towards him, concern showing.

                    BIRANI PEMBA
        Bad?

                BILLY BOB MASON
        Bad enough, maybe kill her within
        hours Birani.

(Curious)
When did you see us, we were careful?

BIRANI PEMBA
Old Freddie smelled you coming 3
hours back. Then we felt you in the
ground. Couple of hours ago we saw
you make camp. Your Granddaddy with
the Straw Hat is with you huh?

BILLY BOB MASON
Yep.

BIRANI PEMBA
You after Bunyip Billy Bob?

BILLY BOB MASON
Yep.

Billy Bob felt the change in tension take place
between them as if a door closed.

He waited and considered the situation. He was
not surprised that native Australians were in
the vicinity. This was a known spiritual place,
but only to those locals who knew the area
intimately and were part of the protective
secrecy that surrounded much of Aboriginal
culture.

He and Birani had been childhood friends, but
there had always been an unspoken cut-off point
where Birani could range freely into his cultural
landscape, and Billy Bob had been left behind.

BILLY BOB MASON (CONT'D)
What's here Birani? Is it a female?

                    BIRANI PEMBA
Yes.
          (A beat, slowly)
We have an egg Billy Bob. We had two,
but one died on us. We...

Birani made an effort to continue speaking, then
didn't. Billy Bob waited several beats.

                  BILLY BOB MASON
Say what you have to say Birani, we
have enough history to deal with
whatever comes.

                    BIRANI PEMBA
It was you Billy Bob, you started all
this. I know you was protecting your
cattle.
          (A beat)
Nobody blames you mate.

Billy Bob was silent for a long time. Birani
allowed the silence to draw out.

                  BILLY BOB MASON
The Bunyip I shot. It was the male,
right?

Billy Bob thought it through, he began to put
it together, blowing a long outward breath.

              BILLY BOB MASON (CONT'D)
So, it was you Birani, at Port Augusta
Hospital? You cut the corpse open for
the eggs?
          (A beat, slowly)
So, I shot the male, you stole the
meat and grew eggs in somebody? FUCK!

(A beat)
Who?

                    BIRANI PEMBA
It was nobody you know Billy Bob. An
Aboriginal man called Jandi, and a
white guy called John Cantrell.

Billy Bob's head was buzzing, the whole chronology
beginning to make sense.

                    BILLY BOB MASON
You have one live egg left you say?
Just the one?

                    BIRANI PEMBA
Yep.
        (A beat)
We got two eggs from Jandi. He died.
We got the eggs out of him, but one
of his eggs went cold, it died on the
way here.

                    BILLY BOB MASON
And the other feller, the white guy
who was a carrier, this John Cantrell?

                    BIRANI PEMBA
We don't know where the fuck John
Cantrell is. No-one does. There's at
least one egg in him, that is if he's
still alive.
        (A beat)
We don't know shit about this feller
right now.

                    BILLY BOB MASON
I saw his wife on TV, she's a gold
digger I reckon.

Birani nodded, a grimace.

                    BIRANI PEMBA
     Yes, that lady had some Bunyip
     meat deep froze, we don't know what
     happened to that neither.

Billy Bob stood up, his rifle barrel down.

                    BILLY BOB MASON
     I'm going back to check on PJ Birani.
     She needs Bunyip meat soon or she
     will die. You get that?

                    BIRANI PEMBA
     Yes mate, I get that loud and clear.

                    BILLY BOB MASON
     I don't care if I have to take the
     egg, or I have to kill that female.
     It doesn't matter to me either way.
               (A beat)
     You hearing me Birani Pemba? My
     daughter comes first for me.

Birani also stood. The darkness immediately
behind him moved. Waru Iluka and Freddie Buna
stood silhouetted silently against the starlight.
They nodded to Billy Bob.

A low hum of wind moved across the ridge,
bringing the iron smell strong for a moment
and falling stars whooped silently in the black
celestial sphere.

                    BIRANI PEMBA
               (Emotional)
     I'm sorry about your daughter mate,
     really sorry.

                    BILLY BOB MASON
But...

                    BIRANI PEMBA
I can't allow you to kill the female
Billy Bob or take the only egg we
got to continue the line. Neither way
works mate for us mate. I'm sorry.
          (A beat, broken)
PJ is my friend, I'd do anything to
save her, except this.

Your way can't happen Bill.

                    BILLY BOB MASON
          (Sadly, accepting)
I hear you Birani.

                    BIRANI PEMBA
We got but one chance now, fail, and
the Bunyip is gone from our Dreamtime,
and gone from all of the Aboriginal
people for all time.

Billy Bob stood stock still, recognizing the
scale and magnitude of the awful impasse facing
both of them. His three friends stood a few feet
away, but a vast spiritual and cultural chasm
had opened between them.

                    BILLY BOB MASON
PJ dying is not an option for me. I
will not and cannot accept it Birani.
          (A beat)
I will kill anyone who stands in the
way of that.

                    BIRANI PEMBA
          (Resigned)
     I know that, Billy Bob.
          (A beat)
     I know.

                                        FADE OUT

**EXT. THE ABANDONED HOLDEN. NORTH OF
TIBOORURA. NIGHT.**

Andrei, Dmitri and Igor hunkered down around
a crackling fire that spat a stream of red
sparks upwards, mixing with the stars. They had
plundered Cowboy's provisions and cooked bacon
wrapped around twigs over the flames.

Dmitri consulted a oil stained Bell 47 manual
leaning into the firelight. Around them the
black silhouettes of the helicopter, its rotor
blades drooping sadly without its centrifugal
force under power.

Andrei was hunched in a blanket, his chin down
to his chest, silent and unapproachable. Igor
lay back, his belly full, watching the endless
display of shooting stars. Eventually Andrei
stirred, glanced across at Dmitri.

                    ANDREI LEBOV
     You going to be OK with flying this
     thing Dmitri?

                    DMITRI OLVO
     Yes Boss. We can get going at first
     light. I never flown a chopper in the
     dark, sorry Boss.

                        389

Andrei didn't respond. Pushed himself upright and got into the Holden, shutting the door and sliding the seat right back.

FADE OUT

EXT. BUNYIP LAIR. SIMPSON DESERT. EARLY MORNING.

Michelle Rogan opened her eyes, lying still, blinking in the soft pre-dawn, her head momentarily as uncluttered and empty as the sky above her. She felt as small as an insect in the vastness that surrounded her, it felt as if she lay suspended in the pearlescent centre of an opal, misty white, indistinct.

She lay, motionless, unhurried, not wanting to destroy the perfection and stillness of the moment as deepening colours slowly spread through her personal opalescent world, and her camp companions began to stir.

She turned her head to one side, reaching out to touch Billy Bob. He was not there. She withdrew her hand back into her blanket as she desperately tried to stop the starkness of inward flooding realities.

She lifted her head, Billy Bob sat, in her eyes he seemed profoundly wise and assured in his preferred environment, cradling a rifle, several feet away looking out over the hazed desert-scape rolling out below them culminating in a ragged pale blue mountain range lost in distant mist.

He felt her gaze and turned a faint smile towards her, then looked away, the muscles across his back taut, his stance watchful and alert.

Straw Hat Man walked from somewhere into her view, stood beside Billy Bob, they both scanned the desert, eyes slitted.

                    STRAW HAT MAN
          You hear something?

                    BILLY BOB MASON
          A chopper, somewhere, way off.
                    (A beat)
          Gone now.

The two men watched the endless infinity of the desert as the edge of the sun rimmed the massive dark rocks behind them with blazing red. Way below them, shadows raced away along dunes, then disappeared, hollows began to fill with orange light.

A momentous day beginning.

                                        CUT TO:

EXT. THE BUNYIP LAIR. BIRANI'S CAMP. EARLY MORNING.

Birani waited in plain sight.

There was little to be gained by trying to ambush Billy Bob Mason, not that he even wanted to. Billy Bob was steeped in desert lore and at least equal to any Aboriginal hunter that Birani ever knew.

Billy Bob was also highly skilled with firearms, and even though Birani fully accepted that he may not live out the day, he had no intention of wasting his life needlessly, maybe hit by a ricochet or by someone else's mistake.

He felt a momentary rhythmic movement in the air and turned his head, looking for the eagle, but saw nothing, the movement faded, but left him alert.

To his right he saw Billy Bob appear from shadow 30 meters away. He watched as Billy Bob leaned against a rock facing the Bunyip cave entrance, placing a shoulder pack beneath his rifle, binoculars and water bottle within reach. Billy Bob tugged down his hat against the glare, looked momentarily in Birani's direction.

> BILLY BOB MASON
> I do not want to shoot you Birani Pemba, or Waru Iluka or Freddie Buna. You have all been a part of my growing up, and my family has known your families for long time.
> (A beat)
> My intention is shooting the Bunyip to wing it, not to kill her.
>
> This I will do, and I want all of you to trust me in this, I will do that.
>
> The alternative I do not want to consider, but if you force me to, I will die trying to save my daughter, and I will take as many of you down with me as I can.

Billy Bob turned slightly to look across again at Birani.

> BILLY BOB MASON (CONT'D)
> Now, I will wait here Birani.
> (A beat)
> I will shoot the Bunyip if it appears, if that shot goes wrong and the Bunyip dies, then you Birani will be my next target.
>
> I know that Freddie is behind me, to my right with boomerangs. Waru is behind me and left.
> (A beat)
> Your task, if you choose it, is to wait to see if I can pull off the wing shot on the Bunyip.

Billy Bob tuned slightly; his voice raised.

> BILLY BOB MASON (CONT'D)
> (Calling out)
> You hearing this Waru, Freddie?
> (A beat)
> We are all in this now, no-one goes home the same after this. If I kill the Bunyip by a bad shot, I will kill as many of you as I can. That's it.
> (A beat)
> So, my old friends, give me your spiritual power to make the wing shot, if it is offered to me.

Birani was suspended like the yolk of an egg in albumen between his Aboriginal heritage and his emerged western identity. He held his breath out until he couldn't hold it any longer and then took an explosive inward breath.

He leaned back and took the gamble that Billy Bob offered. He waved assent to Billy Bob and his friends up on the rim.

CUT TO:

EXT. THE BUNYIP LAIR. STRAW HAT MAN'S CAMP. MORNING.

Mish sat beside PJ, holding her hand as she slept fitfully. She kept trying to raise herself upright in her delirium as her fever escalated. Mish met Straw Hat Man's eyes, and they shared the oncoming inevitability of the loss of this remarkable young woman, even though she still clung tenaciously to life.

> STRAW HAT MAN
> (Eyes glittering)
> She will make it Mish; I guarantee she will. She is his daughter. She was raised bloody tough.

Michelle nodded, biting down on her bottom lip to stop it quivering.

> MISH ROGAN
> Where has Billy gone Bruce? Do we just sit here and wait for something to happen?

> STRAW HAT MAN
> He's gonna try to wing the Bunyip Mish, not kill it. Big gamble, but it's all he's got.

Straw Hat Man looked at Michelle's silent wide-eyed disbelief. She looked away shaking her head helplessly. He turned and watched the gap in the massive rockfall where Billy Bob had disappeared an hour ago.

EXT. BUNYIP LAIR. CAVE ENTRANCE. MORNING.

The sun was well up. The mouth of the cave was deep impenetrable black, yawning like the jaws of hell. Billy Bob watched it over the open bullhorn sight of the Marlin rifle. He was glad of the open sights; a telescopic sight was useless for a fast moving or unexpected targets. The cave was 45 meters away over slightly falling open sand. He knew he must shoot low and expect to hit high.

Inside the mouth of the cave, he could see as far as the edge of the black pool of water, some 15 meters inside. He felt a movement in the earth and quickly looked across at Birani, who also reacted. He focused back to the pool inside the cave mouth.

The water moved, rippled slightly. Inside the pure blackness behind the pool, he sensed something incredibly huge that moved, then became motionless. He looked along the sights, keeping his barrel held low, his breathing speeding up, forcing it down.

There was the sound of water. This time the light caught the small waves. The blackness behind the water coalesced into a shapeless form, then a hideously repulsive creature raised the dripping maw of its mouth up from the black pool and stared into the blazing light with eyes that were as dead white and sightless as the eggs of spiders. It swung its head low over the surface of the water, cascading it, as if to take the scent of something, its explosive outward breath rippling and burbling the surface.

The massive body moved forward towards the light and Billy Bob dropped his head to the scarred wood stock of his rifle. The Bunyip crouched in full view, strangely vulnerable, pale and naked. Its skin soft, ragged hair hanging in clumps, other parts of its body mottled and translucent, its organs, bowels and thumping heart showing as faint movement along its bare flank.

It swung its grotesque head from side to side, scenting the air, taking another lumbering step into the pitiless light, giving out a long low moan like a petulant child that trailed away into a long outward wheeze.

Billy Bob waited his shot. He could have shot the brain that pulsed in the dull glass hairless bell of its skull, but that shot would have eventually killed them all. He needed a rear flank shot, but the Bunyip stood stock still, its head inclined upwards towards him, seeing something that he could not see, and did not dare to look for.

There was thunderous roar, and the world went to hell. Dust flew everywhere and small rocks and debris scattered in every direction as a Bell 47 helicopter hovered then settled into the flat area between Billy Bob and the cave.

The creature yowled into the sky, turned, and lurched away, then loped soundlessly back into the deep blackness beyond the cave lake.

Billy Bob staggered back, buffeted by a gale of stinging dust and stones. The Bell settled, its engine cutting, and Billy Bob was vaguely aware of men running stooped, away from the spinning rotor blades.

Rubbing his eyes, Billy Bob looked around for Birani, saw nothing. He crouched down behind the rock, levering his rifle, feeling dust grate in the mechanism. The rotor blades slowed, then gradually stopped, drooping like dead eagles' wings.

EXT. BUNYIP LAIR. STRAW HAT MANS CAMP. MORNING.

Michelle and Straw Hat man rose out of their cover in total shock as the helicopter suddenly thundered low over their heads, roaring and scattering gales of flying dust and debris, obliterating the landscape.

Mish staggered against a boulder, momentarily blind. She heard Straw Hat Man cursing and shouting but couldn't hear what he said. The dust cleared slightly, and she saw the shape of the helicopter, white against the red rock formation, swinging its nose around, a huge blue number 47 along its flank. The glass sides were open, and she saw a man holding a rifle. Straw Hat Man hit her from the side, his weight bearing her down onto the sand, heavy on her, his Colt 45 held towards the lowering helicopter.

STRAW HAT MAN
Oh, fuck look at that...

She heard him curse and looked where he was looking.

PJ was lurching upright 40 meters away in the settling dust, her back bright red, glistening with fresh blood, staggering drunkenly towards the gap in the rocks where Billy Bob had gone earlier.

The helicopter descended from their view behind rocks, it's roaring thunder becoming muted.

                                        CUT TO:

EXT. BUNYIP LAIR. CAVE ENTRANCE. MORNING.

Billy Bob kept low. His rifle was locked solid with dust and debris. He cursed, struggled with it, sweat running freely in his eyes, working the under-lever in small widening arcs, gaining a little each time.

                    ANDREI LEBOV
               (Calling out)
          Hello the rocks.

          My name is Andrei. We have a very
          simple mission. We are here to collect
          and protect the Bunyip egg for the
          Australian Government.
               (A beat)
          I'm sorry for the dramatic entrance
          here today, but we had to land
          somewhere.
               (A beat)
          Whoever has the egg, if you could
          please step forward where we can see
          you, a substantial payment will be

made to cover your inconvenience, and
then we will be gone.

No worries.
      (A beat)
We have guns here, but as you know,
they are for protection against snakes
etc. We have no intention of harming
anyone.

Billy Bob had got the under-lever working more
loose but was still unable to close the sliding
breech of the rifle to chamber a cartridge. He
ventured a look over the rock.

A tall well-built man was holding a handgun to
Birani's neck, his knee cruelly pushed into his
back, holding his face down into soft sand. The
man was looking around, scanning the rocks.
Another man was inside the helicopter, alert,
holding an automatic rifle.

Billy Bob stood up. The man holding Birani saw
him immediately, motioning to another man. That
man levelled an automatic rifle at Billy Bob.

                 BILLY BOB MASON
      I don't who you are, but you need to
      let that man breath. His head is in
      the sand.

                 ANDREI LEBOV
      Well, good morning to you Sir.
            (Looking down)
      Yes, I believe you may be right. My
      apologies.

Andrei pulled Birani upwards, and he rolled over on his side coughing and retching. Andrei kept the handgun on him.

ANDREI LEBOV (CONT'D)
(To Billy Bob)
I don't know who you are Sir, but

someone here has the Bunyip egg. I need to retrieve that egg safely, then we can all go about our business. To expedite things, I am going to shoot this man here in a couple of minutes.
(Politely)
Do you Sir, have the Bunyip egg?

BILLY BOB MASON
No mister, I do not. But if you shoot that man, you will not make it out of here, I guarantee that.

Andrei laughed with genuine mirth.

ANDREI LEBOV
Well sir, I like you. I take it this man here is your friend.

Are you going to help me?

BILLY BOB MASON
I told you. I do not have the egg.

ANDREI LEBOV
Well, we are at an impasse and cannot move forward, so I will shoot him anyway if someone else does not step forward.

Billy Bob stood, an automatic rifle on him, his rifle useless, held loose in his hand, the under lever jammed open. His friend living out his last moments of life, his daughter dying. His instincts telling him these were serious men facing him.

All options closed down.

> BILLY BOB MASON
> (Calling out)
> Freddie, step out here and give this man the fucking egg.

Billy Bob saw a movement in his peripheral vision and turned. He saw two things immediately. In the gap in the rocks, PJ appeared. She was staggering drunkenly towards the helicopter. From time to time she fell, then got up again.

Andrei's man saw her, his rifle coming to bear instantly.

At the same time, Freddie appeared from behind a rock. He was shaking and frightened. Clutched protectively to his chest, he held a large pale blue egg. He stood uncertain what to do next.

Andrei's man swung his rifle from PJ to bear on Freddie. Billy Bob was 35 meters away with a jammed rifle, helpless.

Freddie stood for a beat, then broke and ran towards the gap in the rocks and towards PJ. Andrei's man tracked him with the rifle.

> BILLY BOB MASON (CONT'D)
> No.... don't shoot.

ANDREI LEBOV
Igor, put down your rifle, do not shoot.

Igor shot. All motion slowed down.

SLOW-MO SEQUENCE

Freddie ran full tilt towards PJ, his hair flowing backwards, his pupils dilated with fear. PJ stopped, getting her balance, she stared at Freddie in delirium, somehow a vague recognition flaring in her eyes.

PUMP JOCKEY
Freddie, oh my God, is that you?

Freddie's face changed from fear to hope. One hand clutching the egg to his chest, the other reaching out forward to PJ.

He was within 3 meters of PJ when Igor's bullet hit him in the small of his back. Freddie crumpled, his head arcing backwards as his spine was severed. The bullet erupted from his lower chest, passing through the egg and exploding it like a grenade.

The blast from the Bunyip egg and Freddie's bloody body parts hit PJ like a cyclone, taking her down with Freddie's broken body in a cloud of blood fragments and orange dust.

The two bodies lay still as dust slowly settled.

END SLOW-MO SEQUENCE.

Billy Bob dropped to his knees in total horror. He bawled his anger and despair into the stone orange sky, his arms raised as if in supplications, his head back, throat arched.

Dmitri, knowing the World had shifted in that instant, started the helicopter, its rotors immediately gathering speed, raising dust all around.

DMITRI OLVO
(Screaming)
Boss, get in here, now, I'm taking off.

Andrei stood in disbelief, dust swirling around him like a maelstrom, his eyes wild. Behind him the helicopter began to lift, the ramps inched off the ground.

ANDREI LEBOV
Igor, you stupid...

Andrei lifted his handgun and shot Igor several times until his gun was empty. Igor's body jerking with each impact, he fell like a broken doll, the rifle flying into the air.

Billy Bob launched himself towards Andrei in blind rage. He began to run the 40 meters towards the helicopter, still clutching his rifle. Andrei turned his handgun on Billy Bob, its firing pin clicking on empty, the slide back. Andrei dropped it and clambered into the helicopter, falling on the floor as Dmitri gave it full power, rising in a storm of dust and flying gravel.

Billy Bob fell back as the dust storm hit him, covering his eyes, he turned away, working the lever-action frantically, swearing incoherently.

The helicopter rose vertically, swinging around, its nose downwards towards him, Andrei scrambling upwards into his seat, grabbing seatbelts. A wild grin breaking behind his shades as he looked down at Billy Bob.

Billy Bob freed the Winchester, levering the damaged shell away, another new shell sliding into the breech. He swung the bullhorn sights onto Andrei's distorted image behind the curved glass and shot.

He saw the glass star with the bullet impact, and Andrei sat back in his seat shock on his face. He levered the rifle again shifting his aim to the pilot. The next shot glanced off the glass as the chopper swung away at a sharp angle. The chopper then settling into forward motion, accelerating.

Billy Bob levered again, taking his time. Birani climbed to his feet, standing next to him.

                    BIRANI PEMBA
        Slowly now Bill, you have the time,
        bring that fucker down.

Billy Bob focused on the tail rotor as it caught the sunlight. He led the shot forward with the motion of the aircraft, pulling the barrel upwards to allow for bullet drop. He took the shot, knowing that it was good. He saw glittering fragments of tail rotor spin away catching shards of light.

The chopper went into its death spin, the main rotor roaring with the sudden surge of power as the tail rotor fragmented. The spinning chopper whirled away across the landscape, its tail whipping around hitting the top of a boulder in a cascade of sparks and dust, then clearing the mountain and spinning out into the heat haze high above the desert floor, spinning faster and faster, loosing height.

It crashed down in a balloon of rolling flame and orange dust 3 kilometres away in flat hardpan scrub. It burned fiercely, a spiral of black smoke rose diagonally from the wreckage, drifting to the right in the haze.

Billy Bob looked at Birani, who nodded.

Billy Bob turned, reality hitting, his world collapsed and over. He walked, his head down, towards the gap in the rocks, then looked up, hardly believing what he saw.

PJ was sitting up, her face pale and covered with blood and gore from the egg. She was feeling her wound, a look of wonder on her face. Michelle ran and knelt beside her, her hands inside PJ's bandages, a look of total incredulity on her face.

Mish looked up at Billy Bob. Her face questioning.

MISH ROGAN
The egg Billy Bob. The fucking egg.

Straw Hat Man running, came to a stop, stood to one side, then walked over to Birani, just as Waru came out from some nearby rocks. They stood together by Freddie's body, hands clasped in friendship, the moment drawing out. Birani walked up.

                    STRAW HAT MAN
        I'm sorry Birani.
                (Hand to his shoulder)
        Sorry mate.

PJ climbed painfully to her feet. She was
covered with a mess of blood and broken egg,
but miraculously she was healed. She stepped
into Billy Bob's open arms. He held her gently,
looking over her shoulder at Michelle, his eyes
soft.

THREE HOURS LATER

Billy Bob collected their paraphernalia together
and they stood in an awkward group, no one
wanted to speak first.

                 BILLY BOB MASON
        What do you want to do with Freddie?

                  BIRANI PEMBA
        We will deal with Freddie Billy Bob.
        We will take him into the Bunyip
        cave.

        Its what he would want.

Michelle stepped forward to Birani, her hands
outstretched, eyes glittering and soft.

                  MISH ROGAN
        We never actually met yet Birani
        Pemba. My name is Michelle Rogan,
        I wish I could have got to know you
        better.
                (A beat)
        I doubted you Sir, and I'm very sorry.

Her eyes slid to Waru Iluka, he returned her
gaze impassively.

> MISH ROGAN (CONT'D)
> (To both men)
> I not only doubted you, but I doubted
> everything that you stood for. I
> doubted ten thousand years of history,
> and I scorned and poured contempt on
> things that I didn't understand.
> (A beat, voice breaking)
> Please forgive me Birani, Waru, and
> try to forgive all the others like me.

> I'm sorry that you lost the Bunyip
> egg, and I'm so sorry about Freddie.

Waru looked downwards, shuffling his feet. PJ
stepped up, taking both Birani's and Waru's
hands. She pulled Mish, Birani and Waru into
a group hug, holding them all for a long time.

They separated, Birani and Waru kneeling with
a blanket to administer to Freddie.

Billy Bob, PJ, Straw Hat Man and Michelle walked
down the mountain slope towards the hardpan
desert floor, heading towards Cordillo Downs.

EPILOGUE

EXT. BUNYIP LAIR. CAVE ENTRANCE. NIGHT.

Birani and Waru carried Freddie in a blanket into
the Bunyip Cave. Waru was holding a long stave
of wood with a tattered strip of cloth wrapped
around it. It was lit and burning, casting a

flickering red light that danced shadows along the jagged cave walls.

They passed the small lake, going deep into the cave interior. Birani nodded to Waru.

                    BIRANI PEMBA
          This will do here.

They collected fragments of wood, then used the torch to light a fire. They lay Freddie nearby and began their ancient ritual. They built a platform of wood collected from the cave floor, and laid Freddie on it, tightly wrapped in the blanket and bound with strips of cloth.

Both men stripped naked, then began a slow dance ritual circling around the fire and Freddie's body. There came a sound in the darkness, human steps swishing towards them in soft sand. It came closer, they stopped. The sound came towards them, the silhouetted form of a man gradually shambling into the light.

Horribly deformed and barely recognizable, John Cantrell shuffled up to the fireside. His clothes were in rags, his face ravaged with folds of skin hanging loose in sheets and his stomach distended into a massive pregnancy that he had to support with an old leather belt around his neck.

                      JOHN
          Hello Birani, Waru.

Both men were shocked beyond words. Birani was the first to recover.

                    BIRANI PEMBA
        John.

John Cantrell sat down in a rush as his tottering
legs gave way. Both other man involuntarily
moving towards him. Birani felt his stomach,
then looked at Waru's questioning face.

               BIRANI PEMBA (CONT'D)
        Its hot.

Waru got behind John, cradling him, looking
over his shoulder at Birani.

Behind them the darkness moved massively as
a huge translucent form shambled into the
firelight. The Bunyip swung its immense saliva
dripping snout towards John Cantrell, taking
huge snuffling inward breaths. Its eyes opaque
white-grey marbles, unseeing in the darkness.
The Bunyip rolled over laboriously onto its
side; every movement painful. The massive head
lolled back. Its jaws open, rows of jagged teeth
showing, its stinking breath filling the cave
air with a foul iron smell.

John Cantrell stirred in Birani and Waru's
arms. He pushed away their hands and climbed
painfully onto his hands and knees. The Bunyip
moaned, a long siren sound that quivered away
into a ragged breath.

John Cantrell crawled towards the Bunyip holding
his distended belly with one hand, supporting
it with utmost care like a mother.

The Bunyip moved, opening its legs wide to
accommodate him.

John Cantrell curled his body gratefully into the Bunyips massive translucent belly in a foetal position, his back pushed inwards against the quivering translucent skin, the Bunyips enormous legs then curving around him protectively.

John Cantrell closed his eyes in ecstasy, his timeless journey completed.

FADE TO BLACK

---

6 MONTHS LATER

CHANNEL 9 NEWS:

RUMORS OF A MASSIVE COBALT DEPOSIT IN THE SIMPSON DESERT HAVE BEEN DENIED TODAY BY CANBERRA AS THE INFLUENTIAL GOVERNMENT AGENCY 'ALTERN' IS FACING SHUTDOWN.

ENVIRONMENTS MINISTER ARTHUR MCCLOUD IS FACING DIFFICULT QUESTIONS ABOUT ALTERN'S ILLEGAL ACTIVITIES DESCRIBED AS 'WAY OUTSIDE THEIR REMIT' BY THE NEWLY APPOINTED MINISTER FOR ABORIGINAL AFFAIRS, BIRANI PEMBA.

MINISTER PEMBA, PREDICTED BY SOME, TO BE A STRONG CANDIDATE FOR AUSTRALIA'S PREMIERSHIP IN THE 2024 ELECTIONS, IS DRIVING FORWARD POLICIES OF SOLAR ENERGY CAPTURE THAT WOULD MAKE AUSTRALIA INDEPENDENT OF FOSSIL FUELS WITHIN TEN YEARS.

OTHER NEWS:

A DOUBLE MURDER IN AN ADELAIDE HOTEL APPEARS TO BE PART OF AN INTERNATIONAL DRUG CARTEL WAR. A

LONDON BASED CRIMINAL HAD TRAVELED TO AUSTRALIA ON A VENDETTA THAT CULMINATED IN HIS DEATH IN A STOLEN HELICOPTER NEAR TIBOORURA, NEW SOUTH WALES. SOUTH AUSTRALIAN AND NSW POLICE ARE WORKING IN COLLABORATION WITH INTERPOL. THEY REPORT THAT INVESTIGATIONS ARE NOW CLOSED.

AND FINALLY: THE BUNYIP?

THE ALLEGED SHOOTING OF A BUNYIP SEVERAL MONTHS AGO MAY HAVE BEEN A LARGE DINGO CROSSED WITH A KANGAROO.

ANTHROPOLOGISTS FROM NEW SOUTH WALES UNIVERSITY ARE RESEARCHING CROSS BREEDING ACTIVITIES IN A REMOTE CAPE YORK PENINSULA COMMUNITY THAT HAS ALLEGEDLY PRODUCED A TWO-METER-HIGH DOG-LIKE CREATURE THAT HOPS ON ITS ENLARGED BACK LEGS, AND BARKS.

THERE HAS BEEN A NUMBER OF REPORTED BUNYIP SIGHTINGS OVER MANY YEARS AND THIS MAY FINALLY BRING THIS VEXED ISSUE TO A CLOSE.

CONTINUOUS

INT. CORDILLO DOWNS. KITCHEN. EVENING.

Michelle Rogan reached across the stained kitchen table and switched off the old black and white TV. The silence descended like a blanket and after several beats she began to hear the ticking of clock on the mantle in the hall.

There was a creak from outside. She looked towards the door with its curtain of motionless hanging beads. Around her was 200 years of history with sepia photographs, coils of leather tack, glinting brass, a gun rack, Spanish leather boots falling over at the ankle, and on the table, a chipped brown jug with the legend 'There'll be more in the larder.

She rose and stepped out through the bead curtain. The heat of the day still lingered. Along the veranda she saw the red tip of a cigarette arc outwards, cascading in a shower of sparks.

Billy Bob Mason swung his boots off the rail and stood to meet her as she slid into his arms. He held her, his chin in her hair, breathing it, as he watched the last iridescent purple-orange streaks coalesce against the ragged rim of distant black mountains.

Somewhere in the east where the sky was pure black, a dingo yowled. A long quavering sound that rose impossibly to a high point, then trailed off to nothing.

Mish pulled closer to Billy Bob, making a small sound on her outward breath.

THE END

Printed in the United States
by Baker & Taylor Publisher Services